Melody Segal ⟨ ......que diamond-and-emerald-encrusted necklace nestled in a weathered, powder-blue velvet jewelry box not long after her grandmother's murder. The treasure flashed bolts of light within the confines of Nana's eerie bank vault. Wafts of scents, sounds, and sights drifted into Melody's consciousness, conjuring enchanting visions of winter white, the icy feel of snowflakes, the jingle-jangle of sleigh bells, the woodsy smell of Siberian pines.

Why had she never seen this gleaming heirloom before? Or known about it? The attorney handling Nana's estate had presented her with the key to the safe deposit box where the jewels had been stored for who knows how long. Not long enough to lose their luster.

The box yielded not only the necklace but an unfamiliar diary. She flipped through the book, written in Russian, and pulled out a translated copy in Nana's hand. But Nana didn't know Russian. In fact, she hated all things Russian. She once joked that the closest she ever got to Russia was St. Petersburg when she went to visit her best friend Bessie at her beach condo in Florida.

What other secrets had her grandmother been hiding?

Praise for Marilyn Baron

"Marilyn Baron's *STUMBLE STONES* grabbed me from the start ... named so for the plaques laid in tribute to victims of the Holocaust, [it] possesses the best qualities of historical romance. Baron knows her settings and her history, and her characters, those both contemporary and in the past, are well-drawn and convincing."

~*Georgia Author of the Year Judge*

~*~

"*THE ALIBI* is...filled with Southern, small town mystery, intrigue, suspense, murder, and a bit of down-home charm. ...and an absolute enjoyable read."

~*Gabrielle Sally, The Romance Reviews (5 Stars)*

"Baron has a compelling and entertaining story...a superb job with character development and credibility. ...the story [is] fun and enticing!"

~*Turning Another Page, Book Unleashed (5 Stars)*

"Marilyn Baron brings a unique style to her quirky and fast-paced stories that keeps readers turning pages."

~*New York Times Bestseller Dianna Love*

"A treasure trove of mystery and intrigue...."

~*Andrew Kirby*

~*~

STRACCIATELLA GELATO: MELTING TIME

"A quick and fantastical read. Which of us hasn't dreamed of traveling back to a special time or a special place that's lingered in our hearts and minds?"

~*Laura Hartland (5 Stars)*

"Fast, enjoyable read...has gotten me in the mood to read again. Thanks to the author for that gift."

~*GerriP (5 Stars)*

The Romanov Legacy
A Novel

by

Marilyn Baron

Nancy,
My dearest friend.
Marilyn Baron

The Romanov Legacy
A Novel

Cover Art by *The Wild Rose Press, Inc.*

The Wild Rose Press, Inc.
PO Box 708
Adams Basin, NY 14410-0708
Visit us at www.thewildrosepress.com

Publishing History
First Edition, 2021
Trade Paperback ISBN 978-1-5092-3593-3
Digital ISBN 978-1-5092-3594-0

Published in the United States of America

Dedication

I dedicate this novel to my creative, talented mother, Lorraine Anne Meyers, who passed away in July 2020. She instilled in me a love of reading and writing at an early age and a sense that I could be anything I aspired to be. Although I objected, she also insisted I take a typing course one summer, which turned out to be the best thing I could do as a writer. I am what I am today because of her.

Part One

Downingtown, Pennsylvania, to Zurich, Switzerland,
2021

"Love is an emerald.
Its brilliant light wards off dragons
On this treacherous path."
~ Rumi, Persian poet

"Round and round, like a dance of snow
In a dazzling drift, as its guardians, go
Floating the women faded for ages,
Sculpted in stone, on the poet's pages."
~Robert Browning, Women and Roses

Chapter One

Downingtown, Pennsylvania

Melody Segal discovered the dazzling antique diamond-and-emerald-encrusted necklace nestled in a weathered, powder-blue velvet jewelry box not long after her grandmother's murder. The treasure flashed bolts of light within the confines of Nana's eerie bank vault. Wafts of scents, sounds, and sights drifted into Melody's consciousness, conjuring enchanting visions of winter white, the icy feel of snowflakes, the jingle-jangle of sleigh bells, the woodsy smell of Siberian pines.

Why had she never seen this gleaming heirloom before? Or known about it? The attorney handling Nana's estate had presented her with the key to the safe deposit box where the jewels had been stored for who knows how long. Not long enough to lose their luster.

The box yielded not only the necklace but an unfamiliar diary. She flipped through the book, written in Russian, and pulled out a translated copy in Nana's hand. But Nana didn't know Russian. In fact, she hated all things Russian. She once joked that the closest she ever got to Russia was St. Petersburg when she went to visit her best friend Bessie at her beach condo in Florida.

What other secrets had her grandmother been

hiding?

Tentatively reaching out to touch the necklace, Melody was reminded of the tale about young King Arthur pulling the sword so easily from the stone to seal his birthright. She fastened the priceless piece around her neck, pulled an illuminating powder compact from her purse to study the sparkling stones against her skin, and wondered again how the gems had come into Nana's possession.

The magnificent necklace was so brilliant Melody was afraid it would burn a hole in her handbag when she placed it there to take it for an appraisal. But discovering its monetary value wasn't her top priority. Finding the answer to the mystery might hold the key to her true identity. The few lines she'd skimmed in the translation hinted at a hidden Romanov heritage, courtesy of Nana's great-grandmother, Melody's third-great-grandmother. An ancestor too far removed to contemplate.

She was even more curious to learn about the rose gold charm necklace worn around Nana's neck when Melody found her still-warm body in the kitchen of their home. Was it only three months ago? Nana had been wearing that necklace ever since Melody could remember. And she still had it on after the attack. Apparently, it wasn't considered valuable enough to steal during the robbery. The charm had lost its sparkle but was equally precious for its close connection to her grandmother. In the diary was a faded picture of a rosy-faced girl she didn't recognize. One of Nana's ancestors, no doubt. Dressed in a heavy woolen coat to ward off the biting wind and frost in some frozen wasteland, the same gold charm graced the girl's neck like a talisman.

In addition to taking a life, the murderer or murderers—for there was evidence of more than one perpetrator—had trashed the house, leaving drawers open and clothes tossed about in tornadic disarray, searching for valuables. The gems, perhaps? The diary? What had they been after? Another mystery that remained unsolved. It was like Nana always said, "You won't find what you're looking for until it's ready to be found."

Her eyes were still red from crying over only cursory glances at the translated diary passages. The words seemed as real on the page today as when they had been written a century earlier, the journal writer as alive as if she had just closed the book to stretch and relax her hand. In fact, Melody and the young Russian girl who had poured out her heart had a lot in common.

Instinctively, she shook the diary—and discovered a hidden pocket in the back. Tucked into the pocket was a letter addressed to her, written in her grandmother's hand.

Nana's final words, hastily written in ink pen, as if she knew the end was near, still echoed in her mind. *"Protect this secret with your life. Trust no one. Pass it on to your daughter so when the time comes, she'll be ready."*

But ready for what? Nothing that came before in her life had prepared her for this.

Driving home, as the sun began to set, the spreading darkness reflected her melancholy mood. She slid the high metal entry fence back with an automatic gate opener and pulled into the circular driveway of the Tudor-style house, thinking it looked more like a fortress as she pushed the button to close the gates behind her.

Languishing in self-pity, she wandered the living room aimlessly in the shadows, searching for traces of her beloved grandmother. But no amount of searching would bring her back. Nana was lost to her forever, and with her, the answers she sought. The thought of Nana brought a fountain of fresh tears to her eyes.

Her mood was only lightened by the joy and laughter her daughter Katya had brought into her life. For Katya's sake, she couldn't let Nana's death consume her. She couldn't afford to be swallowed up by a tsunami of sorrow.

Nana had been her lifeline since her parents had perished in an auto accident when Melody was only six years old. She was the sole survivor of the crash. It had always been Nana and her against the world. And now Nana was gone when Melody needed her most. Why had she hidden this information about her birthright? Was she doing it to protect her granddaughter? Was she ever planning to tell her the truth? And if so, when? Melody had a million questions and no one on earth left to answer them.

First, she needed to have the words on the back of the charm translated. The front of the necklace was etched with the familiar image of the Ten Commandments, encircled by an olive branch, with Hebrew letters on one side. No mystery there. The words on the back of the tarnished disk were the puzzle.

She didn't speak Hebrew, despite the years of Hebrew lessons or the fact that she'd had a Bat Mitzvah. Suddenly, it became imperative she know the meaning of the words. No one she knew spoke fluent

Hebrew. No one except the new rabbi. Melody had an appointment with him tomorrow at the synagogue.

****

The next morning, as she prepared to leave on her errands, she kissed her fingertips and touched them lightly to her daughter's warm cheek as she lay peacefully asleep in her crib, curled up like a chubby cherub in a Michelangelo masterpiece. Katya was her favorite work of art.

Miss Natalia Cormier (pronounced the French way—Cor-mee-yay), the nanny, her eyes bleeding contempt, looked exasperated as Melody issued her instructions for the day, as if she were dying to say, "You've already told me that a thousand times." Well, she'd tell her a thousand and one times if she had to. Katya's well-being was too important for her words to be misinterpreted. She blew her baby another kiss before she turned her back on the enigmatic, frostier-than-thou, uber-capable Miss Cormier.

Looking in the mirror, with her back to the Gorgon, she assessed the battleax that was her babysitter—the short, squat figure, shaggy, straight mop of ink-jet hair, pinched mouth, and frightening demeanor. Everything about the woman was unsettling, off-putting, immovable. But Nana had given her stamp of approval, and Nana was rarely wrong about anything.

Hiring this particular nanny had been her grandmother's idea. She'd made the arrangements to recruit Miss Cormier in anticipation of Katya's birth. But then Nana's life was cruelly, violently cut short. The police had no leads, no clue. It was the work of professionals. Nana was in her late seventies, but in Melody's mind, she was immortal. She'd never imagined a world without Nana in it. She still hadn't completely processed the fact that her grandmother was gone.

Curiously, Miss Cormier showed up the day Melody brought Katya home from the hospital. There were no terms to her employment. Nana had apparently taken care of her salary for the next year. Melody could hardly complain. She'd left college early, so without a degree she was unemployable in her field. Besides, there wasn't much of a market for a Russian history major in Downingtown, Pennsylvania, or any other city. Melody spent every spare moment trying to find work, and with no family to watch Katya, Miss Cormier was a godsend. At first.

"Her credentials and references are impeccable," Nana had observed, perusing the resume. "She's certified in Krav Maga. She speaks six languages. You never know when her particular skills will come in handy. She will be a fierce protector."

Miss Cormier was more than a bit overqualified for the job. But over the years, Melody had learned that second-guessing Nana never paid off.

Melody picked up a framed photograph of her grandmother. In her day, Nana had been a regal beauty. She had never remarried after Grandpa died, but men came to call, men with thick foreign accents and even thicker mustaches. Melody was always afraid her grandmother would run off with one of them and leave her behind, but even more afraid Nana would go off with the men and whisk her along into an unknown and shadowy world. She was never allowed to stay for those meetings. One look was all the visitors were allowed before Nana hustled her out of sight.

As Melody attempted to tiptoe out of the nursery, a piercing howl assaulted her ears. Katya was a light sleeper. She sensed her mother was leaving.

Her first instinct was to run to her daughter. She headed back toward the crib to pick her up, soothe her, and wipe away her tears.

But Nanny Goat Gruff blocked the way.

"You mustn't give in to her every whim or you'll spoil her," admonished Miss Cormier, shaking her head. "Now look what you've done. You've woken the Grand Duchess." Miss Cormier placed a firm and practiced hand on Katya's back until she shifted positions and slipped back into slumber. A final pronouncement—"The royal baby needs her rest."

The nanny was stuck in some absurd Russian fairy tale. Why she persisted in calling Katya the Grand Duchess, Melody couldn't even imagine. She was the most magnificent child ever born, *her* princess, but she was not truly royalty.

Melody was determined to get rid of the nanny and replace her with a more pliable, less threatening caregiver. When she got around to it. When she got up the courage to let her go. Truth be told, she was deathly afraid of the nanny. The woman acted as if Melody was a threat to her own daughter. Miss Cormier was ultra-possessive, but she seemed to genuinely care for Katya. That's why Melody was keeping her around, for now. But she could not let her latest insubordination go unanswered. She gathered her courage.

"Are you trying to tell me how to raise my own child?" Melody ventured, her knees unsteady, her voice quivering. She couldn't quite believe the words tumbling out of her mouth.

Dismissing Melody, the nanny turned on her heels. "You may leave. I'll watch over the Grand Duchess."

Frankly, Miss Cormier's constant presence made her feel incompetent. She never let Katya out of her sight. She hovered like the Hindenburg, slithering like a spirit, haunting the hallways of the house, a malignant Mary Poppins. Melody was sure the nanny wanted to poke her in the ribs with what was probably the poisoned tip of her umbrella. Thankfully, it wasn't raining that morning.

Was she jealous? Possibly, but only of the time the nanny got to spend with Katya. And, off-putting as she was, she was a link to her grandmother. So, for the time being, the nanny stayed.

Reluctantly, she left her child in Miss Cormier's care. She drove twenty minutes to Temple Beth Tov, a place with which she wasn't exactly on intimate terms. She had occasion to see the inside of the sanctuary only a few times a year, on the requisite High Holy Days—Rosh Hashanah, Kol Nidre, and Yom Kippur.

The rabbi was new to the congregation. The temple had held several welcome get-togethers for the members to get to know him, get-togethers Melody hadn't bothered to attend. So she didn't really know Rabbi Shmueli Rosenberg, who she understood liked to be called "Slick." An appropriate nickname for a hip former Houston oil trader, a wunderkind who made his fortune and then found religion. And now he was determined to deliver religion to his new congregation, whether they wanted it or not. The last time she'd seen a rabbi was at Nana's funeral and again at her daughter's naming ceremony. But that rabbi had moved to Israel. And now she was about to become acquainted with Slick, The Slickster, or should she call him Shmueli? No wonder he preferred a sobriquet.

Slick rose to meet her when his assistant ushered her into his spacious office. He was beanstalk tall, all legs, in tight-fitting blue jeans and a body-hugging long-sleeved blue chambray sports shirt, his jacket, his only nod to formality, tossed carelessly on the seat back. His white cowboy hat hung on the coat rack behind him. She guessed it was to symbolize he was from Texas, or that he was one of the good guys, or both.

Holy Heaven. He looked better than a rabbi had a right to. In fact, she had to look away to keep from blushing—or worse, fainting dead away. Her thoughts were bordering on sacrilegious. His sexy smile and twinkling green eyes completed the devastating package that was Slick. She imagined he was used to women falling at his feet. Rumors were that all the single women in the congregation had the hots for him. And many of the married ones. Up close and personal, Melody could understand what all the fuss was about.

But she was immune to the rabbi's charms because she'd sworn off men. Katya's father in particular. A man she was trying her best to forget. Geesh. But she wasn't so rusty she couldn't detect when a man was interested in her. And Slick was definitely interested. He held out his hand. "I'm Slick."

You sure are.

"It's n-nice to meet you," she mumbled. "I'm Melody. Melody Segal."

"A pretty girl…" Slick began to sing.

Her confused look prompted him to continue.

"…is like a melody. You know, like in the song."

Shmueli thought she was pretty? Doubtful, since she had barely shed her extra pregnancy pounds. Her figure was closer to what an artist would refer to as Rubenesque. Evidently, some men preferred women with a little meat on their bones. And her limp, although slight, marred her appearance. He hadn't noticed that yet, the gift that kept on giving from the accident.

So the hunky rabbi was corny, too. Sweet. Nana used to sing that song to her. Tears threatened to spill over, so she quickly grabbed a tissue from her purse to stave them off.

"Is everything all right?"

"Allergies," she sniffled, wiping the dampness from her eyes.

Slick indicated the seat in front of a desk that was as large as the Lone Star State. And not a moment too soon. She slid into the chair, hoping the puddle of hormones she was melting into didn't slide on the leather fabric. She tried to fight the instant connection she felt for this man and the curious sense of peace his presence offered.

"Congratulations," he said.

"For what?"

"On the birth of Ekaterina." He must have done some checking on her after she'd made the appointment. Either that or he was unusually omnipotent. Which she supposed was possible, since he was a rabbi.

"Oh, yes, thank you." Katya was her favorite topic of conversation. She was tempted to pull out her cell phone to show him a photo or two, or twenty, but that was not why she was there. She took a deep breath.

"What can I do for you?" the rabbi asked, sensing

her discomfort.

"I need this translated," she said, unfastening the thin gold chain and the solid heavy rose gold charm from around her neck and handing it to him.

The rabbi studied the piece in silence.

"I've never seen a piece like it. On the front side are the Ten Commandments, of course, in Hebrew. But on the back, well, it's not Hebrew. It's Russian. My Russian is a little rusty, but it says, 'To our daughter, Ekaterina, as a memento from her parents.' There's a street address but no city name." He rattled off the address, wrote it down on a pink telephone message slip, and handed it to her.

"That's impossible."

"That's what it says."

"But I'm not Russian. I mean, I think my great-grandmother might have lived in Alaska at one time, but then the family relocated to Nashville. We moved around a lot before we got to Downingtown." Too much information to volunteer to a man who hadn't asked for it.

"Well, whoever had this necklace made apparently was. Did you name your daughter after this relative? Perhaps your mother suggested the name?"

"My mother is dead. My grandmother raised me. But no."

"What about the father? Is he Russian?"

Melody's cheeks reddened. Maybe this rabbi was also a mind reader. Katya's father was, in fact, Russian.

"He's no longer in the picture," Melody managed, nerves loosening her tongue. "He didn't even know I was pregnant, and I want it to stay that way." She didn't want to think about sleeping with Count Nikolai

Kinsky, her college Russian history professor, her *married* college Russian history professor, and that embarrassing period of her life. And she'd just imparted more information than she'd intended to a perfect stranger. Who was obliged to keep her confidence, wasn't he, being a confessor, of sorts?

"That bad?"

This was shaping up to be an inquisition.

Rabbi or not, if Slick thought she was going to unburden herself to him, he was delusional. She didn't need a shrink, just an interpreter.

"No, I already told you I'm not Russian and neither was my mother or my grandmother."

"You don't look Russian," Slick observed, examining her a little too closely.

What he probably meant to say, what everyone said when they discovered her religion, was, "You don't look Jewish." She always joked with Nana that her dirty blonde curls and blue eyes must have come from some random Cossack who'd had his way with one of Nana's ancestors.

That usually set off the predictable tirade, "I told you, we're not Russian."

Nana repeated her mantra when Melody relayed her decision to major in Russian history in college. She was like a fish in water when it came to languages. She could speak a smattering of Italian, French, Spanish, and German, but when she indicated an interest in learning Russian, her grandmother became almost unhinged.

"You are not majoring in Russian history, and you are definitely not learning to speak *that* language." But it seemed the more Nana steered her away from anything Russian, the more she gravitated toward it.

"My grandmother couldn't have named my daughter. She knew I was having a girl, but she died before Katya was born."

"Are you a spiritual person?"

What a question to ask a congregant. "Well, I never really thought about it."

"Perhaps someone was communing with you from beyond the grave."

Now the man was a medium. And this conversation was bordering on the bizarre.

"You don't really believe in all that, do you?" she said, shifting in her seat and crumpling the damp tissue in her fist.

"Yes, I do, but the question is do *you*?"

"I have no idea. I studied Russian history in college, but when my daughter was born and it came time to put her name on the birth certificate in the hospital, the name just came to me. I've always liked the name Ekaterina, like Catherine the Great. But her Hebrew name is in memory of my grandmother. Which reminds me, I have another errand to run before I get back to my daughter." She reached across the table and grabbed the necklace from the palm of the rabbi's hand, which generated sparks. She quickly withdrew her hand, threw the necklace into her purse, and rose to leave.

"There are a lot of things in the universe we can't explain, Melody. God communicates in strange ways. I think you were blessed, that you received a message from heaven."

She didn't want to be rude, but Slick had obviously been drinking the Kool-Aid—or the Manischewitz.

Next thing she knew, he was going to levitate the desk. She needed to get out of there as fast as possible before she fell hard for his soft-spoken Texas charm. Shouldn't a rabbi be wearing a suit? The fact that he was so casually dressed was disarming, putting her at ease, when her first instinct was to be wary. His eyes appraised her as if she were an expensive piece of jewelry, a piece he coveted.

"Well, th-thank you, Rabbi. You've been a big help." She swayed on her feet.

"Are you okay?" he asked again with genuine concern.

"I'm fine. I just need to get going."

"Will I be seeing you again…at services?" he asked, rising from his seat, hope sparkling in his eyes. "I'm new here. I haven't met that many people."

"Aside from the two hundred congregants and their families?" she answered.

"Women, I meant. *Beautiful* women. Single women."

Was Slick seriously trying to pick her up in a synagogue office? That was borderline creepy. Or maybe he was just lonely. She'd give him the benefit of the doubt. She could relate to lonely. Or horny. She could relate to that, too.

"You'll probably see me next Rosh Hashanah," she said, thinking he would unless she could concoct a believable excuse to skip services. "And what makes you think I'm single?"

He looked at her ring finger, her *naked* ring finger.

She hid her left hand behind her body and started to back away, like she was leaving the presence of a king. But he wasn't a king. He was a rabbi. Just a man.

Maybe it was her turn to put him on the spot. Because she was curious.

"As long as we're getting personal, may I ask why you left Texas if you were so successful?"

"Money isn't everything. I needed a change. And a wife. Actually, I was going to call you."

His remark stopped her in her tracks. "Call me? Why?"

"Your grandmother thought we'd make a good match."

"You knew my grandmother?"

"No, but your grandmother and mine were friends. They had our futures mapped out."

"Nana never mentioned you." She looked up into his green eyes and suddenly felt faint. In an earlier century, she would be having the vapors. She grabbed the edge of the chair for support. There were a lot of things Nana never mentioned.

Melody jutted out her chin. "I'm surprised your grandmother would want to set you up with an unwed mother."

"When you've experienced as much of life as I have, you learn not to judge."

"You don't believe in all that matchmaking hocus pocus, do you?"

"It's old-fashioned, I admit. But I don't discount anything. I believe there is such a thing as meant to be—*bashert*. I mean, I didn't believe it at first. But then I saw you."

She flushed.

"Loneliness can make a believer out of even the most devout skeptic," Slick continued. "When the person who knows you best says someone would be good for you, you tend to listen."

"I have a hard time believing you're lonely. You won't stay single for long in this congregation. I'm sure all the unattached women in the synagogue are standing in line to keep you stocked in briskets and matzoh ball soup."

"I'm not looking for a brisket, Melody." His serious eyes held hers, and he inched closer, coming out from behind the desk.

Soon he was close enough to kiss. She was tempted to taste his lips.

"All I ask is that you not reject me out of hand."

She edged away from him toward the door. He was radiating serious pheromones. In fact, his pheromones were humming. And hers were trying their darnedest not to dance to his tune.

"May I call you? We could go out to dinner or a movie."

"Katya keeps me pretty busy."

He reached into his pocket. "Here's my card. If you change your mind, I'll be here waiting."

Since when did rabbis have business cards? What was this world coming to?

Slick took her hand in both of his, and the jolt of their connection unnerved her.

She pulled her hands from his grip and rushed out of the office, without saying goodbye, before she drooled all over him, limp or no limp. Who cared? She was never going to see him again. Reaching the safety of the temple parking lot, she unlocked her car and plopped her head on the steering wheel, breathing heavily after that close call. Her heart was still galloping. She had to calm down. She was not going to fall for another inappropriate man. Last time she let her heart rule her head, nothing good came of it. Well, except Katya. How could she regret that union if the result was the best thing that had ever happened to her—her daughter.

And how could whoever had worn that tarnished charm also have a daughter named Ekaterina? That was Katya's name. She didn't pick it, like an apple, from some family tree. Or derive it from some DNA test on AncestorsAreUs. She didn't even know anything about either her mother's family or her father's, and even less about Katya's father's background. She had come to realize that everything the professor had told her about himself was probably a lie. The name was just a coincidence. Had to be. Katya was Katya. Her Katya, nobody else's.

If Nana was communicating from the great beyond, then why didn't she talk about her family while she was still alive? Or for that matter, why didn't she mention the hot new rabbi? Melody trusted Nana's judgment implicitly. Why did she leave her with all these unanswered questions swirling around in her head? Questions about Nana's death, questions about her heritage, and questions about Nikolai, her deceitful and unavailable Russian history professor. The answers had fallen into the big black hole of the universe, forever out of reach.

The interior of the car had grown warm from the beating heat of the sun. She started the vehicle and switched on the air conditioning. She'd be at her favorite jewelry store in time for her appointment with the appraiser. Maybe he could tell her more about Nana's necklace and the diamond-and-emerald piece.

Despite the rabbi's pronouncements, the charm was probably just a worthless trinket of no significance. When she got home, she was going to throw it in a drawer, forget about it, and file away all inappropriate thoughts of Slick.

The problem was she couldn't entirely discount fate and mysticism, but she didn't want any evil spells or spirits to mess with her or her child, the light of her life. And she was not Russian. That was preposterous.

She was just a plain old college dropout from Downingtown, Pennsylvania. The girl with the limp. Her surgeon said there was no physical explanation for the limp. Her orthopedist couldn't correct it. Her therapist suggested she might just be hanging on to her impediment as the last vestige of the accident, the last connection to her parents. That it was all in her head. She was not going to let Slick get inside her head. Or her pants. Been there, done that. Actions had consequences. Case in point—Katya.

She pulled up in front of Goldstone's Jewelers. A salesperson escorted her to a room at the back of the store, the appraiser's office, where he was waiting for her. Like Father Time examining an expensive watch, he looked like a wizened wizard with a jeweler's loupe strapped to a sheaf of white hair sprouting from his head, a caricature of his profession. He laid the timepiece on a velvet cloth at the edge of the table. Melody gave him both of the pieces she'd brought with her. He studied the charm with great interest. But what most excited him was the diamond-and-emerald necklace.

"May I ask where you got this?"

"It was in a safe deposit box I inherited after my

grandmother died, um, was murdered, actually."

"When I got the photograph of the necklace in your email, I did some research," the jeweler began. "A friend of mine who works at the US Geological Survey Library in Reston, Virginia, consulted the library's rare-book collection and found a volume called *The Russian Diamond Fund*. That book catalogs the imperial regalia of the Romanov family. 'Russia's Treasure of Diamonds and Precious Stones' is considered the most complete inventory of the Russian crown jewels. It includes a photo of an item that was not described in the official 1925 inventory of the collection. I'm certain this is one of the missing pieces. At any rate, it is no longer part of the Russian Diamond Fund jewels on display in the Kremlin in Moscow.

"This is a remarkable historical artifact," he pronounced, walking over to the fax to pull off the report.

"This was part of a collection fashioned specifically for Empress Maria Feodorovna of Russia, the mother of Tsar Nicholas II and wife of Emperor Alexander III. A piece that has been missing from the royal jewelry collection since the 1890s."

"Are you absolutely sure?"

"There's no doubt. There's not another piece like it in the world. It disappeared without a trace in the nineteenth century. The question is how did you get it—or rather, how did your grandmother come to acquire it?"

Shaking her head, she replied, "I have no idea."

"It's an heirloom piece. And the gold on this charm is from a Russian mine, most likely in Siberia. It is carved with the coat of arms of the Russian empire. The insignia indicates this was the property of the Tsar at the time."

The Tsar? She had barely started the diary. Maybe it held a clue about the origin of the necklace and, more specifically, Nana's origins, therefore her own origins. When she got home, if Katya was still down for her nap, she'd read the diary and find out what other secrets Nana had been keeping.

****

As Melody pulled into the driveway, she noticed Miss Cormier's black Lexus SUV was missing. She looked at her watch. They should be home by now. She tried reaching the nanny by cell phone, but no one answered. No answer to her texts. They could be at a nearby park, or on any number of errands. Or maybe they were out of diapers and Miss Cormier was at the supermarket to refill the supply. Miss Cormier was nothing if not efficient and as resourceful as she was sullen, aloof, and judgmental. But it was getting late. And Melody was getting worried.

It had been a long day. Her head ached and she was tired. She drifted off to sleep on the living room couch, cell phone in hand, hoping for Miss Cormier's return call. And she dreamed. It was a nightmare, really. She was on one side of a glass wall. Katya was on the other. She pounded on the glass and tried to break it. She could see Katya, but her child couldn't see her. However, she could see Miss Cormier, hovering over her daughter like a sinister crow. She shot off the couch like a rocket, heading for the tall, narrow multi-paned glazed windows that overlooked the driveway.

But this was no dream. The nanny's car was still missing. And so was her child. She couldn't help but be concerned. But her mounting anxiety had more to do with her intense distrust of the nanny, which was growing deeper by the second. She returned to the living room couch, thumbed through a fashion magazine and tossed it carelessly on the coffee table. She stared at the cell phone, but it didn't ring or buzz. Where could they be? Why hadn't Miss Cormier called? Had they been in an accident? An accident had changed the course of her life once before. Was history repeating itself?

She didn't like where her thoughts were going, but could the disappearance of both Miss Cormier and Katya be related to Nana's death? Maybe Katya had been kidnapped? Should she go to the police? Something was not right. She couldn't dismiss the helpless sense of danger invading her soul. But what evidence did she have? Her nanny was a meddling shrew? No, they would likely dismiss her panic and fear as typical of new motherhood jitters. Her babysitter was an hour late, and her mind went right to abduction. Maybe she was jumping to conclusions. The police could issue an Amber Alert. But what if it was a false alarm? Considering Nana's recent murder, it had to be more than coincidence. None of the TV network detectives believed in coincidences. And neither did she.

Melody picked up the phone to call Miss Cormier. Again. No answer. The next time she saw the nanny, she was going to give her a piece of her mind. And hand the insolent woman her walking papers. She was perfectly capable of protecting her own child. And she'd delivered her precious baby into the hands of a total stranger. A gnawing feeling of dread gripped her heart and squeezed it. She desperately missed her child. Would she ever see Katya again?

She was not religious, but she prayed for Katya's safe return. She must remain calm. There was nothing to do but wait for Miss Cormier to contact her or bring her daughter home. Better to occupy her mind with something else—Katya's father, Nikolai, who was never far from her thoughts.

Chapter Two

Slipping in and out of consciousness, slumped on the couch, Melody was suddenly overcome with exhaustion. Her mind was hazy. She could barely force her lids apart. When they fluttered open, Nikolai was standing there watching her.

Am I dreaming him? How long have I been asleep?

Nikolai was standing as close as he was when she had first seen him in her Russian history class. She'd been absently sketching her professor, staring at him dreamily, for months as he stood in the front of the room. One day, after class, he called her into his office and instructed her to close the door.

"You are one of my brightest students," he began. "I've had my eye on you from the beginning of the term."

And I've had my eye on you, she thought, stifling a giggle.

"Have you thought about what you wanted to do after you graduate?"

"Not really," she'd replied.

"I'd like you to consider graduate studies. I've got some material at my condo. I could bring it in on Monday or..." He hesitated. "If you had time to stop by this weekend..."

The professor was propositioning her. It's what she'd been waiting for.

"I could swing by tomorrow," she offered.

"Excellent. You won't regret it."

And she hadn't. She arrived at his door, and he drank her in with his eyes. He must have recognized a similar hunger in hers. He exhaled in anticipation, and Melody signaled her permission. He reached out, and once he touched her, once their lips met, it ignited a flame that could not be extinguished. Their joining was like a bullet train. Nothing could stop it. They'd lain naked, sated, cocooned in Nikolai's bedroom night after night for almost the remainder of the school year. They couldn't get enough of each other. Until she found out he was married, with a wife stashed away in a castle in Switzerland.

How could she have been so naïve? Just a silly college senior entangled in a hopeless relationship with her much older, more experienced professor. How many other female students had he seduced? He'd sworn he loved her. He never wore a wedding ring. When she discovered he had a wife—another of his spurned lovers couldn't wait to tell her about that and his prodigious sexual appetite—she dropped out of college. When Melody found she was pregnant, she confided only in her grandmother, never revealing the identity of the father, but Nana had guessed, correctly.

Melody never told Nikolai about the baby. She never wanted to see that man again. Never wanted him to know about Katya.

"What are you doing here?" Melody demanded.

"There will be plenty of time to talk later," Nikolai assured.

"Where's Katya?" she asked alarmed, fighting to stay awake. But her mind was muddled.

"Miss Cormier has gone ahead with Katya. She is safe away in Switzerland, which is where we're going."

Nikolai had told her about his castle in Zurich, above the city center, at the edge of the Adlisberg forest. From the pictures she'd seen, it was more of a fortress. The rooms had a fantastic view over the bay, the city of Zurich, the lake and the mountains, accessible to visitors only by a cog train. It sounded like a fairyland. Nikolai had promised to take her there one day. But not against her will. Could they be headed for Kinsky Palace?

"So, she *has* kidnapped my daughter. How do you know Miss Cormier, if that's even her real name?"

He folded his arms. "It is."

"But her stuffed bear," Melody protested. "She can't fall asleep without it."

"Katya will have everything she needs."

"She needs her mother," Melody pleaded, on the verge of tears. "She needs me."

"We hope you will cooperate," he said, his voice rising. "But if not, we still have Katya. It's up to you. You are now dispensable."

"What do you mean? Tell me what you are doing here!"

"Serving my country."

"Which country, The United States or Switzerland? Or Russia, perhaps?"

"I have many allegiances."

"How can I believe a word you say? You never told me you were married."

"You never asked."

"I was your student."

"My best student."

"You seduced me. You made me fall in love with you when all the time you were lying to me. You had no right. You were a married man."

"A marriage of convenience. It means nothing. I care very deeply for you. You must know that. I've been waiting for you for a long time. I tried to hold off. But I couldn't resist you."

"Are you even a count?" she wondered bitterly.

"I am."

Nikolai gazed at her with a distant look.

"What are you staring at?"

"You have to know you look just like her."

"Like who?"

"Like Anastasia. I saw it the first time I laid eyes on you."

Melody had noticed the resemblance, too, every time she picked up her Russian history book. The count was obsessed with Anastasia, the Grand Duchess of Russia. The way he spoke of her in class, with such longing for something that could never be, such nostalgia for lost hopes, crumbling tradition, Melody had taken a closer look, researching her, until finally she even wished she were Anastasia so Nikolai would fall in love with her. She even had her hair colored and styled to look like the Grand Duchess.

She loved paging through the grainy pictures of the Romanov sisters, always together, all dressed alike as if in uniform, the four of them lined up in a row, in their wide-brimmed straw hats festooned in silk, strolling in the garden or running up and down the deck of the *Standart*, the imperial yacht—a floating palace. She'd found the book hidden away in a drawer in Nana's room. When Nana caught her ruffling through the pages, she'd slammed the book shut and closed the door. When she'd checked back later, the book was gone.

Nikolai reached over to caress her cheek. She pulled away.

"Take the compliment, Comrade."

She recoiled at his familiar term of endearment. How many times had he called her Comrade while they made love.

"I want answers, now."

"We had to preserve the bloodline."

"What are you talking about?"

"You will understand in good time. Sleep now, my love," he soothed, and she felt a tiny prick in her arm.

She woke up later to a low humming noise. Her head was throbbing. Her mouth was as parched as the desert sand. She felt a distinct vibration. She looked around. She was on a private jet, above the clouds, thousands of feet in the air. Not a commercial flight. How did she get on this plane? Where was she going? There was one other passenger. He looked a lot like Nikolai. But that wasn't possible. Was this another dream? Was it really Nikolai? Her heart soared beyond flying altitude. Nikolai was taking her to Katya. She would soon be reunited with her daughter. The rocking of the plane and the rumble of the engine lulled her back to sleep.

Chapter Three

Kinsky Palace, Zurich, Switzerland

A jackhammer pounded away at her brain. She could hardly lift her head off the pillow as she struggled to surface from a deep, drugging fog.

She heard a man's voice somewhere above her. "You must be hungry. Breakfast is being served downstairs."

She was thirsty and starving, but breakfast was the last thing on her mind. The deep, penetrating voice registered on her personal Richter scale. It sounded a lot like Nikolai's voice. But she hadn't seen Nikolai in more than a year, since she'd left the university. Other than in her frequent and fevered dreams.

She'd forgotten how good-looking her former professor was, how mesmerizing.

"We've waited a long time."

It was Nikolai's voice again. Was she still dreaming? Or was she mistaken?

She pushed herself up from the bed. "What do you mean?"

"We've been planning this."

"For how long?"

"Decades."

"Why are you doing this?"

"Think of me as your protector. We did what was

necessary. I don't have to remind you of your Russian history."

She was puzzled. She examined the man. It *was* Nikolai.

She hid back under the thick, luxurious duvet cover. She was dressed in a silk negligee that she didn't own. How did she get into it? She was practically naked. Nikolai had seen her undressed, countless times, but that was before he had become a virtual stranger, her own personal Rasputin. The Devil himself.

"Why are you holding me prisoner?"

Nikolai whispered, "It is you who hold me prisoner." He skimmed his fingers across her cheek. She batted his hand away.

"So I'm free to go?"

"You have a choice to make. We're hoping you won't want to go."

"We? Who exactly is 'we'? What choice do I have? Why am I here?"

"The simple answer—to learn how to be an empress. All the rest in good time."

"What does that mean?"

"Oh, to be specific, lessons on comportment—how to walk and talk and act and think like an empress— wardrobe fittings, Russian language courses, Russian history studies, politics."

"And who's going to teach me?"

"Me, of course."

Nothing was making any sense. Melody looked around. The room was sumptuous, decorated like a palace, with ceilings that scaled the sky. Through the large picture windows the scenery was on parade—a winter wonderland. The snow was coming down in torrents. She could see the Dolder Grand Hotel in the distance. So, they were in Zurich, in the mountains. It would not be so easy to escape in this terrain at this time of year. Melody wondered where Katya was and how fast she could get to her. She didn't think Nikolai would hurt a child, especially if he knew Katya was his. But he didn't know, and she was determined to keep it that way.

Here she was, trapped in this fairy tale castle, with a handsome prince, well, a count, in a place she'd been longing to see, and it had turned into her worst nightmare.

"You're wondering where your daughter is." *Your daughter.*

Melody exhaled. So he doesn't know. But he has lied about other things.

"I want to see Katya," she demanded.

"If you do well in your lessons, that will be allowed. And don't even think of leaving us. We're high on a mountaintop, surrounded by soldiers with orders not to let you slip away. And, if I remember correctly, Comrade, you can't tolerate the cold."

The memory of Nikolai's strong hands rubbing her feet, keeping her warm, came unbidden. Of Nikolai massaging her leg, then running soothing kisses along the sore limb, assuring her she was beautiful and perfect in his eyes.

"Your leg. You will never make it. You'll freeze before you get ten feet. Katya will never survive."

She raised her hand to slap him, and he grabbed her wrist.

"Comrade," he whispered.

"Stop."

"You used to like it when I called you that. Remember our role playing?"

How could she forget? Their lovemaking was wild, and it was forever imprinted on her brain. It had been a long time since she had been with him that way, and she was still susceptible to his touch. Every pore of her body hungered for him. Still burned for him. Worse, he could read it in her eyes, the bastard. But she would no longer allow that. She would not be manipulated by a man who would separate her from her daughter.

"Take me to Katya, this instant, or I'll scream."

He laughed, settled himself on the bed, and pulled her on top of him, holding her in an iron grip around her waist.

Her breath came in uneven spurts. Trying to wriggle out of his grasp, to make a break for the door, she found he tightened his grip and her movements only further inflamed him.

"Easy, there, Comrade," he said softly.

She remembered how Nikolai used to calm her down whenever she was unsettled. He rubbed his fingers across her lips. That was how it started, and she knew what would follow.

If she didn't stop him this minute, he would not relent in his torture. He loved the power he had over her body. She could fight hard to escape him, but the harder she fought, the tighter his hold on her would become. She could scream, but who was listening in this remote hideaway? She hated him. She wanted to bite him. She didn't want to show her emotions, but her body would undoubtedly betray her, again. She could almost feel his satisfied smile. And she could feel something else, lower down.

She tensed against his bulging erection. He'd better not even try to go further.

"You have no right."

"I have every right. You left me, remember? Without a word. And it didn't take you long to replace me. I'd like to take you over my knee and…"

Melody tensed.

"Don't worry. I just wanted to calm you down. It has always worked in the past when you were being obstinate. If I release you now, will you promise to behave and not to bolt?"

Grinding her teeth, she seethed, "Where would I go if I did?"

"That's my girl."

"I'm not your girl," she spit. But her mind was still muzzy. He must have drugged her again. Otherwise, she never would have allowed him to…overpower her this way. But she couldn't deny she had missed the nearness of him, his musky smell, the tone of his voice.

He nuzzled her neck in a familiar way, licked it and kissed it, then gnawed on her skin as if he was going to take a bite, branding her like a vampire, but slowly he released his hold.

She jumped out of his clutches.

"It would be easier if you just relaxed and enjoyed our time together."

She heard a low growl and was surprised to find it was coming from deep inside her. He had reduced her to a mewling animal. He always had that effect on her. He knew her body as well as she knew it herself. And he was taking every advantage.

"I expect you to be dressed and downstairs for your first lesson." He paused for emphasis. "Your majesty."

She wanted to claw his eyes out, but she lacked the strength and coordination.

"Don't call me that."

"What else would I call you?"

"You could try Melody."

"That's not even your real name. The name on your birth certificate is Maria Tatyana."

The man was a serial fabricator. So why should she start believing him now?

"How could you possibly know what's on my birth certificate?"

"I know everything about you. Have you actually seen a copy of your birth certificate?"

She hesitated.

"I can show it to you. It's all part of the public record, or the record that will be made public once you are coronated."

Coronated? The man was delusional.

"Surely, your grandmother told you—"

"She never talked about life before the accident. When I questioned her about my parents, she always changed the subject. She was reluctant to talk about them."

"So, we will go back to your legal name, Maria Tatyana. That is what everyone will call you when you are introduced into society. Now get dressed. There's a gown on the chair. I trust it will fit."

His certainty implied that he knew her measurements. He should. He had touched and tasted every inch of her body.

He turned abruptly, stood, and walked away.

She wanted to strangle him. Did he think she would just follow his orders like a lackey?

But the dress was magnificent. Made for an empress. Nikolai was right. It was a perfect fit. Had he purchased it at a vintage shop? She looked at the French designer label. This was no knock-off. It was authentic. This could have been Anastasia's dress. How had Nikolai managed to procure it? She wriggled into the dress and looked in the mirror. The gown was fashioned in the empire style, of the finest gray silk. A woman came into the room to do her hair. When she had finished her handiwork, Melody had to admit she did look like…the Grand Duchess Anastasia, complete with elbow-length white silk gloves.

Yes, that's where she'd seen this dress before. In the history books. In one of Nikolai's history books. He was a foremost authority on Russian history. And on Anastasia. She walked over to the closet. There were more original gowns hanging there. Somehow, he had managed to salvage or duplicate the Grand Duchess's wardrobe.

She would follow his rules until she could find Katya, and then they would escape, somehow, as soon as she formulated a plan. In the full-length gown, she glided down the staircase like a queen, the folds of the fabric disguising her limp, until she came face to face with her captor.

"Where's Katya?" she demanded again, glaring at him as she paced the floor relentlessly.

"We would never harm Katya. She is as precious to us as she is to you. As you are to us."

"Then you do have her." His silence all but confirmed the fact.

"Calm down."

"I won't calm down until I see my daughter."

"All in good time. Trust me."

"That's the last thing I will ever do. Why are you doing this to me, to us?"

Nikolai scowled. "You are thinking only of yourself. You must learn to think of others. Of the Russian people. Your people."

"They are not my people," she said hotly.

"You can continue to fool yourself. But it is time you faced facts. You do not understand the changes that are happening in Russia. Economic pressures are mounting. The Russian economy is weakening. The Russian Federation is imploding. The price of oil is dropping...so the implications for the oil market are immense. The value of Russian assets is diminishing. Since the end of the Soviet Union, the oligarchy has been crushing the spirit of the people. Russia is less than a superpower. Greed has seeped into the system like a sewer and contaminated it. The society is corrupt and has been for some time."

"Why should I care about any of that?"

Nikolai continued as if she hadn't objected. "If you read the newspapers, you'd know that the relationship between Russia and the U.S. is deeply strained. The legislature is pushing through with new sanctions. Maria Tatyana, are you even listening? Oh, that's right. You don't care for politics. Well, that, my dear, will have to change after the revolution and the formation of the New Russia."

"And will the New Russia be the same as the old Russia?" she challenged. "Corrupt at every level? Another failed experiment? Yes, that much I know."

"No, the change will be major, transformative, exciting, and nonviolent. Thomas Jefferson said, 'Every generation needs a new revolution.' "

Melody tugged at her gloves and held them in the air by her fingertips for effect.

"Wasn't it Joseph Stalin who said, 'You cannot make a revolution with silk gloves'?"

"Touché. Hopefully, we've learned from our mistakes."

"You sound very sure of yourself, but Russia already has a leader, one who seems to have no intention of going anywhere."

"That's because we're prepared," Nikolai said. "We've secretly infiltrated the SVR and the FSBI. We control the armed forces and the private security armies of the Russian oligarchs, including the current president. And our people control the banks."

Nikolai paraded around the room and continued his monologue. She pretended to listen but was interested in one thing only—finding her daughter and escaping.

"The country is ripe for another revolution. The people are not satisfied with the status quo. The United Russia Party is losing popularity. They only got elected by a narrow margin. And you could hardly call that a fair election. There was only one viable candidate—The Bear—who has been in power for what seems like an eternity. And now his legislative changes have extended his term. Muscovites are fed up with their government and are finding ways to express their frustration. Uprisings are becoming more widespread and visible. Every day you read about all the pro-authority backlashes."

"Now you sound like a pompous professor."

"Rightly so. You have a lot to learn."

Melody covered her ears with her hands.

"Russia is a corrupt, autocratic kleptocracy," Nikolai expounded, parading up and down the room, hands clasped behind his back. "The oligarchs have all the dollars and the dachas, acquiring artwork and private islands, while the ordinary people fight to make a living. We will restore the monarchy, and you will be the face of the New Russia."

Melody threw back her head and laughed. "The face that launched a thousand ships? It will take more than my face to turn the Red tide. If I remember my history lessons correctly, the people hated the Tsar. That's why he had to abdicate. And when he did, the people danced in the streets, rejoiced at the end of a three-hundred-year dynasty. Why would they welcome back someone who looked like the daughter of the Tsar? Your beloved Anastasia."

"It's a dynasty that never should have ended," Nikolai said. "With your help, it will be just a century-long pause in history."

"What does all that have to do with me or Katya?"

"Everything, if you would please pay attention and stop your childish displays."

"You can't just bring back the Tsar like a Houdini because you will it so, and how do you know the people even want another Tsar?" Melody asked.

"The Tsar and his family were officially rehabilitated as 'victims of political repressions,' " Nikolai noted. "Attitudes have shifted. The people want to restore the Romanovs. They want to go back to the way it was. People are nostalgic about the past. They're filled with regret and what-ifs. They wonder what would have happened if the King of England had saved his cousin when he had a chance, or at least rescued the

Romanov family. If Lenin had demonstrated an ounce of humanity and not ordered them to be executed. The beautiful daughters could have been married off to royalty. Bred another generation of Romanovs. We've been waiting a century. The time is now."

"And how do you intend to pull off this violent coup?"

"Oh, it won't be violent at all. Our people have access to the Big Bear's bank accounts, personal and corporate. Once we present him and his cronies with the alternatives—leave the country with their necks and net worth intact, or have their private wealth drained and leave the fate of their private parts to the people—it will be an obvious choice. You might remember what happened to Mussolini and his mistress at the end of the second world war. They were literally torn apart, strung up for all the world to see."

"Fight or flight?"

"Exactly. And these bullies are nothing but cowards underneath."

"And then do you and your people plan to funnel the country's vast wealth into your own pockets and personal bank accounts the way the revolutionists did with the Tsar's money and the oligarchs continue to do?"

"No," Nikolai objected. "It will finally be a fair system."

"In theory at least. If you can be believed, which I doubt. But what part can I play?"

"The leading role."

Melody shook her head. "Why me?"

"You are a direct descendant of the last tsar of Russia, the result of an affair little-known but well documented. The royal blood of Tsar Nicholas II flows through you and now your daughter. You are the true heirs to the Romanov throne. You have the power to change history."

"I don't know where you get your information," Melody argued. "I am certainly not Russian. And surely, there are other Romanovs in the world who could assume this public face."

"Of course. I have Romanov blood running through my veins. Every family tree boasts of Romanov relations. Even the British royal family has Romanov ties. But those Romanovs are on the radar, in the spotlight, under constant surveillance. Not many know of your existence. Your grandmother did an admirable job of hiding you in plain sight, locking you up in a fortress in a small Pennsylvania town, of all places. We finally tracked you down when you registered for the Russian Studies degree program at University of Pittsburgh. You represent a new world of possibilities. Yes, there are dozens who would love to take your place. But no legitimate male-line heirs. There are descendants of the Tsar's sisters, but you are our last direct link, our best hope, you and Katya, of course. So, it will be either you or Katya who wears the crown. Your choice."

"So, if this tale is even true, we are to give up our lives because of an accident of birth?"

"It will be worth the sacrifice."

"That's easy for you to say. I don't have any grand aspirations. I just want to live a quiet life with Katya."

"You have a responsibility to your people."

"My only responsibility is to Katya. And I find it hard to believe that, even under the worst conditions, the Russian people are suddenly just going to revolt."

"There is nothing sudden about our movement," Nikolai reasoned. "We have been planning and hoping for this day for a century. We have a network of supporters and sympathizers all over the world. People waiting to rise up in literal and figurative terms. We have allies in place in positions of power. People who are prepared to give their lives, though threatened with imprisonment or worse, for our cause, if it comes to that. Just waiting for our signal."

"How do you know this?"

"It's our job to know this. You and Katya will be the new Russian royal family. And if you agree, I could serve as your consort, to guide you through this perilous process."

"Ah, now I see what's in it for you. This is all arranged so you can grab power. You need me. I hate to disappoint you, but I would never have you as my consort or anything else. And anyway, you're married."

"As it happens, that will not be a problem. My wife and I have a very open relationship."

"Oh, so you can stay married to her and have me on the side. Like when we were at the university. How can I believe anything you say?"

"You'll have to trust me."

"As it happens, I don't. And even if I were to agree, it sounds dangerous. I would never put my daughter's life at risk."

"Of course, there are risks, but there is no longer another option. We have to move quickly."

"What is the big hurry?"

"When your grandmother was murdered, we were motivated to move up the timetable."

"What does my grandmother have to do with this?"

"Everything. She is your link to the past, to a line of mothers and daughters who were born to wear the crown. We have just been waiting for the right moment in history. This is our moment."

"Who exactly are you? Modern day White Russians?"

"What do you really know about White Russians?"

"I prefer margaritas."

"You're smarter than that. You know what I mean."

"Only what I learned from you."

"Yes, of course, you were my star student."

"Teacher's pet," she managed dryly. This reminder of their time together ushered in all the memories, good and bad. She was so naïve, so in love—until Nikolai's deception split her world apart.

"It's true, we're descendants of the White Russians," Nikolai explained. "Now we're called Guardians."

"Guardians of the Galaxy?" Melody laughed.

"Guardians of the Romanov legacy. A responsibility I take very seriously. A responsibility I was born to uphold."

"The scenario you're describing sounds like an expensive proposition. Who will fund this pseudo revolution?"

"In a word, gold. The Lost Gold of the Tsar. We've been looking for that shipment of gold bullion for a century. It is part of the Russian Empire's gold reserves."

"Well if it hasn't been found by now, perhaps it never will be. Or maybe, it was never there in the first place."

"That's where you're wrong. There are rumors the gold was on a train on the Trans-Siberian Railway, transferred from the Kazan Bank vaults and heading east to the port of Vladivostok, when it crashed into Lake Baikal. Some thirteen crates disappeared without a trace. Other sources place it in Omsk or Irkutsk. It might be buried in the woods or a forest or hidden in a monastery or a church basement or in a tunnel. But it's more than a legend."

He paused and looked at her pointedly. "We think you might know the location."

Melody began to back away out of the room.

"Where are you going?"

"To find my daughter. And you can't stop me."

As she ran, she collided with Miss Cormier and felt a sharp sting in her shoulder. She collapsed into Nikolai's arms.

"No need to be so brutal," he admonished as she began to slip out of consciousness.

"We have to take precautions until we know where her loyalties lie," she replied. "The silly girl doesn't even believe who she is. She doesn't deserve this honor."

"She'll find out soon enough. She'll cooperate, once she appreciates the importance of our mission."

"This is our moment," Miss Cormier echoed. "We have no time to lose."

"*We* know that. She will soon understand her place."

"I don't know what you see in her. My Katya is the one destiny has chosen."

"She's not *your* Katya," Melody wanted to scream

but her mouth wouldn't move. She could hear the nanny and the count's words, but she couldn't respond. Her body was immobilized.

"Your problem is, you're in love with a ghost," Miss Cormier stated.

"You have eyes, don't you?" Nikolai accused. "Look at her. She is Anastasia in the flesh. How can you doubt it?"

"I have a feeling her *flesh* is all you are concerned with, Nikolai. I see the way you look at her. Like a man with a fever. This is no time for lust. Remember, you are not just playing a role. This is for real. Don't get caught up in fantasies and frivolous talk of love."

Nikolai grimaced.

"She is forbidden fruit. You shouldn't be laying your hands on her. Rotten fruit will spoil. If you continue to let your emotions get in the way of your duty, I will report you."

"You forget your place," Nikolai yelled, still cradling Melody in his arms.

"And you forget yours. No one cares if we accomplish our goals with the mother or the child. If you choose her, you will be on the losing side. The child is young. We can shape her."

"I will make Maria Tatyana understand. She will be with us."

"You care nothing of our mission. You're in love with the idea of the Grand Duchess. This has become personal for you."

Melody was back in her bed, listening to warring voices—hers, his. None of it made any sense in her current state of mind. There was only one thing she was sure of. She must get to her daughter.

"Katya." She sobbed, trying to claw her way to consciousness.

"She's not ready to listen," Miss Cormier said. "That's why I had to put her under again."

Melody was hallucinating. The nanny assumed the form of a slithering snake, her tongue darting in and out, a hungry serpent capable of consuming her and swallowing Katya whole.

"Katya," she screamed, trying to raise her arms, but they might as well have been stuck in cement. "No!"

"We don't have time for her drivel."

"Katya," she screamed again.

Though she was dazed, she recalled a conversation with the nanny while she was still breastfeeding.

"It's time for Katya to go on the bottle. I don't believe in coddling children. She will need to be on her own soon."

The nanny had been in on the plot from the beginning. Her need to wean Katya from the breast was all part of the plan to separate mother and child. How could Nana have known? She had died before Katya was born. She tried to imagine her grandmother's face. But all she could see was Katya.

When she came around again, she was dressed in her gown, Anastasia's gown, lying prone on the bed.

"Now, will you come down to breakfast?" Nikolai pleaded. "You've slept through the night."

"Do I have a choice?"

The count's eyebrows rose. "You have to eat. And there's no reason we can't still be friends. We can be more than friends, if that's what you wish. That would be my preference."

"What I wish is to see my daughter."

"I'm afraid that's not possible at the moment."

"How long have you been targeting me?"

"*Protecting* you."

"Do you deny you made me fall in love with you?"

Nikolai hesitated. "Do you remember the first time we made love?"

Her face colored.

"It was the night of the lesson I taught about the execution of the Tsar and his family. Among the tears and the disbelief, you captured my heart. That was not supposed to happen. Yes, I was supposed to put you under our protection, and only that, but instead, I fell in love with you. We had a lovely year together, and then you left me, just disappeared, and got yourself pregnant. We had to find another way in. To ensure your loyalty."

"And Miss Cormier, was she part of the plan?"

"Yes."

"Did my Nana know?"

"Of course. She put us off for the longest time with one excuse or another. You were too young. You were not ready. We couldn't believe our luck when we found your college application. I arranged for the teaching position and made sure you were in my class. Loving you was not part of the plan, but I couldn't help myself."

"I didn't know our love was on a timetable. So, it wasn't fate, as you kept saying."

"I would never leave anything so important to chance. I was protecting you from them."

"And who exactly do I need protection from?"

"The people who would see you and Katya dead—like your parents."

Melody sat up and leaned against the satin headboard.

"My parents died in a car accident."

"It was no accident. You were supposed to die in that crash with them. After their deaths, your grandmother refused to cooperate with the Guardians. She hid you away. You, and now Katya, are the true living heirs to the Romanov throne, as was your grandmother. But she was past her time. The Russian government and their spies know all about you and want you dead. They would kill you if they could find you. Execute you like they did the Tsar and his family, without a second thought. Like they killed your grandmother."

"What? The Russian government killed my grandmother?" Melody's outrage was followed by tears that would not stop. Suddenly, her grandmother's death was beginning to make sense. Nikolai put his arm around her shoulders to comfort her, but she swiped it away.

"Anti-Guardian factions in the government, yes, and you were the next target," Nikolai explained. "That is why we had to extricate you and Katya. You are on a hit list. You would never see it coming. Perhaps it would be a needle with a poison tip, or radiation, or you would just disappear. That's why your grandmother tucked you away in Downtontown and changed your name all those years ago."

"It's *Downing*town," she corrected.

"As I said, Downingville."

"Downing*town*."

"Either way, it's an inconsequential speck on the map. We think our network has been compromised somehow. That someone in our organization is working with them. Your grandmother thought she could protect you. But the opposition is too powerful."

"And who will protect me from you?"

"I would never hurt you."

"It's too late for that."

"History repeats itself," Nikolai said.

"What do you mean?"

"You will learn soon enough."

She stuck out her lower lip. If he wanted a fight, she would give it to him. She would do anything to protect her daughter.

"You still don't trust me."

"Is it that obvious?" She paused. "I have a lot of questions."

"And I have the answers, if you will just be patient."

Nicholas handed her the diary.

"Where did you get that?" she asked, arms crossed, facing him.

"In your purse. I've skimmed through it. You'll find some of the answers in here."

She dismissed him. "You had no business going through my things. And besides, this was written a hundred years ago. Who is this girl to me?"

"Just read it. I will have your breakfast tray brought up."

Melody glanced out the window at the endless blanket of snow covering the frozen ground. They might as well be in Siberia, she thought. She had nowhere to go and was getting nowhere with Nikolai. She had nothing but time on her hands and everything to lose. Eventually, she would rescue Katya. For now, she must appear to cooperate, although everything in her screamed rebellion. She could be patient. Settling on a lounge chair, she opened the diary from her grandmother's bank vault and forced herself to start reading the tale of a Katya from long ago, hoping to find the answers she needed.

Part Two

Ekaterina's Diary
Omsk, Siberia, to St. Petersburg*, Russia, 1891-1918

"Those who cannot remember the past are condemned
to repeat it."
~Spanish philosopher George Santayana

*Renamed Petrograd in 1914

Chapter Four

Omsk, Siberia, 1891

I was born in Siberia, in a town called Omsk. Nothing much happened in the harsh winters and frozen tundra of my birthplace. My most exciting adventure was when I turned seventeen and traveled with my parents to the capital city of St. Petersburg. My mother had a special dress made for me, fashioned of the finest gray silk, worthy, she said, of a Grand Duchess, since I was to be presented at court to Tsar Alexander III. My father ran the mine that supplied the Tsar's gold, and he was bringing the latest shipment of the precious metal to the palace along with some of the Empress's jewels, brimming to the edge of the chest, straight from the bank vault in our hometown. It was an important mission. My father was one of the Tsar's top advisors— his eyes and ears in this far-flung place. The Tsar trusted my father and depended on him because he spoke the truth when the Tsar's other advisors often held back.

"You remember my daughter Ekaterina," said Papa when we arrived at the palace at the appointed time.

"Of course," said the Tsar as he appraised me. "She's a real beauty." In turn, he presented me to his wife and to his children—Nicholas, Alexander, George, Zenia, Michael, and Olga.

The Grand Duke, Nicholas, turned his head toward me, and his eyes met mine. I curtsied and looked away.

"Nicky is just home from a world tour," the Tsar announced.

Nicholas moved closer to me. I drew in a breath and faced him.

"This can't be little Katya."

I smiled at him, dipped my head, then looked back up into his eyes.

He took my hand in his. His hand was warm and fit perfectly into mine, like the tumblers of a lock clicking firmly into place. My heart leapt; my body overheated like a furnace, though the material of the dress was fully breathable. How many times had I dreamt of this moment, of reuniting with Nicholas, or Nicky as everyone called him, as I used to call him when we roamed the halls of the palace? I was touching the future Emperor of All Russia—the heir to the throne. No wonder my hands were shaking.

"It's Ekaterina," I corrected, blushing. Did he think I was still his little playmate? I was seventeen years old.

"The same little Katya who used to chase me from room to room at Gatchina Palace until I caught her?"

I smiled and forgave him for continuing to call me by my childhood nickname. So, he remembered me. I had never forgotten him. How could I? He wasn't particularly tall, his shoulders were narrow, and he had short, stocky legs, but he was very handsome and charming. One of the most eligible bachelors in Europe. He had just turned twenty-three. I'd met him again in 1884, when I was ten years old, at his coming-of-age ceremony at the Winter Palace. He hardly remembered me then—a stinging disappointment since I was nursing a serious crush on him.

All hope of my unrequited love sailed away later that year at a wedding in St. Petersburg, when the sixteen-year-old Tsarevich met the bride's younger sister, twelve-year-old Princess Alix. Five years later, in 1889, the Princess visited St. Petersburg again, and rumors of a more serious attraction flew. They'd had occasion to meet at other family events. However, Princess Alix was a devout Lutheran and refused to convert to Russian Orthodoxy in order to marry Nicholas.

Nicholas's voice pulled me out of my reverie.

"My little Katya has blossomed into a beautiful woman."

I blushed. *His* little Katya? I wasn't used to compliments. Men's eyes frequently leered at me when I went to bring Papa his lunch down at the mine. Disrespectful eyes that undressed me as I passed by. With one exception, Pyotr, who stared at me longingly, his puppy-dog eyes following my every move. His feelings for me were on display, like sugar cakes in a bakery window. His raw emotions could be detected in his voice and his touch when our fingers brushed as I delivered the lunch pail to take to my father. But his hands were rough from mining. He was not bad to look at, and I was flattered, but he was not Nicky. There would be no other man for me.

"Come, walk with me," Nicky said when the Tsar began discussions with my father about mine output, disease outbreaks, and the riots and strikes breaking out across the land over the famine that was ruining the crops. My mother flashed me a disapproving look, which I chose to ignore. I was seventeen, after all. I didn't need a chaperone. I was a fully grown woman. Decorum or not, who was I to refuse the Grand Duke?

"Your daughter has grown into a beautiful girl," noted the Empress, Maria, as we walked away. "No wonder Nicholas has taken an interest in her. He was determined to marry that German/English princess. And my son is very stubborn. But she is a strange one. She doesn't have the soul of a Russian. And she won't change her religion, so that obstacle can never be overcome, although he continues to correspond with her. Our Nicky is a hopeless romantic. If Ekaterina can help him forget the princess and his current mistress, I'm all for the diversion."

My mother pursed her lips. She would never say it out loud, not in front of the Tsarina. It was impolite. She bit her tongue. She was no doubt thinking, *My daughter is nobody's diversion.*

Nicholas kept my hand tucked protectively in his as we strolled down the corridor, out of earshot of our parents, and out of sight.

"Come to my room tonight," Nicky whispered. "There is something I want to show you."

"I love surprises," I said, smiling.

He massaged my hand with his thumb in a circular motion, and I thought I would melt into a puddle of feelings. Nicholas took his leave, and my eyes followed him down the hall. My heart leapt. I felt feverish. My mother was hot on my trail. I had a secret. I hoped she didn't notice.

"Ekaterina, what were you thinking, wandering off alone with the Grand Duke that way?" Mother scolded when she finally caught up. "He has a reputation with women, and not a good one. The ballerina is his flavor of the month. And then there's Princess Alix. He only has one thing on his mind. Don't disappoint me. Come along, at once, and stop this foolish behavior with the Grand Duke."

When Omsk freezes over, I thought to myself.

Then I laughed. Omsk was permanently frozen over.

Frankly, I didn't care what anyone thought. I was unleashed, ready for the thrill of the spring thaw. I wouldn't miss this assignation at any cost.

****

"You came."

"I wasn't aware you could disobey an order from the Grand Duke," I said lightly, playing the sophisticate, not revealing how difficult it had been to evade, and lie to, my parents.

Nicholas chuckled. "I wish all women were as compliant as you."

Everyone knew about his torrid affair with the ballerina. But she wasn't here now.

"What does a young lady such as yourself do for fun in the frozen tundra?" he asked, walking me down a dim passageway lit only by hall sconces.

"Read, mostly."

"Ah. So, you are studious." He stopped and lifted my chin with his finger. I shivered at the nearness of him and hungered for more of his touch and his smell, so welcoming, like a cool pine forest.

"I like to have fun," I protested, biting my lip, trying to remember the last time I'd had fun in Omsk. Fun was in short supply in my desolate corner of the world.

He placed his hand softly on mine and pulled me farther into his quarters. I could smell the tang of wine on his breath. "And what does my Katya do to keep warm on those cold, cold nights in Omsk?"

"My bed is piled high with quilt blankets and furs," I mused brazenly. Living in the frozen tundra, I hadn't had much practice with flirtation.

"So is mine. We could snuggle under them to keep out the cold," Nicky said, with a twinkle in his eyes.

I blushed, screwing up the courage to ask about his latest lover. "What about your ballerina? Everyone knows you are involved with the prima ballerina Kschessinskaya."

Nicky frowned. "Old news. That affair is over."

Everyone, even in Siberia, was also talking about how Nicky wrote letter after letter to the ballerina, who was jealous of his attentions to Princess Alix.

"And everyone is talking about how you fancy Alix, the Princess of Hesse-Darmstadt," I continued. "That you may marry her one day."

"I wasn't aware that my life was an open book." Nicholas scowled, clasping his hands behind his back. "My parents would like that, certainly. They think they can arrange my life. Who I choose to love or not to love is not their business. And besides, they are not overly fond of Alix. I am my own man."

"Who would be free to love another woman?"

"If I choose. Pay no attention to rumors. Don't believe everything you hear."

"I would like to hear the truth." I hoped I didn't sound too demanding. But I had to know where I stood, what I meant to this man.

"The truth is neither woman holds a candle to your beauty."

Nicholas's hand wandered to my shoulder. I

shivered and sprang back.

He cornered me against a wall.

"You are super-sensitive. No need to be nervous. You are safe with me. Now close your eyes."

I did as ordered. But my heart was thudding. From fear or anticipation?

I heard a clicking sound like a box opening. Then I felt Nicky's fingers fasten something cold and heavy around my neck.

"Now open them." He guided me to a gilded Venetian mirror in the hallway.

The sight in the looking glass stole my breath. "It's stunning. This is one of the pieces my father brought from the bank vault to the Tsarina."

"Yes, I know. And my mother gave it to me to give to the woman of my choice when I marry. I choose you."

I couldn't believe what I was hearing. Could it possibly be? I was certain this piece was meant for Princess Alix as an engagement present. It was so extravagant. It was worth a Tsar's ransom.

"To my parents, I'm a pawn. But I am a man and I won't be manipulated."

"You should be free to be your own man," I agreed, fingering the exquisite piece.

"You see. I feel as if I could tell you anything and you would understand."

We approached his bedroom. The two guards out front leered at me and hailed Nicky in a mock salute. They were Nicky's age, and by the looks that passed between them, they were obviously close compatriots. How many times had they seen their friend bring a woman into his bedchamber?

"Keep your eyes and your thoughts to yourselves," Nicky warned the guards, as he waltzed me in, closed the door, and pulled me toward his bed.

I stumbled, and he caught me in his strong arms.

"Don't be frightened. No harm will come to you in here."

My nerves were on display. How unsophisticated I must seem to him.

"Why are you giving me this necklace? Surely, your mother meant for it to go to Princess Alix."

"She'll never miss it. She has dozens of diamond brooches and rings. She'll think it's been lost."

He lifted the heavy piece, accidentally brushing his fingers across my breast, dipping them down the front of my dress, like a spider weaving his silky web.

I dared not move. Was his touch accidental? Or was he trying to seduce me? Should I move his hand or let his fingers continue their journey? I shivered. But the last thing I wanted was for him to stop.

"How does that feel?"

Was he talking about the weight of the necklace on my chest? Or his touch?

"The necklace," he said, smiling as if he were a mind reader. "And all that goes with it. Don't worry. We're quite alone."

"Except for the guards outside the door."

"Sergey and Ivan? They're my guardians. I trust them with my life. They're more like brothers than bodyguards. I can't go anywhere without them, ever since the assassination of my grandfather. So you see, I'm trapped. We're trapped."

I remembered that day ten years ago. My family and I were in the capital when Tsar Alexander II,

Nicholas's grandfather, was assassinated and Nicholas, who witnessed the attack, became heir apparent when his father ascended the throne. Nicholas and the rest of the family had been in the Winter Palace in St. Petersburg, but for security reasons, the new tsar and his family relocated their primary residence to the Gatchina Palace, outside the city, where I had first met Nicholas. I'd been dreaming and daydreaming about him ever since. Weaving fantasies about our life together. Silly, unattainable dreams. But what if...?

He placed his hand fully on my breast. I panicked. But at the same time, I couldn't deny I liked the solid weight of his fingers splayed across my chest.

"Your heart is hammering like a captured dove. When I saw you this evening, I thought I'd never seen anything more ravishing. I love beautiful things. I knew I had to have you, and I generally get what I desire." He pulled me into his arms and stared soulfully into my eyes.

"Come over here by the firelight. Let me see how the necklace sparkles."

When I did, he pressed his lips to mine and held them. Right then and there I knew I would pay the highest price for his gift. It was a price I desperately wanted to pay. Whatever that entailed. I had never been with a man. My virtue was about to fly out the palace window. And I didn't care.

Instinctively, I pressed myself against him and wrapped my arms around his neck. This might be my only chance to let him know how I felt. He pulled his lips away, but only for a moment, and then increased the pressure when I groaned for more. He smiled and reached down the front of my dress again, first encircling my nipple with his finger, then pulling down the fabric of the gown for better access, wetting one nipple, then the other, with his tongue. My breath caught in my throat. No man had ever taken such liberties. No man had ever touched me that way before. But this was Nicky, my Nicky. And it felt so good to be near him.

He pulled me back toward the bed, tightened his hold, and slowly pulled down the rest of the fabric of my gown and then slipped off my undergarments. He weighed my breasts in his hands like they were bits of gold on a scale, like I had seen Pyotr do down at the mine.

"You are a perfect fit for me," Nicky whispered hoarsely. Then he suckled me, like I had seen baby pigs suckle from their mothers on farms in Omsk, tugging on my nipple until I felt a flood of moisture in my private parts. His hand fitted over my bottom.

"You are ready, my love. Primed and ready."

"Ready for what?"

"I thought you liked surprises. Just lie back while I pleasure you." He laid me gently back against a pillow. His hand trailed from my stomach down to my leg in a slow, tortuous trail.

Is this how love feels? I wondered. If so, it was glorious. I was sure I was in love. But was he in love with me?

"You are so sweet and innocent. Let me taste you." Was he going to go down my body with his mouth? Yes.

My jaw dropped in shock like a gasping fish pulled out of a lake. Could this be the way between a man and a woman? Was this part of making love? Nicholas was so much more experienced. But surely not this?

"I c-can't, I mean I c-couldn't," I sputtered.

"You must obey your master," he cajoled.

Did young men and women of the court behave like this? It was outrageous. My mother would be horrified. But I am seventeen. It is my body. Did the ballerina do this for him? Certainly not Princess Alix. But Princess Alix was not in the Grand Duke's bed. Neither was the dancer. I was. In the end, I followed his direction as if in a fog.

"Your body is spectacular. You were made for me. Have you ever been with a man?"

I shook my head and pushed him away. It was all happening so fast. I wasn't sure what was coming next.

"As I thought." He halted his seduction. "A bad case of nerves. Perhaps you should have some sweet wine first."

"I don't drink."

"Just one glass," he coaxed. "You'll like it. I promise."

"Just one, then," I agreed reluctantly, hoping this interlude would bring me to my senses. He reached over to a side table, filled a cut-crystal goblet, and brought it to my lips. He cradled my head as I drank, his other hand never leaving my body. I drained the glass, and the liquid warmed my insides. Nicky was right. It was sweet and delicious. Another rite of passage I had been missing.

"Now another," he whispered. I drank from the wine cup in his broad hands. He removed the cup from my mouth, placed it back on the bedside table, then positioned me among the feather comforter and fur blankets.

"Are you relaxed now?"

"Mmm," I purred.

"Now touch me, down there."

My eyes widened. "I...I..."

"Katya," he whispered, coaxing me in an exaggerated warning.

I let out a deep breath and followed his orders.

"Yes, yes," he sighed, his voice strangled, his eyes rolling back. "Just like that."

In turn, he placed his hand firmly over the center of my private parts. "How does that feel?"

It felt like heaven, and I couldn't speak.

Then he covered his body with mine and sank his manhood into me, withdrawing and re-entering in a continuous rhythm. I winced.

"It will feel uncomfortable the first time, but then, the next time, you will grow to like it."

So there would be a next time?

When it was over, we relaxed against the pillows.

"How long are you staying in St. Petersburg?"

"A month," I reported.

"Then you and I will be spending the next month of nights together, cocooned in this cozy room, our private paradise. Would you like that, my little one?"

That sounded wonderful. For one month, the world would drop away, and everything would be blocked from my mind. Everything but Nicholas.

"But my parents..."

"You'll come to me at night when they're asleep."

And that's how it began. That night we talked of everything and nothing. He made promises to write when I was gone, and to see me. Promises of love. Promises I believed.

Outside, I could hear the guards talking in low voices. I could barely make out their words.

"The Grand Duke's little playmate has grown up quite nicely."

"Filled out quite a bit," the other joked.

"No wonder Nicky is interested. She's a delicious morsel."

"She's warming his bed well, I imagine."

"She's a virgin, I'll wager."

"How do you know?"

"The walls have ears, and when she screams his name…"

"I wouldn't go spreading that around unless you want to lose your ears or your head."

"What happened with Kschessinskaya?"

"Yesterday's news. They had a lover's spat. She stopped talking to him when he went to Germany to see Princess Alix. He's written letters, but she won't answer. He's still obsessed with Princess Alix, longs for her. But a man of his voracious appetites doesn't like being alone, and Princess Alix is in Germany. He has to occupy his time. The winters are quite cold in St. Petersburg."

"Surely, Kschessinskaya realizes Nicky can't marry her."

"I hope this peasant girl realizes it, too."

"She's hardly a peasant. She comes from a prestigious, wealthy family."

"A *Jewish* family. The future Tsar of imperial Russia cannot marry a Jewish girl even though the family is the closest thing we have to Jewish aristocracy."

"She's hardly a princess. And she's going back to

Siberia. Although she's a real beauty. She will service him, and he'll tire of her like he does all the others. She's just a diversion."

"The Tsar and Tsarina don't have much use for Princess Alix, but Nicky is strong willed. No one will force his hand. In the end, he will marry his German princess."

"Personally, this wench is more to my taste. Perhaps I can have Nicky's leftovers. The princess is too bony by half."

"But he can have his fun on the side before he has to do his duty. His father will be on the throne forever."

The men laughed and shouted in tandem. "Long live the Tsar!"

Chapter Five

Omsk, Siberia, 1892

Outside, the snow was falling, steady and silent. When was the snow ever *not* falling in Omsk? It was a scene so familiar it invaded my dreams. Inside, my mood was just as bleak and lonely. My heart was frozen over. Although nothing stirred in the garden, my body was beginning to show signs of new life. I waited in vain for a message from Nicky, sending for me, but no letter came. If I could get word to him that I was carrying his child, I knew he would rush to my side, make me his wife.

While I waited, my mind was filled with treasonous thoughts. Nicky in bed making passionate love to his ballerina, or making practical marriage plans with Princess Alix or some other appropriate princess of another royal kingdom. He could have his pick of European princesses. So why would he settle for me, a commoner? All I knew was that I was truly in love with him. He'd claimed to love me. He'd gifted me with a precious necklace to cement his commitment. But as the weeks slipped by without a word from St. Petersburg, I had to face the truth. I was just a plaything, while Nicky was in a holding pattern between his mistress and his duty to marry someone worthy of his position. Or any desirable woman at court who was in proximity and caught his fancy.

I knew the Grand Duke was a prize every woman coveted. His sexual appetites were legendary. I was just one naïve woman in a long row of more experienced women, felled like a tree in the forest, a mere conquest. Perhaps even now he was laughing about me with his comrades, his *Guardians*.

When I first discovered I might be pregnant, I convinced myself it was just a stomach sickness, hoping that was the explanation. But when I failed to get my menstrual flow for two months in a row, and the vomiting arrived with the dawn every morning, I knew something was wrong. I knew the signs. I touched my swollen breasts and my sore and sensitive nipples. My clothes no longer fit my body, so I wore heavy outer garments, ostensibly to fight off the cold. Those signs confirmed what every farmer's wife in Omsk knew. I was with child. Nicky's child. The child of the Grand Duke of Russia. And there was no one I could confide in. I didn't really have any friends. My parents had kept me isolated for my own protection. I wasn't allowed out by myself in this rough mining town.

What was I going to tell my mother? Could I tell her anything? And the thought of my father finding out—that was incomprehensible. What could I do? I couldn't just leave Omsk on my own. Not in my condition. I would bring shame on my family. I couldn't imagine how my parents would react. Would they throw me out or forgive me? What I had done was unforgivable. I didn't have money of my own.

I could sell the necklace, but then I might get arrested for theft. And the diamond-and-emerald necklace was a constant reminder of the love I still felt for Nicholas. I would not easily part with it. I hid it among my undergarments, taking it out to admire it when I had a moment to myself. Tried it on, wearing only the diamonds and emeralds against my naked skin, remembering how and where Nicky had touched me. Imagining he was there in my bed. The necklace was exquisite, but when I wore it, all the memories of our month of nights cocooned with Nicky, listening to him whisper words of love, came flooding back.

That brief period of ecstasy was followed by a long period of silence. When we left St. Petersburg, no more words were spoken. No promises were kept. No commitments fulfilled. I was hopelessly in love with the Grand Duke, but he held out no hope. I knew now the affair was only that, an affair. Were his words of love all lies? Was he bound by tradition to marry someone else all along? The heir apparent could never marry a non-royal.

I lay in my bed naked, daydreaming of Nicky. In my colorful dreams, I floated above the palace in a gossamer gown, every inch a Grand Duchess. We walked hand in hand throughout the gardens, rode horses like the wind, spent endless nights of love on the cool, silky sheets in Nicky's bedroom.

"Wake up, sleepyhead. What's wrong? Why are you still in bed? You didn't come down to breakfast." At the sound of my mother's voice, I was jolted out of my reverie. The thought of food made my stomach heave.

I threw back the quilts and coughed up some bile.

Mother took one look at my newly rounded naked body and shook her head in disbelief. The changes in my body were finally on display for her to see. There was nowhere to hide.

"What—I—this can't be—Ekaterina, are you with child?"

I hung my head as I wiped away the bitter greenish-brown fluid with the coverlet.

"How did this happen? When did it happen? Who is the boy? Who did this to you? Was it one of the miners? Were you attacked?"

I shivered with cold and shame and could barely choke out the words.

"Who have you been with?"

I considered lying, but that was out of the question. My mother knew me too well.

"It was N-Nicholas."

My mother shook her head in disbelief. "The Grand Duke? How is that possible?"

"I love him."

"You love the Grand Duke?" She looked at me in puzzlement as if that scenario were as likely as the possibility of catching a shooting star.

I sighed. "I've always loved him."

"Why is this the first I've heard of it? When did this happen?"

"When we were at the palace."

My mother rose in anger. "Right under our noses? That was months ago. How could you behave that way? Like a common camp follower!"

I sprang back like she had slapped me.

"He said he loved me," I protested.

"He loves you? Then why does he continue to bed his ballerina? Why is he promised in marriage to the German princess? We're not so far away from St. Petersburg that I don't hear the rumors."

"He gave me this," I said, opening a drawer, rustling through my lacy garments and thrusting the diamond-and-emerald necklace into my mother's hands.

Her jaw dropped. "My God. What are you doing with this? This belongs to the Tsarina. We brought it to her for the Grand Duke to give to his future bride."

"He gave it to me as a token of his love."

"And you fell right into bed with him. The Empress will think you stole it. What are we going to do?"

My mother choked on her anger. Tears pooled in my eyes.

"How will I tell your father?"

"Don't tell Papa," I pleaded.

"Don't tell Papa? Of course I will have to tell him. He will have to fix this. The Tsar trusts him. If they find out—"

"Maybe Nicky will marry me."

"Maybe the winter snow will melt in Siberia and it will be endless spring. And rubles will fall from the sky. Are you out of your mind? He must marry a royal. Surely you know that."

"But it could happen."

"The Grand Duke marry a non-royal, a Jewess, at that? You know how the Tsar feels about Jews. Your father was an exception, but now? How can we explain the unexplainable? Your father will lose his position, his freedom, maybe his life."

My mother paced the room, refusing to relinquish her anger. "Go back to bed," she directed. "Cover yourself. Does Nicholas know?"

"No. We have not been in contact since we left St.

Petersburg. I was sure he would send for me."

"Foolish child. You sold yourself for a bunch of diamonds and emeralds?"

"It wasn't like that. I love him."

"Does anyone else know?"

I shook my head.

"I blame myself. I tried to protect you by keeping you away from boys, and you crawl into bed with the first man who comes along. You gave up your most priceless gift."

"That's not how it happened. You don't understand."

"Understand this, young lady. You will stay locked in this room until we come up with a solution to this problem," she ordered, holding the necklace in her trembling hands. "No one must find out."

As soon as she left, I broke down in tears, all hope extinguished, buried in mounds of grief as heavy as the snow surrounding our house.

Between whimpers, I heard shouting voices that shook the house to its very foundation. Papa's. Mama's. After about an hour, the raised voices died down. The silence was even worse. They had come to a decision. What would they do to me? What would become of me and my child? Would we be cast out in the cold?

What seemed like hours later, my mother swept into the room like a winter storm.

"Get dressed," she commanded.

"Nothing fits," I said softly.

"Squeeze into something. Fix yourself up. Pyotr is coming to call. We are going to see the rabbi."

"The rabbi? Why is Pyotr coming over?"

"To ask for your hand in marriage."

"Mama, no, you can't do this. I don't love Pyotr."

"Love has nothing to do with it. Pyotr works for your father. He will do anything your father tells him to. He is being given a nice promotion at the mine and a handsome sum in gold."

"You're selling me to Pyotr?"

"You are in trouble. By God's grace, Pyotr is in love with you. Have you not noticed how that boy's eyes follow you whenever you come into sight? How he moons over you whenever he's around? He is willing to overlook your little *problem*. Do you know how lucky you are? He's not who your father and I would have chosen for you. But we are out of options. And we are out of time. You must never tell him about the child's paternity. Tell no one."

"I can't marry Pyotr," I screamed. "I don't love him."

"What does love have to do with anything? The matter is out of your hands. Your pregnancy is beginning to show. People will talk. You will marry Pyotr or you will leave this house and never return. And you will be an obedient wife to him in every way. Is that understood?"

The meaning of my mother's words was crystal clear. I would be giving my body to a man I didn't love. Pyotr wasn't Nicky. How could I do the things I did in bed with Nicky with Pyotr? But I would have to. If I married him, I would no longer be in control of my own body. That was the bargain.

"Where's my necklace?"

"In safekeeping. Let's not mention it again."

Without the necklace, there was no tangible proof that Nicky and I had been together, except for the baby growing inside me.

****

I was seated in a chair covered in precious furs to keep out the chill in the air. But no number of furs could keep out the cold or cover up my shame. Mother had arranged my hair and pinched my cheeks to make my pale face look presentable before Pyotr.

"Ekaterina," Pyotr said, looking at me with adoration, holding a fistful of flowers he must have picked on the way to my house. Flowers in winter in Omsk? He must have searched far and wide. Or he must be a wizard to have plucked signs of spring from this vast frozen wasteland.

"How did you happen to find flowers this time of year?"

"These wildflowers grow year 'round. When I saw them, I thought of you."

"Because they're wild?"

"Because they're lovely, like you."

"They're beautiful. Thank you." I looked down. "Pyotr, you don't have to do this."

"I *want* to marry you. When your father told me you were in love with me, I felt like I held the moon and the stars in my hand. I've loved you from the moment I saw your face. I had no idea you felt the same way. It is more than I could have hoped for."

"And did he also tell you that you are getting damaged goods?" I pointed to my swollen belly. It seemed enormous to me, like it had grown immensely since that morning.

"Don't ever say that. You are the purest, most beautiful girl I've ever known."

"I'm hardly pure. And will you still love me when I

grow as big as a house?"

"Yes, because there will be more of you to love."

"You're crazy."

"Crazy in love. You're shaking."

"It's the cold."

My parents came out of their bedroom in their finest clothes and walked toward us. Pyotr lifted me to a standing position and tenderly wrapped my hands in my fur muff. The two of us followed my parents to the tiny synagogue down the road, like a funeral party or a condemned man marching to his doom.

The rabbi was ready. He performed the ceremony, saying the words according to Jewish culture. We stood under a makeshift *chuppah*, the wedding canopy, sipped the wine, recited the blessings. Pyotr stomped on the wine goblet as dictated by our tradition. The shards of broken wedding glass symbolized the tempering of joy, to be mindful of the sadness that exists in the world. The fragility of human relationships. My life was certainly filled with sadness. My hands shook when I signed the *ketubah*, the marriage contract. But there was no fanfare, no music, no guests to celebrate with us, just secrecy and shame. I wondered how much the rabbi had been told.

Pyotr, standing close, dressed in his finest garb, wrapped in a prayer shawl, looked proud, like he had won the greatest prize on earth. I was in shock. But at least my child would be protected from gossip. I wondered what kind of lover my new husband would be. When he touched me, would I imagine it was Nicky touching me? If my husband was inexperienced and clumsy, I would teach him where and how I liked to be touched. Nicky had prepared me to please a man, but could I do what we did with another man?

Father shook hands with Pyotr to seal the deal and officially welcome him into the family. I stood there, frozen in place. Mama pushed me toward my new husband, no doubt anxious to get rid of me. She had put out some delicacies at the synagogue. I was too traumatized to eat. It had all happened so quickly.

My parents took their leave. I was left alone with my new husband to start a new household, a new life. I was not nearly ready.

Something pulsed inside my head. I was wobbly and feeling nauseated.

"Are you ill?" Pyotr asked solicitously.

"I want to go home," I admitted. He led me away from the synagogue. But something was not right. We were walking in the wrong direction to the wrong side of town. And then it dawned on me. I could not go home. My new home was with Pyotr.

****

Pyotr carried me over the threshold, and then it was just the two of us alone in his house. I looked around. It was a spare dwelling, much smaller than our grand estate. Pyotr looked embarrassed as he saw his home through my eyes.

"It's not much," he admitted. "I will buy you a nicer house, a house you deserve."

Pyotr was wrong. I didn't deserve anything, though he could have afforded to move me into a dacha on a country estate, with all the gold my father must have pushed on him. I was resigned. So it was not the Winter Palace. Is that what I expected? There was no cook; there were no maids. This was not the life I had imagined.

"There will be plenty of room for our new family," he assured.

Our new family. Talking about the baby that obviously was not his was awkward. But if Pyotr wanted me, the baby and I came in a package.

Pyotr leaned over and kissed my lips, tenderly, then more urgently. It was nothing like kissing Nicky. Nicky had taught me well during our month of nights, so I knew what was coming. Life as I knew it was over. I was facing a lifetime prison sentence. Pyotr was now the master of my body. My jailer. I could only hope he would be merciful.

But try as I might to remain stiff, my body responded to Pyotr's touch. My breasts were so large they almost overflowed my gown, and when he pressed my body against his, he sighed, and I felt his manhood expand.

"Pyotr," I called his name, rubbing against him. I would give him what he wanted, what he expected. That would be the way of it, then. I would whore myself to my husband. Perhaps I was no better than a camp follower. I certainly felt that way.

My husband stared at my nipples straining against the fabric of my gown, and I took his hand gently and brought it to the swell of my breasts. He touched them as if he were handling precious jewels. He was entranced. He was ecstatic, blinded by love. I knew how it felt to be in love, and that is the way my new husband looked at me.

As he lay me down on the bed and began to kiss me again, I could tell he wanted more. If I was honest, Pyotr was not hard to look at. He was big and muscular. He had to be, to work in the mines. And he was smart.

My father said so. I slid my arms up and down his rippling shoulders. He took that as a sign I was ready. He rose from the bed, removed his clothes, and folded them neatly on a chair. Then he returned and began to undress me, planting kisses up and down my body, molding my breasts in his hands like he was weighing precious ounces of gold.

He rubbed his rough hands over my nipples until they hardened, then took one in his mouth, then the other. Soon, I would be suckling a baby. Was he thinking of that as we made love? By the look of him, he was beyond thought. He touched my swollen belly reverently, then kissed it. Then, he moved his hands lower, readying me with his fingers, one, then another. So, he came to our marriage bed experienced. I wondered who he had lain with.

What was I expecting? Would he be gentle? If he wasn't, there was nothing I could do. I could hardly complain to my mother. I could not play the frightened virgin. Pyotr knew I was no longer a virgin. Evidence of that fact was on parade between our bodies. Would he take his time with me? Would I ever get used to his rough, sunburned hands against my soft, smooth, pale skin? He seemed oblivious to the contrast. He was in ecstasy.

He drew back his fingers, wet with moisture.

"You are ready for me," he whispered, bringing my hand to his engorgement.

I did not want this man, but he wanted me, and my body betrayed me.

I remembered how Nicky had instructed me to touch him, just so, and I performed all my wifely duties. And Pyotr loved it. When it appeared he could no longer hold his seed, he cried out my name, shuddered, and plunged into me again and again. And I cried out, not wanting to lose control but losing it anyway.

He lay there half spent, looked into my eyes, rubbing his hands across my breasts, circling my nipples in a gentle, lazy rhythm, then slid his hands down across my stomach and lower, making me come again.

"Was it good for you?" he whispered.

My breathing slowed almost to a stop. "Couldn't you tell?"

"I'd hoped to be the husband you desire and deserve. But never did I imagine you would be so responsive, so spontaneous. And I love the way you pleasure me, wife."

I could tell he wanted me to say more. How did he rate compared to my first lover? He wanted reassurance, like any man, I suppose. How would he feel if he knew my first lover was the heir to the Russian throne?

"Do you want to talk about it?" he coaxed.

I absolutely did not.

"No," I said simply, holding back the tears, but failing.

"Please, don't cry. Was it so bad, then?"

I licked the tears from my face.

"Did he hurt you when he forced himself on you?" What tales had my father told? What lies had my mother spun?

"It wasn't like that."

"I would never hurt you, never force myself on you."

"I know."

"It will get better," he promised, releasing me. Words I'd heard before from Nicky.

He respected my wishes. He couldn't compare to the way Nicky made love. There was no magic, no delight, but he was a considerate lover. He did his best to satisfy me. It could have been worse, much worse. He could have been cruel. My father could have chained me to a beast, who forced me to do his will, hated me for carrying another man's child, made me grovel, whipped me, because he'd have a right to, as his property, ushering in a lifetime of misery. But Pyotr would never whip me. He worshipped me. He was a gentle man. Grateful for any bit of attention I paid him. He had given me a home when no other man would want me.

"I still can't believe you're mine," he whispered. "Have I made you happy?"

I raised my hand to his cheek. "Yes."

He covered me with his body. "Then let me make you happy again, my love."

He stroked me softly with his hands, his tongue teasing its way down my body, planting gentle kisses, then more amorous ones, suckling at my breasts, his manhood pressing against me. Grunting, pawing, putting his mark on me, making me his, plunging into me, harder and harder, trying to erase every trace of the man who came before him. But he could never make me forget.

Making love to Pyotr wasn't unpleasant. I squirmed and sighed, on cue, even groaned, screaming out his name, and then he was inside me again, planting his seed. But his seed would not grow because another man has been there before him. He had to know that. He placed a possessive hand gently over my stomach, marking his territory.

That was to be the way of it, then, the way of women with men, down through the centuries. Settling. My body would be available to him day and night. My new husband could not get enough of me, and I was not in a position to refuse him. Whenever he had an urge, I would be there to satisfy him. But there would be only one true love in my life. I imagined I was making love with Nicky when I was in Pyotr's bed. But that betrayal had to stop. Pyotr deserved more. He deserved a devoted partner. And that is what I vowed to become.

Chapter Six

Omsk, Siberia, April 1894

There was no denying it now. All of Russia was abuzz with the news. It was with great fanfare that the engagement of Grand Duke Nicholas II to German Princess Alix of Hesse-Darmstadt was announced. That's when I knew I had lost my Nicky forever. I hated the German princess, just like most everyone else at court. Even Nicky's parents had issues with her. They said she was aloof—a German, after all. She couldn't be bothered to learn our language. But I realized the real reason I hated the woman was because she was marrying the man I loved. Gossip around court was that it was a true love match, that Nicky has been madly in love with his bride for years, which threw me into a great depression. I refused to be coaxed out of it. Did he ever think of me, yearn for me at night? Did he miss our lovemaking? Did he know I had married? That I had his child?

The one true light in my life was Alina, whose name translated to "beautiful, bright." Giving my baby the best name would give her the best start in life. Alina was every inch a royal—her father's daughter. I thought Nicky would be proud if he knew she was his. How I desperately wished he could see her. I felt sure he would dote on her. But she had been cheated out of her birthright.

****

November 1894

Later that year, after the passing of Nicky's father, Tsar Alexander, left his twenty-six-year-old son Nicholas II as Emperor of Russia, his wife, Alexandra Fedorovna, became the Grand Duchess and eventually the Empress. I'd seen a picture of the wedding and the coronation. Whenever I felt forlorn, I imagined myself in Alexandra's place, in the traditional dress of a Romanov bride, looking up at Nicholas, handsome in his Hussar's uniform. And I thought about what might have been. In my mind, I was the woman walking down the aisle of the church with Nicky, being coronated.

But I had to face facts. Nicky had planted his seed inside me and then planted me firmly in his past. Not one visit. Not one letter. I thought of him every moment, dreaming or awake, and every time I looked into our daughter's classic Romanov eyes and fine Romanov features. What would he think if he knew I had given birth to a daughter, *his* daughter?

How many times had I thought of running away, of going to him, telling him? But there was no hope. I was married now, and so was he. He was untouchable, beyond my reach.

****

November 1896

Tsar Nicholas II and Empress Alexandra had their first child, the beginning of their dynasty. A daughter. Only that was not Nicky's first child, though he didn't know it. I'd hoped the Empress would be barren, but she proved to be more than fertile. Three more daughters followed. But no heir to the throne. The

German princess needed a son. And when a son finally did come along, there was something wrong with the Tsarevitch. It was a little-known fact, but my mother and father were privy to court gossip, so they revealed that the royal baby's blood was poisoned with a strange blood disorder, inherited from his mother.

I am sure I could have given Nicky all the perfect sons he wanted. While Alexandra was occupied creating a family for Nicholas, I was also busy performing my wifely duties. Pyotr was insatiable in the bedroom. He kept me permanently pregnant. I could hardly complain. He was a devoted father to my daughter and to our three sons. Pyotr loved my daughter as if she were his own. If he played favorites at all, my daughter was his. And for that, I was grateful.

Chapter Seven

Pyotr spoke often of the District of Alaska, formerly Russian Alaska. He brought up the possibility of moving our growing family there, far away from the temptations of my first lover. He probably thought the more often he regaled me with his tales and dreams of moving to that frozen destination, the more my resolve to stay in Russia would weaken. If I had a choice to move anywhere, it would be to a warmer climate, not a pseudo-Siberia.

I was lying in Pyotr's arms, weary after making love, when he whispered my name, so as not to wake the newest baby, who peacefully slumbered in a makeshift cradle in our cramped bedroom, or the other children snug in their beds in the new outer room Pyotr had added to the tiny structure we now called home. Pyotr was doing well working for my father, but he had big plans to make a success on his own. He wanted to make a better life for me and the children.

"Did you know, Katya, that Russian explorers discovered Alaska in 1732? The Russian merchants were drawn to Alaska for the walrus ivory and the valuable sea otter fur, for which they traded with the local people. Trading was done by the Russian-American Company, the RAC, which arrived in Alaska in 1799. The RAC was started by adventurers—Russian businessmen, courageous travelers and entrepreneurs."

His not so subtle message to me: He would make a fine adventurer. He also fancied himself a courageous traveler and an entrepreneur.

Pyotr reported that the company controlled all of Alaska's mines and minerals. It even had its own flag and currency—leather "marks," privileges granted to the company by the imperial government. The tsars and their family members were among the RAC's shareholders.

"At first, the RAC brought in enormous revenue," explained Pyotr. "But by 1819, they were close to bankruptcy."

"Mmm," I mumbled, trying to feign interest as my eyes fluttered. I had already heard the history of the RAC a dozen or more times. By then I could repeat it by heart. But my husband never tired of talking about it.

"In 1867, Russia sold the Department of Alaska to the U.S. for $7.2 million," he continued. "Imagine that. Selling this valuable land was madness. I will never understand how the imperial officials could have given up such a choice parcel. They say it was an honest deal, but I think the Americans stole that land from us. Russian Alaska was a center of international trade before we sold the territory. In the capital, Novoarkhangelsk, merchants traded Chinese fabrics, tea, and even ice, in great demand by the Southern states before the refrigerator was invented."

"No need of a refrigerator in Omsk." I laughed, nestling deeper under the fur coverlet, trying to block out the words. But Pyotr was relentless. He kept up his familiar monologue.

"Then, wouldn't you know, in August 1896, gold was discovered on a tributary of the Klondike River—

Rabbit Creek. That started the Klondike Gold Rush. My contacts report that Americans are already finding numerous gold deposits underground in the area. Huge deposits. Katya, are you listening? The Americans are mining gold in Alaska." The American discovery of gold in Alaska caused Pyotr's eyes to glitter in the dark.

"Pyotr, I'm too tired for another history lesson. The baby will be up soon and eager to feed. I need my sleep. And there are the chores."

Pyotr lightly touched his fingertip to my nipple and came away with a tiny drop of milky moisture, which he brought to his lips. "I would be eager for the breast too."

"Pyotr," I scolded, raw from feeding the baby. Between satisfying the constant demands of the new baby and the other children, I was wrung out, exhausted, drained dry.

So were the Russian people. Four years of war had taken its toll on my family and had devastated families across the country. When the war started, citizens patriotically rallied around their tsar. Then the sinister influence of Gregory Rasputin over the tsarina wreaked havoc on the royal family's reputation. Nicky was isolated at the war front. Alexandra, with Rasputin, was ruling the home front. Rumors were that the tsar was ineffective. Military disasters and poor morale among Russian soldiers resulted in desertion and widespread chaos. Food and fuel were in short supply, made worse by the cold.

But my parents remained true to the tsar. Workers went on strike, including workers in my father's mine. The Provisional Government and then the Bolsheviks finally wrested control from the 300-year-old dynasty and implemented communist rule. Perhaps leaving the country was the best solution. I was losing my resolve to stay in Russia. Nicky seemed as far away as a distant star to me.

"I could get a job managing the gold mines in Alaska," Pyotr whispered insistently. "Katya, Katya, did you hear me? Katya, my love, are you awake?"

"Yes, my love."

Pyotr pulled me close to him in the narrow bed, the moonlight spilling onto the wooden floors.

"The doctor says you are healed, strong enough to…"

"Make love?" I smiled. "I would welcome my husband."

"Katya, I love you so much. I sometimes wake up and stare at you and the baby and the other children, and I can't believe how lucky I am."

"I am the lucky one to have found you, my darling."

He positioned me beneath him and kissed me hungrily.

"I feel how much you want me." I laughed, touching his engorgement. It didn't take much to arouse my husband. He was an ardent lover.

"When we get to Alaska, I want to build us a great big house and fill it with the laughter of our children."

"That sounds wonderful. But we already have a houseful of children. It seems I get pregnant with just one look."

"I think it took more than a look, my love. Let me show you exactly how it happened."

"As if I could ever forget."

"A repeat performance, then?"

"How many repeat performances does this make?"

"Who's counting?"

Pyotr moved inside of me quietly and pulled out, making me moan, then thrust back in, then slid out. I clung to him, twisting my body and legs to keep him inside of me a moment longer.

"Pyotr," I panted. "Please."

"I'm right here, my love," he said, pulling out again, his thrusts stronger and longer, doing something amazing with his fingers to make me buck, riding me until I could no longer take it. I cried out, and he covered my scream with his hand.

"Be patient, my pet, and hush. You'll wake up the dead."

"Pyotr, if you do not come back to me this instant, I think I'm going to die of wanting you."

Then he rammed into me and we both exploded in ecstasy.

We fell back against the bed and stared up into the darkness, holding hands.

Chapter Eight

Omsk, Siberia, July 1918

Someone was knocking on my front door. I awoke in a daze from another dream about Nicky. He was trying to get to me, but he couldn't reach me. The pounding on the door got louder. It took me a minute to get my bearings. Pyotr was working at the mine. The children were with my mother. This was my quiet time. When I became melancholy, the family wisely left me alone with my thoughts and fancies.

Pyotr attributed my dark moods to my latest pregnancy. I hardly remembered a time when I wasn't pregnant. My body was fertile, and Pyotr loved my body, so pregnancy was my natural state. I waddled over to the door and opened it. A chill slithered into the room. Who could it be? Following the revolution, a knock on the door frequently tolled trouble.

"Ekaterina?"

The man standing before me looked familiar. I had seen him somewhere before, but I couldn't immediately place him.

"You don't recognize me?" The man smiled. And then I knew.

"You were at the palace, guarding the bedroom door."

"Yes. I am a friend of Nicky's. His guardian."

My body was shaking. I was lightheaded. I was going to—

"Madame," the man shouted, catching me before I collapsed in his arms. "Come, let's get you settled." He half walked, half carried me to the couch, where he placed me down gently. He was big, so I felt like a feather in his arms, despite my weight.

"I didn't mean to frighten you. I am Sergey Sergeyevich. I came with a message for your father about a shipment of gold. But I—also came to apologize to you."

"Apologize? For what?"

"For many things. For the way we treated you at the palace all those years ago."

I colored when I remembered the guard's leering looks and the sneering comments I'd overheard.

"You were the Tsar's lover. But what you didn't know was that you were his greatest love."

"I don't understand. Nicholas didn't love me."

Sergey shook his head. "But he did. He wrote you letter after letter for months, hoping for an answer. And when he learned you were married—hastily—he knew it was over. That you could never be together."

"He wrote me letters? But I never got them."

"His mother instructed me not to deliver them, but here they are."

Sergey took a stack of letters tied with a blue ribbon from his jacket pocket and handed them to me. "He learned of your daughter and wondered if she might be his. He asked me to find out the truth. I traveled here before, although you did not see me. I watched you with her. I reported back that she had to be his. She is the image of Nicky, of his daughter,

Anastasia. She has your good looks, but there is no doubt, she is a true Romanov."

My hand flew to my mouth. If I hadn't already been seated, I would have fainted.

"If he loved me, and he knew about our daughter, then why didn't he send for me?"

"It was better that you were hidden away in Siberia. You know how the court would talk. And his wife would never allow it. The Tsar's life is not his own.

"His mother knew about Nicky's romantic tendencies. She said, 'Let him write to her, pour his heart out, but never deliver the letters. He will think she's forgotten him, and he will move on.' She knew your love could never be. It would dilute the bloodline. She thought you were a foolish girl, another in a long line of conquests. But she came to realize how important you had become to her son."

"All these years. He hasn't forgotten me?" I was buoyant with joy.

"Never. His love for you was real. And now, well the reality is that he is a prisoner. I am his guardian, and I can no longer guarantee his safety. Czech regiments are approaching the city, but I fear they won't arrive in time. He wanted to ensure that you and his daughter were protected. He can't save his family, but he sent me with enough funds to guarantee a new life for you and his daughter. I swore to protect Alina with my last breath. To be her Guardian."

A steady stream of tears slipped down my face.

"The country is no longer safe for you. They are rounding up Romanovs in Russia. If they should discover your daughter's paternity, her life would be in danger. I've explained all this to your father. He has his instructions about protecting the Tsar's gold. If he were to fall into the wrong hands, they would torture him for what he knows. And you and your daughter must leave Siberia at once. And for God's sake, never tell anyone about your daughter's lineage. It would be a death sentence."

I blew out a breath and wiped my forehead with the back of my hand.

"This is all too much. How is Nicky? How are they treating him?"

"I would give my life for him, but I can't get near him. My sources say his keepers are vicious. The guards who were sympathetic to the Tsar's family have been replaced. The ones holding the royal family now will kill him, the Bolshevik dogs. It's only a matter of time. One day, we will avenge his death. But there's no time to waste. You must leave at once. You must protect his legacy. Fifty-three of the Romanovs were living in Russia when Nicky abdicated. Eighteen more were murdered and thirty-five escaped. Thirty-six if you include your daughter."

I thanked Sergey. Pyotr would get his wish. Now we had enough money for passage to the Alaska Territory. I would have to live on the other side of the earth from my true love, but I would follow his wishes.

"I apologize," said Sergey, who wore the look of a defeated soldier. "I've regretted my decision and my role in this deception. I want to make it right."

****

"Mama, who is that man Grandpa was talking to last night? It was late when he arrived, and I barely got a proper look at him before we went to bed."

"But he got a good look at you. Grandma told me about the way he was staring. That he almost exploded in flames."

"Mother."

"He is rather handsome, isn't he?"

Alina shrugged her shoulders. "I didn't notice."

"Then why are you wearing your best dress, a sheer white dress that leaves nothing to the imagination? As if you were offering yourself to him on a silver platter. And why have you brushed your hair and let it fall down around your waist like a water nymph? And where are your shoes, young lady? Is that lip color you're wearing?"

"I grabbed the first thing I saw in the closet," Alina protested.

"Alina, I wasn't born yesterday. I was once young and in love like you."

"How can I be in love if I haven't even formally met the man? And I don't even know who he is."

"Sometimes all it takes is one look."

"Is that the way it was for you and Papa?"

"I fell in love with your father the moment I saw him," Katya said, which was both the truth and not the truth. "Your grandfather is thinking of going in with that man on a venture. He has offered to provide an infusion of cash and the necessary contacts when we get to Alaska."

"So he will be around for a while," Alina stated, tossing her head back like she could care less. "And will he be staying with us? I need to know so I can avoid him."

"He'll be staying nearby at your grandfather's, but yes, he will be around. In fact, I am anxious for you two to meet. You are of marriageable age. And I don't see any men who have sparked your interest. Try to be on your best behavior."

"Humph. So I'm supposed to be compliant while you palm me off to the highest bidder."

"We are not palming you off. Just offering choices. You have been rather picky. Some would say a handful. How many marriage proposals have you rejected?"

Alina pursed her lips.

"Too many to count. You're beginning to get a reputation. You scare off every man who comes near you. You're not getting any younger."

"I'm not ready to marry. I don't need a man masterminding my life."

"Marriage doesn't mean being masterminded. Not if you're in love. It's more of a partnership."

"Besides, he's old enough to be my father." Alina pouted.

"Not quite. He is older, but you have to admit, he wears it well. And there's something to be said for an experienced man."

"Mother! I want to do something with my life besides getting married."

"You can be married and do something with your life. The two are not mutually exclusive."

"Like you did?"

"I raised a family, and I'm very happy with my life. Oh, here they come now. Your grandfather will introduce you."

Alina stood rigid, hands folded across her chest, barefoot, legs spread apart in a hostile stance before the two men in front of her.

"Alina, I'd like you to meet Sergey Sergeyevich.

Sergey, this is my granddaughter, Alina."

Alina remained in her fixed position. She deliberately did not extend her hand.

"Alina," her grandfather scolded. "Where are your manners?"

"Well, I guess if you've already bought and paid for this man, I suppose I should be gracious and *grateful.*"

"Alina," Katya reprimanded gently.

"Here, then," said Alina, thrusting her hand toward the stranger. "If I must."

Sergey took her hand in his and bent at the waist to kiss it. An electric charge pulsed through her body.

"Aren't you Prince Charming," she scoffed, trying to tamp down the heat that emanated from his touch, inflaming her to the core.

"Alina," her mother said. "What is wrong with you? Please don't be disrespectful."

"Have I done something to offend you?" Sergey asked, staring at her like a hungry wolf.

Alina swirled around to face their guest, throwing her hands above her head as if in a sultry dance.

"Take a long look at the goods. Do they meet with your approval?"

Sergey's green eyes sparkled, and he mouthed to her alone, "Most definitely." To her grandfather, he said, "It's all right. I like a woman who speaks her own mind."

"It makes no difference to me what you like, sir." Alina turned and pranced out of the room.

Katya shook her head. "I apologize for my daughter."

"Don't apologize. She is even more beautiful than I

had imagined. Untamed and temperamental. Every bit a royal. I imagine she has some very passionate opinions. Does she know who she is, who I am, that I am her Guardian?"

"No," said Katya. "We decided to wait until she was of age before telling her about her heritage. Even my husband doesn't know."

"Obviously, this is not the right time to introduce a long-lost Romanov. But I think it's time she should know the truth so she can be prepared. I came all this way to meet her. And now that I have, there's no doubt in my mind Alina would prevail if called upon. She's quite a firebrand."

"Sometimes impossible to control, I'm afraid," Katya said.

"I have broken in more high-spirited horses," Sergey countered, rubbing his chin.

"Remember, this is my daughter we're talking about."

"I think we will get along just fine." He turned to Katya's father. "This is going to be a most interesting partnership."

That night, at dinner at Katya's parents' estate, Alina glared at Sergey, maintaining a glacial silence, trying her best to freeze out the newcomer. She made a point of sitting on the opposite side of the table, surrounded by her brothers. They talked, they laughed, they bantered as siblings do, but not once did she bring Sergey into the conversation. Sergey's eyes never left her face, except when they dipped dangerously lower. She felt exposed. She was not going to be bartered like some farm animal.

"May I be excused?" she finally asked, getting up

from the table.

"Why don't you show our guest around the property," Katya suggested. "It's a nice night for a stroll."

"Mama, it's freezing outside."

"It's much colder in this room, young lady. Now take Sergey for a walk. Get to know each other."

"Could you be any more crude?" Alina retorted.

Sergey rose and stretched languorously. "Alina, I think we got off on the wrong foot. I would very much enjoy the pleasure of your company. I'm sure we could find something to occupy our time."

"Suit yourself. But I hope you have a warm jacket."

"That won't be a problem," he said, his voice dipping to a whisper that only she could hear. "I'm very hot-blooded."

Alina growled and stifled a silent scream as she walked out of the room, leaving him behind. The man was infuriating. She pulled a fur jacket from the coat rack, slipped into it, and walked out the door, intending to slam it behind her.

"Alina," Sergey said, stopping the motion of the door, taking her arm and wrapping his elbow around it, controlling her so they moved in tandem.

Alina hissed, "I am not for sale."

"You misunderstand." Sergey expelled a breath. You ought to be horsewhipped, he thought. You're a devil in disguise.

"What did you say?"

"I was just remarking how beautiful the night sky is."

Sergey moved closer to Alina. Alina shivered, but

not from the cold. No man had ever made her feel this way. Uncomfortable, out of control. On the surface he was polite. But who knew what lurid thoughts lurked beneath that impenetrable exterior?

"What is it you want from me?" Alina asked as they strolled around the perimeter of her grandparents' property. She tried to put some distance between them, but he maintained a strong grip on her arm.

Only everything, his eyes seemed to say.

"If you think because my grandfather needs your money and my father is desperate to go to Alaska that I would be willing to…that I would even consider…that I would even want—"

Sergey stopped in his tracks, turned to face Alina, and pierced her with his eyes.

"If I wanted you, and I do, when I wanted you, I could have you," he said evenly. "And I will."

"You arrogant bastard."

Sergey smiled. "Let's just get this out of the way."

He pulled her tightly into his arms and gave her a long and passionate kiss. A fiery kiss she felt to the bottom of her toes. He kissed her senseless, until she was completely slayed. She felt lightheaded and might have fainted if he hadn't been holding her up. No one had ever kissed her like that. And she didn't want him to stop.

She clawed at him, scratched him, and clutched his shirt, fighting him but needing to be closer.

He deepened the kiss, then pulled his lips away but held on to her. "And when I get you into my bed and strip you of everything, you will come to me willingly. I want nothing more than to worship you for the rest of your life and to love you. We are fated. I am yours forever. I am your Guardian."

Alina's eyes widened, and for the first time in her young life, she was powerless to speak.

"Have we come to an understanding?"

She sagged against him, expelling a breath, all the fight seeping out of her. He continued holding her against him to steady her.

"There is a lot you don't know. But I will teach you, my love, so you will be ready."

Once he had come face-to-face with this goddess, Sergey knew he could never leave her, would never leave her. He would marry her, love her, keep her content in his bed, continue the bloodline until the world was ready for the next Romanov.

Chapter Nine

"Mama, have you seen Alina? I can't find her anywhere. We need to start packing."

"She rode off on her horse in a huff when she found out we were leaving for Alaska in a matter of weeks. She was in a temper when that man from Petrograd came to meet with your father. I think she was ready to kill the messenger. I fear she resents the fact that we're pushing her toward Sergey. She just needs time to adjust. I don't know who she's waiting for—a prince, perhaps? The girl has her head in the clouds. She doesn't understand why we have to leave in such a hurry."

"That's because she doesn't understand who she is," Katya said, frowning.

"She's almost twenty-six. I think it's time we tell her."

"Sergey agrees, but I don't want to tell her now. Maybe when we get to Alaska, when we're far away from here."

"It's none of Sergey's business. Where were Sergey and the Grand Duke when Alina was born?"

"We've got to find her. It's not safe for a young girl alone in the forest. I'm worried. It's too dangerous in these woods. It will be dark soon. The Bolsheviks are all over, burning, looting, and worse. Sergey said they're killing Romanovs in Russia."

"She'll ride it off. She's like you. When you get in one of your moods, it's best to leave you alone. You sulk in your room. Poor Pyotr. I don't know how he puts up with it. He's so in love with you, he can't see straight."

"He sees clear often enough to find his way to our bedroom," Katya laughed, pointing to her protruding belly.

"Alina can take care of herself."

Katya turned to walk back to the house, holding her bulging belly, but worried about her daughter. She was in no condition to go after Alina. "I'll send Sergey to go after her."

****

Alina rode her stallion into the woods until she was breathless. She pulled up short, dismounted, and tied the horse to a tree. What right did they have to dictate her future? She was destined for something great. She was on the cusp. Finally coming into her own. And just like that, they decide to pull up roots and go to Alaska, that upstart land, chasing gold. Didn't they have enough gold in their mine here in Siberia? What was so great about Alaska? She'd be exchanging one vast wasteland for another. And that stranger, Sergey, was so sure of himself. So sure she was eager to jump into bed with him.

She strode off, furiously trying to shake her foul mood. She hated to be pushed.

Suddenly, a giant shadow appeared to block her path.

"What have we here? A young maiden off alone in the woods?"

Alina turned toward the threatening voice.

Suddenly a second man ambushed her from behind and twisted her arms roughly behind her back.

"I know this one," said the man directly in her path. "Her father runs the mine. Thinks she's better than the rest of us. No man is good enough for her. I think we need to teach this Tsarist sympathizer bitch a lesson. Break her in properly." He sauntered in close to her and ripped her dress down the front. Alina screamed, and he slapped her hard across the face, drawing blood. Then he ripped away her undergarments, and her breasts sprang free into his waiting hands. He pawed her.

"Stop!" Alina screamed again, but she knew no one could hear her.

He slapped her again and his hand came away with blood where she'd bitten him.

"A little spitfire."

"Nice pair," said the second man. "I wonder what the rest of her looks like. Why don't we find out? Hold her down while I show her what a real man is."

Alina spat in the man's face and began kicking him. She tried in vain to break free of the man behind her, but he threw her on the ground. When she landed, the back of her head hit a rock and she blacked out for a minute. When she came to, her skirt was up over her face, her panties were down around her legs, and the man in front was about to mount her. The other man leaned over and began kissing her and his breath stank of liquor. He fondled her breasts.

"Don't worry," said the man on top of her to his comrade. "You'll get your turn."

The man stopped kissing her. She squirmed and tried to twist out of the first man's grasp but he pulled her arms tighter above her head.

"Why are you doing this to me? What have I ever done to you? I've never—"

"What we have here is a virgin." He licked his lips. "I'm going to enjoy breaking you in."

"Please," Alina cried.

"You see, she's begging for it."

"Don't do this."

"Get off her, you Bolshevik pigs!" another man's voice called out in the dark.

"Says who?" the man about to penetrate her asked.

"Let her go! Both of you step away or I'll blow your heads off."

"Hear that? Two against one says you'd better get out of here. Or maybe you want a turn?"

Alina screamed, but she couldn't see the man who had come onto the scene. "Help me."

The next second she was staring into a mess of blood and guts that used to be a face. She kicked her attacker's body away.

The hands holding her down loosened, and as she broke free, she turned to see a bullet tear a hole in his gut.

The man holding the rifle helped her up. Her skirt billowed down around her naked legs.

"Here, take my coat and cover up."

She reached for the coat and put it over her shoulders to cover her breasts.

Then she bent over and threw up.

Her rescuer handed her a handkerchief. She wiped herself off. Then she saw his face in the moonlight.

"It's y-you," she stuttered, shaking. "Sergey Sergeyevich. You saved my life. Thank you."

"You shouldn't be out in these woods alone. Let's get you home." He put his arms around her shoulders and led her gently over to her horse. "Can you ride?"

She nodded.

"Good." He helped her up into the saddle and mounted his own horse.

"How did you know where to find me?"

"I followed you."

"Why?"

"I'm your Guardian."

"My guardian?"

"We'll talk more when we get home. Why did you tear out of your house so fast?"

"My parents think they can control my life. I don't want to go to Alaska. I'm old enough to make my own decisions."

The man smiled, recalling his friend Nicky's conversation so long ago about exerting his independence. "You remind me so much of your father, not only your looks, but the way you look at life."

"My father? I look nothing like my father. Everyone says so. It's like the stork dropped off the wrong baby at my house."

The man kept smiling like he had a secret.

They rode alongside each other in silence for miles. She had plenty of time to steal furtive glances at him, to study him. He was a dashing soldier. Very handsome, much older than she was but still very muscular. A real hero. He had certainly saved her life. If he hadn't come along when he did, she would be shattered. Alina hesitated, remembering the explosive encounter in the Siberian forest, an image she would never shake from her mind—the time when Sergey rescued her from certain ruin or worse.

She gagged just thinking about what could have happened to her. She had saved her virginity and for what? For it to be snatched away by some Bolshevik pigs? Probably deserters. She vowed she was going to make love with the next man she saw. She looked at Sergey inquisitively.

"Are you all right?"

"I am now, thanks to you."

"You were spectacular back there," he said. "A real warrior."

"I was stupid to get myself into that situation. I should have known better." They rode farther before Alina spoke again. "Why are we going to Alaska?"

"To make a fresh start. It's not safe for you here anymore."

"But I don't know anyone there."

"You know me."

"My mother said you'd be accompanying us."

"I'm your Guardian. Where you go, I go."

The idea of a guardian angel, a handsome guardian angel, who had the look of a devil, sounded nice. She looked forward to getting to know this man better. She'd seen the way he'd looked at her with longing, not disrespect, when she was naked and vulnerable. It wasn't the time or the place. He'd been a real gentleman, but he'd wanted her. Maybe he was the one she'd been waiting for.

Chapter Ten

Omsk, Siberia, July 25, 1918

"The Bolsheviks just announced that the Tsar was executed by firing squad. It happened a week ago," my mother reported.

What was I doing a week ago? Did I feel the life flow out of me? Did I have a premonition like an arrow piercing my heart? I felt so connected with Nicky, surely, I would have known when he took his last breath. How horrible it must have been for him. What a betrayal.

Or was it just an ordinary day, among many ordinary days? The world would never be the same. Certainly, my world would not be. My child had lost her father and she didn't even know it. She would never know it.

"What about the rest of the family?" I asked my mother. "The Empress and the children?"

"Soviet authorities reported only the death of Nicholas. They say the rest of the family was evacuated, most likely lost in the chaos of the civil war."

I knew I should be thankful that at least the rest of the family was spared, but I was bereft. I locked myself in my bedroom for days, refusing entry to Pyotr with no explanation. My Nicky was gone. Of course, Pyotr didn't understand. He attributed my behavior to general moodiness and the fact that I was pregnant again. No surprise since Pyotr couldn't keep his hands off me. He kept me warm on the cold Siberian nights when the wind roared into our small dwelling. There was nothing else to occupy the bleak nights.

****

Late August 1918

"Have you heard?" my mother said, running to my house to report the news. "They're all gone. The Empress, her beautiful daughters—Olga, Tatiana, Maria, and Anastasia—and the Grand Duke, and their staff."

"What do you mean they're gone?"

"Executed, along with the Tsar. Massacred in cold blood. The people didn't like the Tsarina. But to die like that? To watch her five children and her husband die? No one deserves that."

"How awful," I mumbled. In truth, I couldn't imagine it.

How chaotic it must have been for the Imperial family in their last horrifying moments. The abdication after the February revolution, traveling in two trains under the Japanese flag as part of the Japanese mission of the Red Cross, taking refuge in their residence in Tsarskoe Selo. Later, the move to the Siberian city of Tobolsk.

Following the Bolshevik uprising, the communist authorities moved the family again. The journey to Yekaterinburg in the Urals, in the hands of the Soviet secret police, where they were held captive at Ipatiev House under the harshest conditions, must have been rough. Rumors circulated that the royal women had been sexually abused by the guards in their final week. Witnesses heard shrieks from the house. Did the captives hope against hope to be saved at the last moment? Did they know they were going to die? What if it had been me and my little girl imprisoned with the Tsar? I couldn't bear it. I couldn't bear losing Nicky again or my precious Alina, the only link to my true love.

"Why did they need to kill the children?" I asked.

"He was the last Tsar. When Nicholas died, the direct line to the throne died with him. They didn't want to leave any loose ends, any Grand Dukes or Duchesses to make a later claim to the throne." She looked at me pointedly. Left unspoken: Alina was a loose end.

"Why didn't the British government bring the Romanovs to England?" I wondered. "Why didn't they provide sanctuary to the family? They might still be alive. His own cousin, the King, should have saved them."

"Who knows why?" my mother answered. "Nicholas was an unpopular ruler. The Russian people did not protest. The Soviet government was concerned about the 'counter-revolutionary' conspiracy they believed wanted to free the former monarch. The Bolsheviks were right to be worried. The Czechs took the city eight days after the Imperial family was murdered. By then it was too late.

"The Tsar's fate was preordained. He was to be shot, on Lenin's orders. But the thought of those beautiful girls, and the young Tsarevitch, murdered... You must leave Russia. The Bolsheviks are hunting Romanovs. They mean to wipe out the entire line."

"But no one knows about my daughter's lineage."

"We can't take that chance. "She's the direct male-line heir to the Tsar. Only you, me, and your father know. And now that man from Petrograd, Sergey Sergeyevich, the one who's been panting after your Alina since he arrived. The one who refuses to leave her side after the episode in the woods. You haven't told Pyotr, have you?"

"No, he doesn't know the identity of Alina's father. I will take that secret to my grave."

My mother placed a gold chain around my neck, fastened with a rose gold charm. On one side were the Ten Commandments. On the other an address.

"What is this?"

"The exact location of the Tsar's gold," my mother said. "Your father had it made with gold from the mine. Never take it off. If something should happen to you, pass it on to Alina."

"Why don't you keep the necklace?"

"Your father is the more obvious target. The gold will be more secure if you're wearing the necklace."

"I will protect it with my life," I said.

"One day, someone will be back for it. If anyone finds out your daughter's identity, they'll be hunting you and the child forever for the gold and for her life. She looks so much like a Romanov—most like Anastasia. That's why we could never bring her to court. People would start talking. You and the children must leave for Alaska right away."

"You are coming too?"

"You will leave first. We will follow soon after. Passage has already been arranged. Your father got a message from the Tsar before he abdicated. We've been planning all this time. Most of the gold reserves have been shifted east into Siberia. Your father is charged with safeguarding the Tsar's gold. If the Bolsheviks come here, they'll torture your father until he tells them the location of the shipment. And if they get a hint about your daughter, his daughter— Your father has already talked to Pyotr. Your father has contacts in Alaska from the former Russian-American Company. And Sergey Sergeyevich will accompany you. With his money and his influence, we will be fine. You've seen the way he looks at your daughter. He devours her with his eyes."

"Alina is very beautiful."

"There was no one appropriate enough for a Tsar's daughter to marry in this barren land. Sergey Sergeyevich would do very nicely, if Alina were interested. She is very particular."

"Oh, she's interested," Katya said. "Have you seen them together? Although he's quite a bit older."

"But handsome. He's a good man. It would be a good match. I heard he lost his wife and child in the riots. He was protecting the Tsar when it happened. He can never forgive himself. He is searching for something or someone, and I think he has found it."

My mother then placed the diamond-and-emerald encrusted necklace in the palm of my hand and clasped her hand over mine.

"This rightly belongs to you. It was given in love."

After I left my mother, I sagged on the bed. Leave Russia? I could understand why my daughter didn't want to go. In my case, Nicky was gone. There was nothing left for me here. If I had been holding out hope, that hope was lost.

I barely had time to breathe, and I had to pack up my clothes and my children's clothes, but I spared a few minutes to read a couple of Nicky's letters that Sergey had delivered, letters I had longed for.

****

My Darling Katya,

I have written to you so many times and still have not received an answer. I poured out my heart and soul to you, my love. Have you forgotten me already? I am longing for you. I should have kept you by my side, never let your parents take you away...

****

Dearest Katya,

I heard of your marriage and the arrival of your child. You broke my heart.

****

Katya My Love,

By now you would have heard the news, even in the far reaches of Siberia. I am to marry the princess from Germany, Alexandra. We have known each other for a long while. We have become friends, and I think she will make a good wife. I have deep feelings for her, of course, but there will never be another woman like you, my Katya. The memory of our times together keeps me awake most nights. Would it be fair to tell you that when I make love to my bride, it will be you I am kissing, you I am touching, you I wish were in my bed and by my side? I fear I shall never get you out of my mind. If only things could be different... You are lost to me now, but not forgotten. Still no letters from you. I can only think that means you are happy with your new husband, Pyotr. Yes, I know all about your new life, your new man. It still wounds me that you would prefer a mine worker over a Romanov. Is he a better lover? Does he bring you more pleasure? Do you think of me when you're in his bed? Why do I torture myself? Because I still hope I will hear from you, that you will come running when I call, but that is not to be. I cannot stop thinking about you, will never stop loving you.

****

My Darling Love,

I have received a report from Sergey. I believe I know the truth about your daughter, our daughter, and why you married in such haste. How can I blame you? A woman alone in that condition, you had no choice. If I were any other man, I would offer you the world. Selfishly, I would bring you to court to watch my daughter grow up and to have you near me, but that would just bring you pain, and I don't think I could bear to see you unhappy or to see you without wanting you. My life is not my own. It was planned out before my birth. There are expectations. But you are with me every day and every night. Our month of nights are seared on my memory...

****

Every time I look at Alina, I'm reminded of Nicky, my greatest love. She is the image of her father.

Alina and Sergey grow closer every day. He has already declared his love to her and come to Pyotr for his blessing. We are more than happy to welcome Sergey to our family. He is a Godsend in many ways. And he can barely keep his hands off Alina. He is never far from her side. If they don't wed soon, Alina is going to follow in my footsteps.

Does he remember his former wife and daughter when he looks at Alina? Does he have ghostly visions, or is he enamored of Alina and grateful that she has filled the empty space within his soul? I wager she makes him as happy as he makes her, judging by the passionate sounds coming from hidden places when they think no one is listening.

Just yesterday I overheard Sergey whispering to Alina. "I can't wait to make you my wife, to create another Grand Duchess, or perhaps a Grand Duke to populate our dynasty."

"Sergey, you're impossible. You know we can't talk that way, can't even think that way. This has to be our little secret."

"I know, my love. But one day, perhaps, one day…"

Now that Alina knows the truth about her birthright, she carries herself like a Grand Duchess. And Sergey treats her like a tsarina. She may never again see her homeland, but with Sergey at her side, she is ready for whatever the future brings. She never tires of hearing about her father, her real father. Sergey is only too happy to fill her head and heart with tales of his exploits with Nicky, with the Romanov history, with everything Romanov. And he is eternally watchful. He will never let anything happen to my daughter or the children they might have together.

****

"Katya, did you hear the news?" Pyotr called rushing into our room. "We're off to Alaska. The White soldier is back for good. He was here to meet with your father, and I sent him to the house for some refreshment. Your mother had the children with her down at the mine. He was staring at our daughter overlong. But your father has asked him to accompany us to Alaska. He has money and contacts."

Pyotr swears his search for gold in the new land will be successful and that he will make us rich beyond our wildest dreams.

I barely had time to hide the hastily read letters with the others in my drawer. If I had received these letters all those years ago, I would have gone to court. As Nicky's mistress, if I had to. I would have found a way. I wouldn't have cared what anyone thought. Just to be near him, to have him know his daughter. But now that can never be.

"Why are you frowning? This is a cause for celebration," Pyotr exclaimed, gathering me into his arms.

I knew what that meant. When Pyotr was in a celebratory mood, he hungered for me. But while I make love to my husband, I will be thinking of another man and our month of nights. I do care for Pyotr. He is kind and gentle and patient. He is a good husband. I know he would protect his family with his life. I am lucky to have him. But still, my mind strays. Should I feel guilty for craving a man who is no longer on this earth? Does that still count as a betrayal?

I'm not in much of a festive mood, and I can hardly hide my feelings from my husband.

Pyotr wiped away my tears. "I know it will be hard to leave your home, but what an adventure we'll have. You'll see. This will be a new beginning for us."

For me it was a bittersweet ending.

Pyotr whispered to me, "Do you think Sergey Sergeyevich is a little heavy handed?"

"Our daughter needs a strong hand to guide her, protect her."

"So you think they make a good match?"

"You wouldn't have agreed to it otherwise."

"Sometimes she seems indifferent to him, almost hostile."

"My darling, you don't know your daughter very well. She is just being temperamental. She's already halfway in love with the man. Or in lust. When I see them together in stolen moments, she looks anything but hostile."

"Was he taking liberties?" Pyotr asked, frowning.

"If he was, she wasn't objecting."

"Should I have a talk with him?"

"That won't be necessary. He intends to marry her. But we may want to move up the timetable or there could be unintended consequences."

"Let's not talk about that now."

Pyotr locked the door and led me over to the bed.

"Come, my love. We may not have much time to be alone. We have a long journey ahead. There won't be much privacy on the ship. Let us take advantage of this respite while the children are with your mother. You grow more beautiful each day."

"And bigger," I sighed.

"That only excites me more."

He began to undress me and cover my lips with drugging kisses. All I could think about was Nicky and what might have been if the world hadn't erupted in such chaos. If we had been just two ordinary people, a man and a woman. I should be worried about the hazards of the journey we are about to take to a new land, the hardships that await us in what will likely be a beautiful but brutal landscape. Alaska—a perfect harbor for my shuttered heart and my shattered dreams.

Part Three

*Zurich, Switzerland, to Bellagio (Lake Como),
Italy, to Zurich, 2021*

"Every generation needs a new revolution."
~Thomas Jefferson

Chapter Eleven

Zurich, Switzerland

Melody put down the diary and rotated her shoulders. Breathless and restless, she felt like a voyeur, intruding on someone's very private life, even though the people she was reading about were long dead. The heat and passion fairly consumed the pages. Reading about the intimacy as the Grand Duke made love to Ekaterina brought to mind her first time in bed with Count Nikolai Kinsky. It had happened that suddenly. He had swooped in, swept her off her feet, sure of himself and his mission. And she'd been off-balance ever since. She had been as naïve as the maiden in the diary, and Nikolai was as experienced as the Grand Duke. She didn't stand a chance of resisting him.

Reading about the deaths of the Tsar and his family was enough to plunge her into a deep depression. Details of the execution weren't revealed in the newspapers until 1926. Details Katya and her family knew because they were so close to the killing ground. And people talked, soldiers who were the last to see the royal family alive, and who took part in their brutal murder, bragged, brought home tokens of the massacre.

The Romanovs had been taken to the basement of Ipatiev House, known as "The House of Special Purpose," where they were lined up against a wall and shot by firing squad. Those who survived the first attack were finished off with bayonets. Then the bodies were thrown into a mine, to reduce any chance that the remains might be found. A brutal way to die. Unimaginable. Especially because the Tsar was more to Melody than a footnote in history.

That's where the annotations in the diary ended. Did Katya finally find true happiness with Pyotr in Alaska or was she forever bound to the memory of Nicholas? Did her parents join them or were they captured by the Red army and tortured? Did Pyotr ever discover the truth about his daughter's paternity? What happened to Nicholas's letters to Katya? Were they destroyed to protect her identity? How did this diary get into Nana's hands? And how did the Guardians track the Romanov descendants all the way to America, one hundred years later? Was Sergey Sergeyevich the first American link to the Guardians? And Nikolai the most recent?

In the diary, there was a hastily drawn family tree, a mention of the long line of Romanov women who fell in love with their own Guardians, birthed daughters, and kept the lineage alive. She felt a strong connection with those women. One thing was certain. Generations of her ancestors had protected the secret. The Guardians had waited a century for their chance to resurrect the Romanovs. The love Katya felt for Nicholas was real and his for her. The death of the Romanov children was tragic. If she and Katya didn't continue their legacy, if they lived out their lives in obscurity, would they be betraying the memory of their ancestors? If she was the true Romanov heir, then wasn't it her duty to own her heritage and protect her daughter's legacy?

She felt a definite kinship with this Katya in the diary. Both of them had become pregnant by their lovers, men not their husbands. Both had been denied true love. Nana must have felt the strong bond with all of the Romanov women too, or she would have disposed of the diary.

The story of Anna Anderson, the woman claiming to be the youngest daughter of the last Tsar—Anastasia Romanov—had surfaced to much fanfare. At the time, the world was captivated by the possibility, the hope, the miracle that a legitimate heir to the Tsar could still be alive. Could she be the last real connection to Nicholas II? Over time, no less than a hundred women had claimed to be the Grand Duchess, but all were proved imposters, all hopes were dashed.

But now, could she and Katya make the impossible dream come true?

Nikolai entered her room, eager to talk. "I see you've finished the diary. We've waited a long time for this moment. I hope you now understand your place in history."

Melody stubbornly repeated her mantra. "I want to see my daughter."

"She's safe. But the world is not. Had the Western powers heeded Winston Churchill's plea to send supplies to the Tsarist White Russian 'reactionaries,' in 1919, the Bolshevik threat—that morphed into Soviet Communism—might have been halted in its tracks and the world would be a better place."

"I don't need a history lesson. I *need* to see my daughter. Now."

"I will take you to her. But first we need something from you." He thrust a grainy photo in front of her face.

"Do you see this, the gold and other priceless metals in the vaults of this Kazan bank?"

"What does this picture have to do with me?"

"As Russia descended into chaos during the First World War, treasures were shifted in 1915 from the capital city of Petrograd—now St. Petersburg—to Kazan, east of Moscow and later controlled by anti-Bolshevik forces, for safekeeping. The gold reserve of the Russian Empire simply disappeared. The Red Army bombed a convoy moving the hold in Kazan in 1918. The soldiers guarding it scattered. The few that were left managed to grab the gold and move it to the forest, hoping to come back for it later. They secured the gold, but then the Reds pushed back the Whites, and all but one were killed by Lenin's forces. That sole survivor was Ekaterina's father. The Ekaterina in the diary. He alone knew the location of the hidden Kazan gold.

"If you recall, the Tsar and his family were under a Red Army guard," Nikolai continued. "The Tsar's forces knew they needed to leave the city, but they were hoping the White movement would eventually succeed. So they hid part of the gold reserves in Omsk."

"Is that supposed to mean something to me?"

"We're counting on it. That gold could help us fund our revolution, do a lot of good for the Russian people. There were many fruitless searches, many efforts to locate the shipment. We believe the gold is still hiding somewhere around Omsk, Ekaterina's home.

"It was called Operation Golden Fleece," Nikolai explained. "The hunt began October 1, 1929, and there was an agreement to share any treasure that was found. It's an intriguing mystery, the whereabouts of the 'hidden' or 'lost' Tsar's gold. A lot of speculation, theories, and claims surrounding where the gold might be stashed. We estimate it could be worth eighty billion dollars at today's prices. We believe you hold the key to the lost gold."

"Me? How would I know about any of this?"

"Your grandmother should have told you. We believe she held on to the secret as a bargaining chip for her safety, for your safety."

"I know nothing about it."

"You may not think you know, but any little clue might lead us to the treasure. You want to keep Katya safe, don't you?"

Was that a threat? He knew she would do anything for Katya. Did he suspect Katya was his? Did she want him to know? Did she trust him? Absolutely not. Nor would she change her mind.

She had been seduced by this man, like Ekaterina had been seduced by Nicholas. Her life and the life of the girl in the diary, it seemed, ran on parallel tracks. When she discovered Nikolai was married, she'd dropped his class and tried to extricate him from her life, unsuccessfully. If she'd told Nikolai his former lover had revealed he had a wife, he would have insisted the woman was just jealous because he had spurned her advances. But that didn't change the fact that he was married. And that he had lied to her, whether deliberately or by omission.

Although she had put distance between them, she had to admit she could not get him out of her mind. The affair turned into the worst mistake of her life, yet it left her with her most precious possession. Every time she looked into Katya's ice-blue eyes and at her golden curls, she came face to face with her past, with Nikolai. How could she love Katya so deeply and not love the man who had fathered her? Fortunately, he knew nothing about Katya's paternity. And she was determined to keep that secret from him.

"I'll be back," he said, striding out of the bedroom. "Take some time to think about it."

With nothing to do but wait, she reopened the diary. Then she pulled Nana's handwritten letter from her purse, the letter she had hidden from Nikolai. Words from the grave. Words she'd been longing to hear. She was desperate for answers. Maybe Nana's letter would solve the mystery, of her birth, of the missing shipment of gold that was so important to Nikolai and his Guardians. Maybe if she helped them locate the gold, he would finally leave her and Katya alone.

My Dearest Melody,

If you are reading this, I am no longer on this earth. There are so many things I've wanted, needed to tell you, but I put off coming to you, like an old ostrich, sticking my head in the sand. I suppose I thought that maybe, if I said nothing, it would all go away.

But that is not how life works. I thought I would have my most darling daughter, your mother, forever, until she was taken from me. And caring for you, loving you, raising you as my own, brought me a lifetime of joy.

No one thought you'd survive the accident. But even at that young age you showed a courageous spirit and clung to life like a barnacle on a ship. You're going to need that strong will to survive now more than ever. I have been hiding the truth for most of your life, but it is time for the story and the secret to come out. I would not be doing right by you or your unborn daughter if I denied your birthright and kept silent. I need to explain your past for your own protection.

I hate to place the burden on you that has been placed on so many of the women in our family and will eventually be placed on your daughter. A burden, yet also an obligation and an opportunity, to fulfill our legacy. You'll understand more once you read the diary.

If you have the diary, then you also have the antique diamond-and-emerald necklace that once belonged to Maria Feodorovna of Russia, the mother of Tsar Nicholas II, and wife of Emperor Alexander III. A priceless gift that was bestowed on my great-grandmother, Ekaterina, one which she passed down from mother to daughter and that has been passed from mother to daughter through the generations. This priceless heirloom along with her words, which I have translated, are tangible proof that Tsar Nicholas II loved Ekaterina and that their love produced a child. You are a descendant of that child.

Throughout the years, the women in our family have been called on to step up, to fulfill our destiny, through the Guardians of the Romanov Legacy. The last Tsar is dead, but his legacy will live on through you and your unborn child. When I came of age, the time was not right for a revolution. But your mother was ready to assume the mantle before she died in a tragic car accident. I know now it was no accident. You were in that car and thankfully you survived. But evil forces were working against the Guardians, forces that wanted your mother and you dead. I agreed to step up, but they wanted someone younger for the face of the new Russia, and the stars were not aligned. I didn't want to sacrifice another daughter, for that is what I consider you, to the cause. So I hid you away. That's why we traveled from place to place and ended up in Downingtown. That's why I never talked about your mother while I was alive. It was too painful.

You are a true Romanov, so naturally your interest turned to Russian history. I did everything I could to stamp out your passion. But you stubbornly prevailed. In the end, it was meant to be. And it was your right. Your birthright.

You never revealed your child's paternity, but I can guess who the father is—Count Nikolai Kinsky. His father was a leader in the Guardians, and he has assumed their mantle. He has been bred for the job since birth. You fell victim to his charms as I did to another Guardian, who swore his love for me, got me pregnant, and left me alone. I tried to disappear with you, even changed your name, but, in the end, they found us. The Count came to me, but I never revealed the paternity of your daughter. That is your decision as to whether you want him in your life. I might have fabricated the truth and mentioned that you had been seriously involved with our congregation's handsome new rabbi.

The aim of the Guardians is and has always been to ensure that the Romanov line continues. I suspect for their own ends. But, whatever the reason, they are committed to that goal. Throughout the generations, the women in our family were seduced, bred for the Romanov seed to continue the line. Yes, even your mother came home pregnant by her Guardian, but luckily she found a wonderful man you considered your father, to make a family. And I found your grandfather, who was the love of my life. I don't consider us to be weak women. Impulsive maybe, romantic yes, but we were targeted.

I tried to get you to leave the university, to forget your dreams to study Russian history, but by the time you met the Count, it was too late. I must admit, he is charming, everything a woman could hope for in a man and a lover. Except for the fact that he was not free to love you. That will only cause you pain, and I'm sorry I won't be around to help you through the inevitable heartache.

That is the way of the Guardians. Count Kinsky was your chosen consort. He spent his life training for the role. It is his destiny as it is yours to take the crown. If he comes to you, that means it is time and that you are worthy. The Guardians are sworn to protect the Romanov heirs. Our futures are tied with theirs. You will have to decide if you can trust him.

But if, for some reason, that scenario doesn't come to pass and the Guardians decide to wait for the next generation, there's someone special for you who is closer to home. I am talking about the new rabbi. I think he'd be perfect for you. His grandmother and I are friends, and we think you could make a good life together. Although I have not met him in person, I have seen photos, and my friend can never stop extolling his virtues.

I know you'll be thinking, 'a rabbi?' But why not?

Melody smiled. So the rabbi was telling the truth about the matchmaking grandmothers. He seemed sweet enough, and in different circumstances, she might have been interested in pursuing a relationship. But meeting the handsome rabbi seemed a lifetime ago. There was a definite spark, a connection between them. But that future was no longer in the stars.

She dried her tears. Her grandmother confirmed what Nikolai had already told her. She was not Melody Segal. She was a Romanov descendant—Maria Tatyana Feodorovna. Ekaterina from the diary was her third-great-grandmother. Alina was her great-great-grandmother. All of these people were merely paper relatives, their thoughts and love stories alive only in the diary. She would have to get more answers from Nikolai, a man she'd sworn never to trust again.

Chapter Twelve

Melody looked up from her grandmother's letter. The puzzle pieces were starting to fit. Nikolai had a legitimate purpose in recruiting her. He was back in her room now, dressed in a military uniform, like pictures she had seen of the Tsar's Imperial Guard. She would never admit it to his face, but Nikolai looked dashing, and his presence was beginning to stir feelings she thought she had buried deep in the crevices of her mind and in the muscles of her heart.

Nikolai picked up a photograph from his desk. It was a picture of a Russian Army officer and Tsar Nicholas II.

"This was the first Guardian, Sergey Sergeyevich. He could not save the Tsar, but he was determined not to fail again. He was a legend. I will not disappoint him."

Was this the Sergey in the diary, the Sergey who made the journey with Alina to Alaska? If so, he would have been her great-great-grandfather.

"Sergey was in the military, so this will be a military takeover?" she asked, cautiously eyeing the sword that completed Nikolai's outfit.

"More like a bloodless coup," Nikolai answered. "Everything is arranged. With the push of a button, money from the oligarchs' private accounts will be transferred back into the public coffers. The current leaders will be presented with a choice: leave with sufficient assets to live in style abroad, or join the rest of the peasants they've impoverished and find out how the other half lives. Or if need be, they'll simply disappear like so many ordinary citizens do on a daily basis. Or maybe they'll be banished to Siberia. We've already infiltrated their military and local police authorities. They think they're in control, but it's just an illusion.

"The current 'Tsar' will call for his guards when we present him a fait accompli, but his guards are our Guardians. They won't come when he calls. We've already seized control of all aspects of the government. When he checks his computer, The Bear will find his myriad bank accounts drained. Hopefully, he will make the right decision for himself and his country. We should put him on trial and execute him. But we are not murderers."

"And you really think the people will welcome a new ruler?"

"We've conducted polls and done significant research, and yes, the people are ready for a change. They would welcome you. You will not wield any true power or have a political role. It will be a constitutional monarchy like the one in the United Kingdom. You'll be a figurehead—the head of state, yes, but without the ability to make or pass legislation. You'll reign, but you won't govern. As the new face of Russia, however, you'll play a very important role."

"A kinder, gentler Russia?"

"Exactly. The people are hungering for it, for an identity. For their past. You are just what they're looking for. There's a definite sea change in economic conditions. Pressure is heightening."

He held out his hand. She placed her hand demurely in his, attempting to appear cooperative. She would play her part, until she located Katya and planned their escape route. Nikolai spun her around the room until she was breathless.

"Let us practice introducing you."

He cleared his throat. "May I present the Empress Maria Tatyana Feodorovna, and the heir apparent, Ekaterina Nikolaevna."

"Nikolaevna?"

"Of course. "I've been meaning to discuss Katya's name with you. She is a blood relative of Tsar Nicholas II, so she should take his surname."

"But shouldn't the child be named for her father?"

Nikolai speared her with his eyes. "And who would that be?"

She looked away, unwilling to answer.

"It didn't take you long to get over me."

"He was just a placeholder, until someone better came along."

Nikolai cast a doubtful look. "Someone to warm your bed?"

"If you like."

"What if I don't? I thought you were in love with me."

"That's when I thought you were available."

"You could have come to me for an explanation instead of dropping out of college and dropping out of sight."

"And what would you have said?"

"I could have explained."

"I'm not interested in your Russian fairy tales. I've

moved on."

"To the new rabbi?"

She would not confirm or deny. Let him wonder.

"Then tell me this. Is the father of your child still in your life?"

The father of my child is standing right here in front of me, she thought. The Count is not the only one who knows how to lie.

Rabbi Slick seemed genuinely interested, so even though he wasn't really in her life she could change that with a little encouragement, if she were allowed to return to Downingtown. But she didn't want to involve him in her drama or jeopardize his safety. She'd been thinking of him a lot lately. Of what could have been or what could be if she could pry Katya loose from this prison.

"He would be if Katya and I were back home. But since you've kidnapped me and my child and are holding us hostage, the answer is no."

"That wasn't our intent."

"Please. Enlighten me. What is your intent?"

"To protect you. I am your Guardian. I'm pledged to watch over you. That is my life's mission."

"Overprotection."

"Maria Tatyana," he said in a soft, deep voice that sounded like he was scolding a child.

"My name is Melody. I haven't decided whether Katya and I are going to participate in your charade. So it costs me nothing if you rename Katya. I don't object."

"You don't have a choice."

"It certainly appears that I don't."

"I don't know why you are complaining. You are

surrounded by luxury."

"I am surrounded by guards with guns in my so-called *sanctuary.*"

"Do you not have everything you need?"

"There's only one thing I lack. Unlimited access to my daughter."

"We can negotiate that. Anything else?"

"Perhaps." She was beginning to warm to the idea. "Will I have a royal yacht like the *Standart*?" She laughed, dancing him around the room.

"If that is your pleasure, your Highness."

"You always were a dreamer, Nikolai. I'm just not as sure as you that this plan of yours will work."

"We have been preparing for this moment for a hundred years. I assure you it will happen just as we envisioned. We were just waiting for the right time and the right conditions. And the time is ripe for a revolution."

Chapter Thirteen

Melody jumped out of bed and paced the length of the room like a caged tiger, which was entirely appropriate because she *was* caged. As she walked, her limp became more pronounced, as it always did in times of stress.

Drawing back the drapes, she looked out the window where she was greeted with a whiteout—blizzard conditions. Even if she could locate Katya in this cavernous castle and they did manage to escape, they would never survive the elements. And Nikolai knew that. He knew they were trapped. And he was depending on that to keep her beholden to him and under his control.

In one sense, Nikolai was right. She had everything she could ever want at her disposal—the finest clothes, sumptuous surroundings, Michelin-worthy cuisine. People to wait on her hand and foot. A library. Everything but her child and her freedom. And her cell phone. She was confined, and no one knew she was here. She couldn't even alert the authorities. For all she knew, the people guarding her *were* the authorities, or the authorities were loyal to the people in charge. Nikolai had thought of everything to keep her in her place in this gilded cage.

Melody explored her options. She could open the windows and jump to her death, but what would happen to Katya? She would be raised by Miss Cormier. She would never let that happen. She could tie the bedsheets together and climb down, but what if the sheets didn't hold? What if she fell? Or froze to death? Then how would she rescue her child?

If she could come to terms with Nikolai, convince him she still loved him, the Guardian might drop his guard. It wouldn't take much convincing. She could sleep with him, but then she would sacrifice her sanity, which was already hanging by a thread. He claimed he was in love with her. But she was just a means to an end. Even if she didn't believe him now, he had been in love with her once. He could be again. And then he would start to trust her, perhaps let her see her daughter. She was going mad missing Katya. It was like a limb had been severed. She was aching to see Katya, to hold her in her arms, to hear her laugh, even her cry. It had been no more than a day or two, but it was the longest separation of their lives.

She rang the little bell on her nightstand repeatedly.

"Tell Nikolai I wish to see him," she instructed one of the nameless attendants who were charged with her care or captivity.

"Yes, Your Majesty."

Unbelievable. These people had actually bought into the idea that she would be the next Romanov empress.

Nikolai walked into the room a minute later and dismissed her attendant, instructing her to close the door. He was out of uniform, wearing a body-hugging gray T-shirt and snug black jeans that showed off his best features. And she knew what was bulging out under those jeans.

"I want to declare a truce," she offered, folding her hands tightly across her chest.

"I didn't know we were at war."

"I've thought about it, and I've decided to go along with your scheme."

"It's hardly a scheme."

"Well, then whatever you call this situation I find myself in. I will cooperate, on one condition."

"Which is?"

"That you let me see Katya. No, that you reunite me permanently with my daughter. There's no reason to keep us apart."

"Hmm." He considered the offer, appraising her, assessing its veracity.

"When you say cooperate…" His eyes settled on her breasts.

Melody expelled a breath.

"That's open to interpretation. If I can trust you, then, I might be willing to restore our former arrangement."

"What we shared was more than an arrangement," Nikolai growled. "We were in love."

"Lovers don't kidnap their enamored and they don't imprison them, and they don't separate them from their child."

"I had to make sure you would cooperate, for your own safety."

"And for your own purposes. Well, you win." She threw up her hands in surrender. "You hold all the cards. But I need something in return. I need your promise that you'll let me see Katya."

He didn't hesitate. "That can be arranged." He was in a hurry to close the deal and the distance between them. He reached out and tucked a lock of her hair behind her ears. He bent down and nuzzled her neck, traced his lips down her face. Then he reached into the bodice of her gown and his hand grazed her breast, just above the nipple.

She shivered.

"I've missed you," he whispered in his gravelly voice.

She bit her lip.

"You're shaking. I would never hurt you. I just want what we once had."

"And you can have it, *if* you let me see my daughter. That is not negotiable."

"You have my word."

She wondered how much his word meant anymore.

Then he kissed her softly, wetly, on the lips.

"Maria Tatyana. I want you. I need you. It's been so long, too long."

She rubbed her breasts against his chest and twined her arms around his neck in false submission, returning his urgent kisses, signaling her consent. She was prepared to sleep with the Devil to get her daughter back.

Could he tell she was only playing a role? It didn't appear that he cared. His passion had taken over. He carried her to the bed. If she didn't stop him, he would undress her, caress her, let his hands play over every part of her body.

"Do you remember this?"

She nodded because she did remember.

If this scene played out the way it had in the past, he would mount her.

She wanted to stick a knife into his ribs, but at the

same time, she loved having him so close. She did remember his touch, and her body responded and fell back under his charismatic spell.

"Comrade," he said gently. "You did miss me. You can't hide it. You can't fake that kind of passion. You want me as much as I want you."

She blew out a breath.

It's just sex, she reasoned. How hard could it be to play the part of the willing lover?

Her eyes roamed his chiseled face. He held her in his strong arms. How hard his body felt against hers. If she didn't stop him soon, it would be too late.

He was right about one thing. She had missed him, missed this. Their joining would be satisfying, just as she remembered.

He was tender, kissed her with all the old passion. He had all the right words. She was desperate for him and wanted more. He sensed her restlessness.

"You want me, Comrade?" he asked.

She nodded, her head nestled against his broad chest.

If he reacted as he had in the past, he would increase his pace until they were both beyond words.

If she didn't stop him first. And she did. She pushed him away gently.

"Not until I see my daughter," she challenged.

He flipped on his back and laid a possessive hand over her breast.

"You are persistent," he said. "But I can outlast you."

She smiled. She had the Count right where she wanted him. And despite the fact that she was leading him on, she did want him.

"You needn't wait to be satisfied if you will just give in to my one demand," she teased.

"It will be hard to wait."

"For me, too," she admitted, wishing it weren't true, removing his hand from her breast and sitting up in the bed, feeling around for her clothes in the dark room. "Now take me to Katya. If you are truly in charge of this operation."

"I'm completely in charge." Nicholas sat up in bed and tried to pull her back into his arms. "Comrade, why are you in such a hurry to get away? We have so much to catch up on. Don't deny how much you miss what we had together. I know you too well."

She smiled and thought, *You don't know me at all.* He didn't know that a lioness would do anything for her cub, however compromising. Including tearing an attacker to pieces.

She rubbed her finger suggestively across her lower lip. It was time to play hard ball. "If I remember, correctly, Nikolai, you are an insatiable lover. And if you want to touch me again, you'll do as I ask."

Nikolai raised his hands in mock surrender.

"Come, we will go see your daughter."

She grabbed her clothes and changed in the bathroom, although Nikolai had seen her naked many times. When she came out of the bathroom, he was waiting for her by the door.

He linked his arm with hers at the elbow and walked her to the elevator.

She counted silently as the elevator rose. So Katya was being kept one, two floors above her bedroom.

They got off the elevator, and he led them up a tiny flight of winding stone stairs. As they got closer to the room where Katya was imprisoned, she noticed a window. They were at the top of the castle, a place reminiscent of the crow's nest situated on the upper part of the mainmast of a ship.

Nikolai noticed her dismay.

"It's for Katya's own protection," Nikolai assured. "It's the best lookout point."

A guard stationed at the stairwell landing saluted Nikolai.

When they walked through the nursery room door, Miss Cormier, Katya's jailer, jumped up to block their way.

"Natalia, it's okay. I am bringing the Empress to see her daughter."

"I've just put the Grand Duchess down. She needs her nap."

Miss Cormier clenched her teeth and sent Melody a horrifying look, a look of pure hatred. How could she not have seen it before? How could Nana not have known it? She rushed by the Medusa and stood over the crib.

"Katya?" Melody breathed easily for the first time since the kidnapping, trying not to wake her daughter but longing to lift her into her arms. "Mama's here."

Katya's blue eyes, so like her father's, unshuttered, and she broke into a happy smile that spread across her face.

"You're awake, little one," Melody cried. "Come to Mama." Melody swept Katya up into her arms, all the while checking the room for a means of escape, and settled them down into a nearby rocking chair. Escape was impossible.

"Maria Tatyana, why are you crying?" asked

Nikolai.

Melody licked the tears as they streamed down her face.

"Because I have my child, at last," she said, rocking her gently and singing an old tune she remembered her own mother singing to her when she was a child. She'd always thought it was Yiddish, but as she recalled the words, she now knew they were Russian. A distant memory of her mother's fading face flitted by. Or was it Nana's face?

Then she pressed her daughter tighter against her body.

"The Grand Duchess needs her rest," Miss Cormier insisted, singing the same old refrain.

"Leave us, Natalia. The Empress is heartsick. She needs to spend some restorative time with her daughter."

Miss Cormier grumbled as she backed out of the room.

Melody continued rocking her child. She could rock her forever. She examined Katya from top to bottom, counting her fingers and toes, satisfying herself that she hadn't been harmed. Katya kept twisting around, straining her neck to see her mother, to make sure she was still there.

Nikolai seemed fascinated by the baby. "She's beautiful, just like her mother," he said.

"There, there, Katya. Mama is never going to leave you again." Then Melody felt her child relax and fall asleep, heavy against her mother's body, her warmth and milky sweet scent enveloping her.

After a while, when Melody was sure Katya was sound asleep, she placed her gently in the crib.

"Come, we must go," Nicholas whispered urgently.

"Not without Katya. I'll stay here with her until she wakes up."

"Maria Tatyana, that is not practical. We have much to accomplish, and she has a host of people to care for her, a nursemaid, and of course, Miss Cormier."

"They are not her mother. I made a promise to my child that I would not leave her. I will not abandon her." *Like my mother abandoned me.*

Nikolai sighed. "I knew this would be a problem."

"Only if you keep me separated from my child."

"Okay, we have a very busy schedule. Katya will remain in her room. But I will guarantee access to her as often as you wish."

She looked into his eyes, trying to gauge if he could be believed. "I'll take you at your word. Thank you."

A tall, slim, regal-looking blonde woman with a dark aura strode into the room, oblivious to Melody's presence. She bent down over the crib to blow silent kisses to Katya.

"A captivating child," the woman observed.

Nikolai stiffened and tried to lead Melody out of room. "Let's go."

"Who is that woman?" she asked.

"No one," Nikolai muttered.

The woman turned to face them. "Nikolai, aren't you going to introduce us?" she asked, but he ignored her.

The woman flashed an evil grin and stared at her, tilting her head curiously. "I am the Countess Juliette Orlov Kinsky."

Confused, Melody directed the question to Nikolai. "Your mother?"

The woman laughed, but for a moment a look of pure contempt froze on her face like a death mask. "I am his wife. And you must be the Count's latest mistress, one of a long line of conquests, foolish women who think they have captured his heart."

Melody's mouth fell open. "Nikolai. Is it true?'"

"I can explain."

The Countess laughed like a hyena. She was enjoying Melody's distress. She edged closer, a cobra about to strike.

"Finally, we meet, *Comrade,*" she said, her voice silky and sadistic. "She's a beauty, Nicky. I can see why you fancy her. Just your type. Curvy and delicious." The Countess lifted Melody's chin with her bony finger like she was assessing a racehorse. Then she ran her fingers slowly down Melody's neck to the top of her breast, stopping short of her nipple, and traversed back up to caress her cheek. She tucked a lock of her hair behind her ear as Nikolai did whenever he wanted to make love. Melody's teeth chattered.

"Take her to bed, my love, she needs warming up. I may join you, later."

Comrade? Melody's heart beat madly. Did this woman have the rooms in the palace bugged? Had she been watching while Nikolai attempted to make love to her, touch her in her secret places, drive her wild with desire, all the while ensconced in another room, their bedroom, observing them like a voyeur? Or did Nikolai reveal their secrets to his wife? The secrets of a naïve, foolish girl who thought she was in love. Was it some kind of private joke between them?

How easy was it for him to traverse the palace from bedroom to bedroom, woman to woman? Was his conscience clear? Why wasn't he saying anything? Why wasn't he denying it? No wonder he wanted to keep her locked up and isolated, prevented from wandering.

Why was she even surprised? She couldn't trust him. The palace was Nikolai's home, so why shouldn't his wife be in residence? She had contemplated the idea of his wife, but being confronted with the woman in the flesh left her cold and furious.

Melody started to grab her child from the crib, to get her away from these morally bankrupt people trying to control their lives. This was nothing but a game to them. And she and Katya were merely pawns to be moved about on a giant chessboard.

Miss Cormier walked into the room and stopped in front of her. Melody fought her with all the strength she had but the nanny blocked her way like a brick wall. She bit and kicked and scratched like a madwoman. She was emboldened with a rage of her own. She was fighting for Katya, too. But she was no match for the nanny. She was overpowered.

"She's a little hellcat, Nicky," his wife observed. Then she waltzed out of the room, her cackling laugh echoing down the hall. She apparently found Melody's plight most amusing.

Nikolai stood there, immobilized.

"Katya," Melody cried. When she tried to slip out of Miss Cormier's grip, the viper plunged a needle into her neck and Melody grabbed onto the rails of the crib, crumpling to the ground.

The last thing she heard was Miss Cormier calling

out to the guard, "Wolfgango, get this woman out of my sight. Take her back to her room and make sure she doesn't leave. I'll have another guard posted in the nursery."

"Natalia!" the count shouted to the smirking nanny.

"You're going to have your hands full with this one when she wakes up. It's best to let her sleep it off while you come up with a story to explain away your wife."

Chapter Fourteen

Days rolled into endless darkness. She was trapped in a nightmare. Her life was no longer her own. But that evening, during a delicious meal, when she and Nikolai practiced conversation at the dinner table, Melody made an attempt to be civil to her jailer.

"What's new in the world?" she asked.

"The yield curve is inverting."

"What kind of dinner conversation is that?"

"The typical kind in this household. You need to learn to hold your own, whether it's talking about the yield curve inversion, macroeconomics, the post-Brexit world, or whether or not OPEC will cut the oil supply. You will be dealing with many world leaders, and you must be their intellectual match."

Talk like that used to impress her, but now it bored her to tears. It was like watching those nature shows or that recolorized WWII series. She was sure she spent more time watching WWII programs on television with Nikolai than the actual war itself lasted.

"Well, what do *you* want to talk about?" Nikolai asked.

"Your wife. I think I have a right to know. After all, she's living right here with us. While you say you want to make love to me, how does that work? Tell me about her."

"There's nothing to tell."

"Do you love her?"

"No."

"Why did you marry her?"

"It's an age-old tale, especially for royals post-revolution. My family had a sterling pedigree—I am a distant Romanov relation, but we were impoverished imperials. She had the proper connections. She had a fortune to spare, and mine was restored when I married her. It is now a marriage of convenience. She only lusted after my title."

"And your body, I suppose."

"You wouldn't be entirely wrong," he admitted.

"So you pimped yourself out to the highest bidder."

"That's harsh."

"But true. She reminds me of the wicked stepmother in a fairy tale or the old krone in 'Hansel and Gretel.' "

"She is bony," Nikolai agreed, smiling.

"And about twice your age?" she wagered.

"That too."

"Then why do you stay married to her?"

"We have an arrangement. As long as we stay married and I meet her needs physically, I maintain my independence."

"Is that code for having other women on the side? No, don't answer that. You made a pact with the Devil. But are you really happy? Were you ever in love with her?"

Nikolai frowned. "Our relationship was tolerable, until I met you."

"What is so special about me? The fact that I am a Romanov? Or that I remind you of Anastasia?"

"It's the whole package."

"So you didn't fall for plain old Melody Segal."

"There's nothing plain about you, and your name was never really Melody. It's Maria Tatyana, and from now on that's how I shall address you."

"So you say."

"I can let you see your birth certificate."

"I have no reason not to believe you." From now on she was going to keep their relationship impersonal. "So what's on the agenda for tomorrow?"

"We'll spend the day in your office going over briefs. When you're Empress, you won't have a political or executive role, but you'll play an important part as the head of the country. You'll give the people a sense of stability and unity. And, of course, you will be the role model for Katya, who will reign after you. It's important that you learn what's happening in Russia and familiarize yourself with the issues of the day throughout the world. I'll be by your side supporting you every step of the way."

"Usurping my power?" she teased.

"That's not the way it's going to work."

Things between them had grown less strained since she'd decided to cooperate—or pretend to cooperate. After all, she reasoned, once she became Empress, if that day ever came about, she would be free to come and go as she pleased and keep Katya with her. She would beat the Count at his own game. She had the upper hand. When she had true power, he would not be able to stop her. She could always banish him or abdicate.

"You are making great progress in the language as well as on all other fronts," complimented Nikolai, who had made a practice of talking to her only in Russian.

"Miss Cormier is also speaking only Russian to Katya, so hopefully she will become fluent. It's only a matter of weeks before we move to the next phase of our plan. We are about to shoot the royal photos. We will videotape your royal statement. You'll even have your own Twitter and Instagram accounts. We'll be setting up the royal household in St. Petersburg, away from prying eyes in Moscow. We've secured a fashionable palace. We'll be very comfortable there."

"We?"

"Yes, we're a team. I thought you knew that. I will be there to help you navigate and perhaps, one day, if you're feeling charitable toward me, as your royal consort or at the very least, a companion."

Melody laughed. "Isn't a consort a spouse? How can you be a consort if you're already married? Unless bigamy is legal in Russia."

"I've already spoken to the Countess. She is aware of my feelings, and she agrees it is the best thing for the Guardians if we separate. She supports our cause."

"What did you have to promise her?"

Nikolai cleared his throat.

"Well, she needn't worry. There's no way I'm ever going to consent to marrying you."

"I'm sure, in time, when you see what I have to offer, you'll reconsider."

"I've already seen what you have to offer," she sneered.

"I know you still have feelings for me, Comrade," whispered Nikolai, making his way around to the desk, lowering his head and kissing her lightly on the neck.

Shivering, she tightened her hands around her shawl.

The Countess entered the room, ushering in a temperature dip of several degrees.

"Suddenly, there's a draft in here. I think I'll head up to my room."

"Please, don't leave on my account," the Countess said. "I have come to tell you how pleased I am with your progress." She looked at Nikolai. "You did it, my love. Long live the Empress." She threw her head back and laughed. "After all these years, you still surprise me. But can she pull it off?"

Melody wanted to shout, "*She* is right here in front of you." They were talking about her as if she were invisible, not standing right here between them. To the Countess, she was a performing seal in a water park, pitiful, powerless. She was not credited for any part of the project's success. They had set the stage, but she was the one left to sink or swim. And she was determined not to fail.

I am the Empress Maria Tatyana Feodorovna, she thought. For the first time, she was excited about seeing St. Petersburg. She had been drawn to Russia her entire life, to what were rightfully her people, her heritage, her daughter's legacy. All along she'd wanted a job that utilized her knowledge of Russian history. This job certainly more than fit the bill.

"She is ready for the final test," Nikolai insisted.

"As you say."

Gathering her billowing skirt, Melody took her leave, wondering what final test she would have to face. "I would like to rest now."

Nikolai placed his hand on her elbow to stop her progress. "Maria Tatyana, wait."

Then, smooth as an eel, he worked his lips up

toward her cheek and pressed them against her mouth, murmuring, "Would you like some company?"

"No." She turned to face the guard. "Wolfgango, please escort me to the bedroom."

Nikolai frowned, narrowed his brows at Wolfgango, who sprang to attention at his Empress's command, looking more like a besotted puppy than a stalwart Swiss guard.

****

What kind of game was the temptress playing? Was she trying to make him jealous, with Wolfgango? Suddenly, she preferred a lowly guard to a Count as her protector? And what of her loyal but smitten soldier? He was playing right into her hands. Who could blame him? He was already bewitched.

Maria Tatyana took Wolfgango's arm and moved closer to him, engaging him in intimate conversation.

"Take me to my room, please," she simpered, looking up at Wolfgango coquettishly, while venturing a smiling glance back in the Count's direction, twisting the knife even further in his gut.

Arm in arm, they ascended the staircase.

The little vixen. The impudent rogue.

He was going to put a stop to this. See how Wolfgango liked returning to babysitting duty.

The Countess waltzed up to him, just in time to see the couple clinging to each other on the staircase.

"I'd watch out for those two if I were you, Nikolai."

"I have everything under control."

"I'd say the Empress has you and Wolfgango under *her* control."

"That's ridiculous," Nicholas stated. "I'm going to

transfer Wolfgango back to the nursery."

"That won't be necessary. We don't need him there. Natalia and I have that job covered. I've become quite fond of the little Grand Duchess."

"What are you up to?" Nicky demanded.

"Nothing that concerns you. But darling, did you ever think what our lives could have been like had we conceived our own child? Katya could be ours, you know. That child has every bit as much claim to the throne as her mother. Maria Tatyana is entirely dispensable. Were something to happen to her—"

She left the treasonous words unspoken.

Nikolai raised his hand in anger to slap her face— but, in an attempt to control his temper, immediately withdrew it. His voice conveyed an unspoken threat. "If anything happens to her, I will hold you personally responsible. We talked about this. I am divorcing you. I plan to devote my life to my Empress, to be there if she needs me."

"Then you will be playing a waiting game. That girl is playing you for a fool. She has more brains than I gave her credit for."

"Maybe. But I am in love with Maria Tatyana and have been for a long time."

"I hardly think she is in love with you. And I'm not finished with you yet. You know our arrangement. Meet me in our bedroom, my love. Suddenly, I am feeling amorous. If you want to invite your little pet to join us, I would have no objections."

Nikolai's jaw dropped. "You disgust me."

The Countess laughed and licked her lips. "I remember a time when the thought of a threesome used to arouse you. In fact, I'm *deadly* serious."

Nicolai scowled. "That will never happen. I'm not in the mood."

"You never are."

Chapter Fifteen

Nikolai paced the office and slammed his fist on the wooden table. What he really wanted to do was smash it into his wife's face and shatter her bones. This charade of a marriage had gone far enough. He had been at his wife's beck and call and in her bedroom longer than he cared to remember. Once, long ago, she'd amused him. She was useful to him. Even challenging. She'd opened up a whole new world to him. But that was before Maria Tatyana had stolen his heart.

He was no longer tempted by what the Countess had to offer. True, her money had made it possible for his family to become solvent again, even to prosper and move up in the Guardian organization. And for that, he would forever be indebted to her. And, more important, her fortune was funding much of the work of the Guardians, laboring to restore a Romanov to the throne of Russia. They were true partners in that venture. But he was through selling his body and soul to that she-devil in the bargain.

Maria Tatyana thought of herself as a prisoner. But he was just as much a prisoner in the palace, subject to his wife's every whim. Which is why he'd tried to spend as little time as possible in that place. He had divorce papers drawn up. But she'd refused to sign, time and again. She threatened the mission if he followed through.

He would do anything to protect Maria Tatyana, even whore himself to his wife if that was what it took. He was sworn to protect his Empress. He would lay down his life for hers. It was his duty, yes, but he was so in love with her he could hardly think straight.

He'd watched her grow up over the years, although she'd had no idea who he was. He'd accompanied his father and uncles and other Guardians on trips to pay respects to her grandmother. He'd seen her blossom into a beautiful young woman, the image of Anastasia. She wouldn't remember him, of course. Her grandmother had always hustled her quickly out of the room when they arrived. But one glimpse had been enough. He could never forget her. She was his to protect and defend, body and soul. And her limp drove him wild. She was perfection itself, and her disability only made her more vulnerable and more desirable to him.

That was before her grandmother had taken the girl and disappeared. Much later, fate had delivered her into his classroom, into his arms, and eventually into his bed, where she was destined to be. While her teacher, he fell deeply in love and lost all objectivity.

But when she discovered he was married, she'd fled back to Downingtown before he could explain that she was the only one for him. Her grandmother intimated that she'd taken up with the small-town rabbi and conceived his child. That man didn't realize what a prize he possessed. She didn't belong to a small-town clergyman. She belonged to him. She was destined for bigger things. He was going to deliver her from her backwater existence and offer her the world.

His wife, on the other hand, was a poisonous spider who spun an evil web and never kept her word. If she acted on her desire to do away with Maria Tatyana and elevate her daughter, she had the power and the influence to accomplish that. She was a force to be reckoned with in the Guardian organization. He saw no alternative but to swallow his pride and enlist Wolfgango's help. And move up the timetable. Take matters into his own hands. Take back his freedom. His love.

Blowing out a breath, he took two stairsteps at a time and threw open the door of the royal bedchamber. There the Empress and Wolfgango were huddled together laughing over some inconsequential private joke.

Maria Tatyana glared at him. "In future, you will knock on my door before galloping in like a raging bull. My Prince Charming has turned into a cheating toad."

Her pronouncement brought Nikolai up short. Maria Tatyana was beginning to act and talk like an Empress, issuing the edict with all the royal authority of a true monarch.

Pulling Wolfgango away from the Empress, he barked, "A word outside."

The Empress laughed.

"What can be more infuriating than two confounding women under the same roof?" Nikolai mumbled.

Nikolai walked into the hallway with Wolfgango and shut the double door.

"Wolfgango…" the Count seethed.

"Have I done something to upset you?" The guard looked at his master warily.

"I told you to keep an eye on the Empress, not to devour her with your eyes and God knows what else. The woman has you under her spell."

"I'm only doing my duty," Wolfgango objected. "I haven't crossed any lines."

"Well, see that you don't. Stay away from her. That is, I need you to protect her, but who will protect her from you?"

"I am no threat to the Empress."

"Well, there is at least one person in this household who does pose a threat. I want you to keep a particular eye out for my wife and her henchwoman, Miss Cormier."

"The Countess and the nanny?"

"I'm afraid one or both of them may do harm to the Empress, favoring her daughter in our chase to the throne."

"Do you really think they would harm the Empress?"

"You don't know my wife. She is not to be underestimated. I'm afraid she and Miss Cormier may be conspiring against Maria Tatyana. I am depending on you not to let anything happen to Her Royal Highness."

"I would lay down my life for the Empress."

Nikolai exhaled and placed a warning hand on Wolfgango's shoulder. "I don't doubt that. Just don't let your guard down. Or your pants."

Wolfgango colored, saluted, and stood at attention outside Maria Tatyana's bedchamber.

Desolate, the Count walked down the staircase and followed the well-worn path to his wife's door. And swore to himself that this would be the last time.

Chapter Sixteen

The Countess was already prone in the king-sized bed, naked, her bony body and surgically augmented breasts on display when he entered the room.

He stared at her, trying to hide his disgust at her sagging flesh.

"You're brooding," she commented.

"What did you expect?"

"I know you prefer to engage in your Anastasia fantasy, but you haven't lived up to our agreement. You've been avoiding me."

"I'm here now."

"Hardly the romantic greeting I was looking for."

"I told you, I'm not in the mood."

"We had an arrangement, and you haven't kept your part of the bargain." She pouted. "I miss my handsome Lancelot. Remember the young buck eager to come to my bed, willing to service me at any hour of the day or night? I crave your hands on my body. Now, get undressed."

Nikolai grimaced, declaring, "This will be the last time."

"How many times have you sworn that to me? Yet you keep coming back."

"I was not in love before."

"You don't know what love is."

"I know I don't love you."

"What does love have to do with it? If you truly value your little Anastasia's life, you will come to bed."

Scowling, Nikolai began removing his clothes.

"Slowly," she mouthed. "I'm in no hurry. I miss watching you undress."

Nikolai obliged and crawled into bed woodenly, entering the hell he called his marriage. He burned with shame.

The Countess rubbed his shoulders, taking liberties with his body, touching it everywhere. She brought his mouth to her nipples and instructed him to lick and suck them. He could barely hide his revulsion listening to her moans and groans and pants. Instead, his thoughts ran to the ecstasy he felt at Maria Tatyana's luscious, pert breasts.

The Countess indicated she wanted him to mount her. She brought his hand to her core. She was bone dry, and he had to work hard to eke out a drop of moisture. She was eager for his firm flesh to pierce her no longer supple skin in the particular place she was most responsive.

Entering Maria Tatyana was like entering a welcoming wooded glen with a cool mountain stream. Entering his wife was like dipping his manhood into the pits of a blazing furnace. A scorched earth. He felt nothing for his wife but pity. Yet he burned for Maria Tatyana, wondered if she would ever give him another chance at intimacy. The two women were a study in contrast. Young and old. Day and night. Light and dark. Good and evil.

He sensed Maria Tatyana was not truly committed to him or to the Guardians. But as long as she pretended, there was hope she would let him back into her life and her bed.

The Countess held on tight while he went through the motions. But he was no longer anchored in her world. He was merely along for the ride.

Chapter Seventeen

When Melody floated back into consciousness, the guard, Wolfgango, was at the door.

"Your Majesty, you're awake."

She studied Wolfgango. He was built like a fortress, but he wasn't much more than her age. He seemed to hold her in high regard, believed she was already the Empress. Perhaps she could use his loyalty and deference to her advantage, cultivate him as an ally.

He must already be familiar with Katya. He had stood guard over her the entire time she'd been in Switzerland. Maybe Katya had already worked her magic on him. She was a remarkable child. How much did Wolfgango know about the Guardian's plans for the Romanovs? He was her only hope.

Her lady's maids spoke mostly Russian or broken English, so they could barely communicate. Perhaps Wolfgango, of all the Count's minions, held the key to her freedom. She would need his help because, even if she did manage to escape and go to the police, who would believe her?

"Officers, I've been kidnapped by a group of White Russians, and they've made me their leader." After a few jokes, they'd throw her out, unless they somehow in league with the Kinskys, and then they would turn her back over to her captors.

"Wolfgango?" she began.

"Yes, Empress."

"Are you Swiss?"

"Half Swiss German, half Italian, Your Majesty."

She smiled. "I could have guessed from your name."

"Let me get the Count. He left strict instructions to alert him the moment you woke up."

"Wait," she exclaimed, holding out her hand to stop him. "Not just yet. You were there in the nursery. You must know I wasn't asleep. Miss Cormier drugged me. I'm being held here against my will. And my daughter is being kept from me. Could you tell me why I am here?"

"For your protection."

"My protection? It seems I need protection against my captors, the people who are holding me hostage."

"I only follow orders."

"Well, if I'm truly your Empress, I would ask that you follow my orders and help me get out of here."

"I would help you if I could. But I work for the Count."

She looked around. She couldn't see any way out of the room without going through Wolfgango, and he didn't appear to be going anywhere. If only she were Rapunzel and could let down her hair, lower herself to freedom. But this was no fairy tale. There would be no happy ending. And what about Katya? Even if she were to escape, she could not leave her child's fate in the hands of strangers.

Katya couldn't make any journey in this cold climate. Melody would have to go and get help and come back for her daughter. But who could she trust? Certainly not Nikolai—a lying rat who kept his wife and his former mistress under the same roof so he could play musical beds. He obviously had the morals of an alley cat. She couldn't stand the sight of him.

"Wolfgango, come closer."

He hesitated but then moved toward her.

"Can I tell you a secret?" she whispered. She had to find out what kind of weapon he was carrying. As he leaned over, she could see a gun sticking out of a holster in his jacket. Would he shoot her if she made a sudden move?

"I'm frightened. I'm frightened of Miss Cormier and of the Count."

"The Count won't hurt you."

"But his wife?"

"She is with us."

"You sound so sure, but I know nothing about their plans. How long do they intend to hold us prisoner?"

"But Empress, you are not a prisoner. Don't you have everything you want? Is there anything more I can get for you?"

"My freedom and my child. If you could grant me those wishes…"

"I cannot let you out of my sight. Those are my orders."

"Well, then look the other way while I walk out the door. Or better still, escort me to my daughter and help us escape from this jail."

"Kinsky Palace is one of the finest residences in all of Switzerland."

"I don't doubt that. But we are being held against our will."

"And I am truly sorry about that. But there are factions that would kill you and Katya on the spot. I

159

can't let that happen. I am ready to lay my life down for you and your daughter. That's how much I believe in our cause."

She expelled a breath. "I'm sure you do. But I don't know who to believe."

Footsteps echoed down the hall. The door opened. It was Nikolai.

"Ah, my Sleeping Beauty is awake."

She gnashed her teeth. "You act as if I woke up from a long nap after being kissed by a Prince, when in fact, as you know very well, I was drugged, *again.*"

"Wolfgango, you can leave us now," ordered Nikolai.

Wolfgango marched off, sparing a backward glance at the Empress.

"Time for the royal photograph."

"What?"

"The makeup and hair people will be down momentarily. We've chosen the gown you are to wear."

"You honestly expect me to do a photo shoot?"

"Yes, this is very important. The people will want to see you and Katya. It will inspire them."

"If I can see Katya, I'll agree."

Ignoring her demands, the Count clapped his hands and numerous people stepped quickly into the room.

"You must be hungry," the Count said. "I've arranged for us to have breakfast here."

A waiter set out a tray, and she fell upon it ravenously. She *was* hungry and, most of all, thirsty. She drank an entire glass of orange juice and tried some eggs and bacon and fruit, followed by a delicious poppyseed muffin. Except for being held against her will, she was getting the royal treatment. Her attendants entered the room.

"Vanessa, please bring her royal highness the gown."

A girl, ostensibly Vanessa, brought a sheer white, empire-waisted gown in a zippered clothing bag from the closet. It was exquisite, with beads, jewels, and pearls, fashioned in the style a tsarina might have worn.

"Is this—it looks like—it's a replica of—"

"No, not a replica, Comrade. You have a good eye. This is the exact gown Anastasia wore."

"Where did you get it?"

"The gowns and what was left of the royal jewels were taken out of Russia after the revolution."

She exhaled. This was all happening with lightning speed. She had no choice but to go along.

The stylist pulled and brushed her hair, snipping here and there, fashioning it so it resembled the style Anastasia wore. When she was through, the makeup artist went to work. Then Vanessa helped her into her gown. The women became embroiled in a conversation about jewels, and Vanessa finally brought over a spectacular diamond tiara, which the stylist positioned in her hair. Then she lowered a long strand of pearls— Anastasia's necklace of choice—around her neck.

"Where did you get this tiara and the pearls?"

"They belonged to the Grand Duchess Anastasia," Nikolai answered.

"I thought the jewels were all housed in the Kremlin after the 1917 Russian Revolution, except for some that mysteriously disappeared without a trace."

"Many of the jewels were smuggled out of Russia by White Russian families for safekeeping. Most ended up in Paris. Now we have them here. They were just waiting for the right time and the right woman to wear them." Nikolai smiled.

The women fussed over her for another ten minutes and then led her over to a full-length mirror.

Vanessa summoned Nikolai. "Count Kinsky, take a look."

Melody looked into the mirror and her eyes flew open. She was transfixed.

"It's a perfect fit, Maria Tatyana," Nikolai breathed, running his hands down her sides and her hips. "You are Anastasia from head to toe." The stylist had worked her magic and transformed her into the living image of the Grand Duchess. Nikolai's fantasy.

She had to admit, he was right. It was Anastasia's face reflected back at her. She was beginning to believe the fantasy.

"Did you know the name Anastasia is making a comeback?" Nikolai said. "That is fitting, as the name is related to the Greek word for 'resurrection.' "

She couldn't help but be caught up in the excitement. For that moment, she felt she was right where she should be.

"And now, Katya," the Count announced.

Melody turned toward the door.

Miss Cormier made her entrance holding Katya. Katya's honey-blonde curls were styled with the traditional Romanov silk headband the sisters always wore in royal photographs, and she was adorable— every inch a Grand Duchess.

"Katya," Melody cried, reaching for her and raining kisses on her chubby face. Finally, Miss Cormier released her daughter into her waiting arms. "You look beautiful." The baby gurgled and smiled, obviously overjoyed to see her mother.

"You may hold her for the royal portrait," Miss Cormier said grudgingly.

If that is what it took to be with her child, she didn't care. Let them snap away.

"Everybody follow me down to the ballroom," Nikolai instructed. "We'll take the photo there. Everything is set up."

They followed the entourage, for that is what it was, so many people, making such a fuss over them. When they arrived at the ballroom, the lights and camera were already in place. Nikolai indicated they should sit in a large throne-like brocade chair already situated in front of the camera. She sat down and placed Katya on her lap.

An attendant smoothed the folds of her gown, posing Katya and Melody just so.

A flash of a thought occurred to her. Was this how the Tsar and his family felt right before they were assassinated? Seated, as if they would be shooting a family photograph, and then, there were shots of another kind. Surely, they would not—

Nikolai spoke. "Vanessa, wipe her Majesty's brow."

Vanessa wiped the perspiration from her forehead.

"Smile, my dear," Nikolai said. "Hold your head up. This photo will be iconic. It will be published all over the world."

She didn't feel like smiling in the least, but she struck a pose. She had momentary happiness with Katya in her arms. That thought fortified her.

Her eyes were light sensitive after being held in captivity and drugged for what seemed like weeks, without the warmth of the sun on her face. The photographer kept shooting. He must have seen something he liked.

Finally, they were finished. Nikolai was speaking.

"Perfect, thank you, everyone. Now leave the Empress alone for a moment."

Apparently, the isolation period didn't exclude Nikolai. He remained as she looked longingly at Katya, who disappeared with Miss Cormier.

"I'm ready," Melody said stubbornly.

"Ready for what?"

"Ready to cooperate. I'm willing to do this under one condition."

"And what would that be?"

"That Katya is returned to me now. We should not be separated. I won't allow it."

Nikolai laughed. "You won't *allow* it? You are sounding more and more like an Empress. Very good."

"I am serious."

"It so happens I agree with you. I imagine Miss Cormier will have something to say about that. She's grown quite attached to Katya."

"Who's in charge here, you or the nanny?"

"She *is* pretty ferocious," Nikolai joked.

"You think this is funny."

"No, I don't. And I'm very happy you're finally seeing things our way."

"I don't see that I have much choice. But I will not work with you unless I'm allowed to be with Katya."

"I'll arrange it."

He placed a broad hand against her cheek and she slapped it away.

"Don't think my cooperation in any way means

you can insinuate yourself back into my life or my bed whenever it pleases you."

"But you know how I feel about you."

"No, I don't. I thought you loved me. But how can that be, when you're married and your wife is living right under my nose. How easy it is for you to move from my bed to hers. She doesn't seem to mind, but I do. Don't you ever touch me again."

"You don't mean that. I can explain."

"I'm not interested in hearing your explanations," Melody ordered, channeling her inner Empress. "Just tell me what I am to do, and see that Katya is moved into my quarters immediately."

Chapter Eighteen

"Before that happens, there is one thing I will need from you," Nikolai reminded her. "Do you recall I mentioned that the Imperial gold reserves went missing in 1918? The country was in a state of chaos. The man responsible for the Tsar's shipment of gold took his family and fled, when he realized that the Red Army aimed to erase any trace of the Tsar's bloodline. You are the sole surviving relative of that man. We have read the diaries and we can find nothing that would lead us to the lost shipment. But we believe you know something. We believe the gold is buried somewhere in Siberia, near Omsk. We must find it. It will finance our revolution, help us restore the monarchy."

"And line your pockets?"

"It will be deposited in the Russian Central Bank. Think of all the good it will do for the people if we find it."

"The people? Somehow I doubt that. But as I told you before, I don't know anything about a lost shipment of gold."

"No, we realize you may not think you know, but there must be a clue, something you can tell us that would help us locate the gold. Something your grandmother might have said, something she left you besides the diamond-and-emerald necklace."

"You have my necklace?"

"It was in your handbag. It is now our property, your property if you're really with us."

"Why don't you use that to finance your revolution? It's priceless."

"It could finance a chunk of operating expenses," admitted Nikolai, "but it's more important as a symbol around your neck." Melody's hand flew to her neck. An Empress could easily lose her head if she weren't careful. Look what had happened to Marie Antoinette.

Melody paused. There was nothing in the diary that she could recollect, except...

Nana's locket. She suddenly remembered the rabbi's translation. He said the back of The Ten Commandments was inscribed with an address, but no city name. Nikolai had seen the disc in her handbag but probably dismissed it as a worthless trinket because he couldn't appreciate its true value. This address in Omsk might solve the mystery. Should she tell Nikolai about that clue? Could it be of importance? She hesitated, then reconsidered. Whatever would get her closer to Katya and freedom was what she needed to do.

"There is something, but it may not mean anything."

He was eager for any information. He moved closer. So close she could feel his breath on her face. His hand gripped her elbow in anticipation.

"My grandmother left me a locket. On the front is the Ten Commandments. On the back, in Russian, is an address, but no city name. The girl in the diary was from Omsk. Perhaps the two are related."

Nikolai could hardly contain his excitement. "Show me."

She grabbed her handbag from the dresser and

pulled out the locket.

"It's a plain rose gold locket," she said, handing it to Nikolai. "It has sentimental value, but I had it appraised, and it's not worth much, according to the jeweler."

Nikolai examined the locket. He read the address out loud.

"This may be it," he noted. "This may be where the gold is buried. You said your grandmother gave you this locket?"

"Yes, she always wore it. She was wearing it when she was killed. There was a picture in the diary of a young girl in a red coat wearing that same locket."

"Passed down from generation to generation," Nikolai mused. "Perhaps it's the missing piece of the puzzle. May I borrow this?" he asked. "I need to make a call."

"Yes, of course. But I want it back. It means a lot to me."

Nikolai called out his assurances as he rushed from the room.

When he returned, he handed her the locket. "We'll soon know if this is the location of the lost shipment of gold."

"How long did you say you'd been searching for the gold?"

"Both sides have been searching since the late 1920s. If we find it, well, nothing can stop us."

"I hope you find what you're looking for." And she meant it. What did she care if they found the gold? As long as she was reunited with her daughter.

"This will guarantee our success in putting you on the throne. It's what we've been waiting for, planning for, praying for. We will finally avenge the death of the Tsar and his family. I've been waiting a lifetime."

The situation began to seem real when she walked in on Nikolai, in the study, surrounded by military men, intent on the television screen hanging on the wall, when a shout arose.

Nikolai noticed her presence and rushed to meet her.

"We are witnessing history here. The Tsar has withdrawn his name from the ballot and announced plans to step down."

And by "the Tsar" she knew he meant the Russian Bear, the longtime dictator.

"Things are already beginning to change. Our candidate, a Guardian, has a reform agenda, and now he is all but guaranteed to win the first free and fair election in our lifetimes."

"And you engineered that?"

"Not me personally, but the Guardian organization, the people who are placed in strategic positions throughout the country. When we confronted the Bear about his frozen bank accounts and he realized we had replaced his operatives and *his* army was now *our* army, the Guardians offered him a choice. He was smart enough to want to survive in luxury, albeit in exile.

"We're making strides to remove the power and influence and money that remains in the hands of a few corrupt oligarchs, who were nothing more than thieves. Between inflation and the growing gap between rich and poor, the Great Recession, followed by the Russian financial crisis, they have managed to oversee the deterioration of the entire Soviet economy."

"I can't believe you pulled off your bloodless coup."

"We've been working on it for a century. We almost implemented our plan in 1991, when Boris Yeltsin came to power after the collapse of the Soviet Union and communism left the Russian Republic in chaos. In every generation, we got closer to bringing our vision to life, but just when we had our chance, your mother was killed—in an auto accident that turned out to be no accident. Your grandmother was too old for the image we wanted to project. The path is clear for you, your Highness."

She shrugged.

"I see you're still skeptical."

"I worry that the people won't accept me."

"They are clamoring for you on social media. We've laid the groundwork. They're waving banners in the streets. They are awaiting the triumphant return of the Romanovs. Time has a way of erasing bad memories. This is our moment."

"Meanwhile, you're holding me hostage in this palace, with nothing to do."

Nikolai dismissed his cadre of guards.

"There is much you can accomplish, if you put your mind to it. For example, how are you coming on that reading list I gave you? You need to become more familiar with Russian history, literature. You must eat, drink, and sleep your heritage. Have you had a chance to pick up a book?"

"In between the times you drugged me?"

"That was Miss Cormier," he said, "mostly."

"Which makes me wonder who exactly is in charge here."

"We're all working together."

"And another thing, how do you know I'm the legitimate heir?"

"We've run your DNA."

She pursed her lips. It occurred to her they could have taken a sample at any time in any number of ways. Probably when she was drugged.

Nikolai observed her from beneath his hooded lids. "I've dreamed of bringing you here to Switzerland. We talked about it, remember?"

"With your wife?"

"Our marriage is a sham. We don't love each other. We just stay together because, well, first out of necessity and later out of habit. I didn't know what real love was until I met you."

She wanted to believe him.

"Nikolai, I need to know the truth. You knew who I was all along. You had the advantage. Did you target me?"

Nikolai flexed his shoulders. "I didn't *target* you. I was recruiting you, grooming you for this role, but I didn't expect to fall in love."

"How can you say you're in love with me, when you separated me from my child?"

"A child I knew nothing about. You say you were in love with me, and yet you ran away from the university, and the next thing I knew, you had a baby. It didn't take you long to get over me. To crawl into bed with another man. I really need to know. Who's the father?"

Chewing on her upper lip, she answered carefully. "The rabbi in our synagogue is very charming."

"The rabbi?"

"Yes, he's very handsome."

Nikolai frowned.

"How did you even find me?" she asked, needing to hear the story again, trying to gauge whether Nikolai was telling the truth.

"Your grandmother knew about the Guardians. She knew we would come for her or your mother or you one day. After the accident, she tried to hide you away, but there are evil forces out there. They were responsible for your grandmother's death. We were afraid they would come for you, too, so we had to take immediate action. You were our last hope."

The story seemed plausible. But she was having a difficult time believing that she really was the lost Romanov, ready to assume the Russian throne.

Chapter Nineteen

She was living in the lap of luxury, but a palace can still be a prison. The only way out was to accept her situation. There were worse fates. After all, who wouldn't want to be an Empress? And to think of those unfortunate children of the Tsar's who were murdered because of their father's actions. The girls never had a chance to grow up, to fall in love, get married, have children, and carry on the dynasty. If she could right that wrong, then why wouldn't she want to? If she could have changed history in those early morning hours at Ipatiev House, changed fate, ensured that the innocent children who were brutally murdered would have a chance to survive into the future, she would. Anyone with a heart would.

She'd been reading and studying about the revolution and the history of the Tsars when reality hit her. She was related to the last Tsar of Russia. His line didn't die out. The rightness of Nikolai's plan was beginning to make sense.

She studied each night until she fell asleep, sometimes with an open book beside her on the bed. Nikolai continued to drill her like he had when he was her professor—correcting her, reprimanding her, driving her. To him, it was more than an education—it was setting the stage, the final fulfillment of his life's goal.

When he felt the time was right, guests began drifting in and out of the palace on a regular basis to get a look at her, like she was some kind of caged animal on display in a zoo or a circus, all the time remarking how much she resembled Anastasia. Nikolai paraded her in front of a host of counts and earls and dukes for inspection. They touched her hair, marveled at her clothes, her jewels. They were enthralled with her, delighted with Katya.

"She's a born Romanov," one visitor said about her to Nikolai as if she were not even in the room. "And the child, she's spectacular."

"Maria Tatyana is a definite royal," said another. "Look at the way she carries herself. She is the incarnation of Anastasia."

They got excited when Nikolai instructed her to model Anastasia's clothes, wear her jewels, make her poor but improving attempt at speaking Russian. On those occasions, he primped like a peacock or a proud papa. And she performed like a pet seal.

After a particularly grueling day, she almost lost the book that was balanced atop her head.

"That's not how an Empress walks," Nikolai admonished.

She'd had enough of posing, enough of his prodding and bullying. The limp she'd tried so hard to disguise was front and center. She had almost tripped, but he caught her before she could tumble.

"Tell me, how does an Empress walk?" she posed, exhausted.

He grabbed the book, placed it on his head, and proceeded to sashay across the room without dropping it.

She laughed hysterically and sang the opening bars of the Miss America theme song, improvising some of the words. "There he goes, Count—"

"I'm glad you find this amusing."

"I find your entire charade to objectify women anything but amusing."

"That was not our intent. That's not what this is about. You will become the most prominent, most talked about, most sought after woman in the world. There is no room for error. The situation demands absolute perfection."

"But I am not perfect, as you know. And I will never be. My limp. From the accident. I try to compensate, but—"

Nikolai enveloped her in his arms.

She relaxed in his embrace, hungered for his approval.

"You're simply tired, my love. Rest a while. Your limp is nothing. It just adds to your charms. To me, you are perfect."

A tear slipped down her face. Of course, he would have to say that. She was his creation. His dream doll Grand Duchess Anastasia all wound up and come to life. He was putting the finishing touches on his work of art. Until, to a person, the Guardians who were gathered at the palace agreed she was ready. Ready to be tested. Ready for her trial by fire.

Chapter Twenty

Zurich, Switzerland, to Bellagio, Lake Como, Italy

The next morning, one of her ubiquitous maids woke her early.

"The household is moving."

"Moving to where?"

"To Italy, to a villa on Lake Como."

"Why?"

"You'll have to ask the Count. I've packed your clothes. We'll be leaving this morning."

Why were they moving to Lake Como? Were they going to be transferred from one prison to another? Would Katya be allowed to travel with her?

As if on cue, Nikolai walked in and sat beside her on the bed. His eyes sparkled with excitement.

"I heard we are moving to Italy."

"That's right. A friend of the family, a Guardian, lives in the Royal Suite on the top floor of his hotel. The place is as big as a palace and right on the lake shore, surrounded by cypress woods and gardens. Have you ever been to Lake Como?"

She admitted she hadn't but had always wanted to see it and the surrounding area.

"It is the most beautiful place on earth. I can't wait to show it to you."

"Why are we moving?"

"We're hosting a ball. Guardians from around the world will attend. They'll all be on hand to celebrate your coming out. And to make sure you're ready."

"I have to pass another test?"

"Of sorts. But you're more than ready. As long as you remember everything we've practiced."

"I feel a little like Eliza Doolittle in *My Fair Lady*. Like I'm your experiment."

"That is not a fair comparison. You are the real thing. You are the Romanov heir. I knew it the moment I laid eyes on you. I just added a little polish and shine."

"But I don't know these people. How do I know they're not enemies?"

"I know them all. There's no place on earth more secure."

"The prospect of a roomful of Guardians somehow doesn't make me feel safe."

Nikolai lifted her chin. "Just last-minute jitters."

"Will your wife be there?"

"Of course."

"And she will be waiting for me to fail."

"You won't fail. And she is as invested in your success as I am."

"Somehow I doubt that."

Her maid—Anushka or Esfir or Evgeniya—their names all ran together—helped her dress for the trip and pack. Nikolai escorted her out of the palace to a waiting private jet.

Observing her prison from the outside looking in was an entirely different experience from being cooped up in splendor.

"Kinsky Palace is beautiful."

"It belongs to my wife, not to me," Nikolai said,

dismissing the compliment.

Melody wrapped the fur coat tighter across her chest. It felt good to be out in the fresh air, no matter how cold. It had finally stopped snowing. The wind had died down. She scanned the empty seats in the jet.

"Where is Katya?"

"She'll stay behind with the nanny."

"Is that safe?"

"She will not harm Katya. You have my word on that. I will not allow it. She will not be needed for this phase of the plan. It will be a very short trip. You'll see her as soon as we return." Melody missed her child already.

After less than fifty minutes' flying time, the jet landed in Milan. A driver was waiting to transport them in a black Mercedes stretch limousine to the elegant Italian town of Bellagio on Lake Como.

An hour and seventeen minutes later, they pulled up to the massive structure, its ochre exterior reflected in the stunning teal water, as it sat right on the lake shore. The property was breathtaking. Reading about Lake Como had not prepared her for the thrill of being there.

"Actually, the area has quite a colorful past," Nikolai explained. "Roman legions conquered the region in the second century BC. It is believed that Pliny the Younger, a famous Roman writer, was born and died here in what was his family's villa. It was once known as a palace, but it was really halfway between a fortress and a villa.

"It was used as a barracks during the First World War," he continued. "But Leonardo da Vinci and Franz Liszt stayed here, visiting, before it was officially a hotel. Important guests through the years included English lords and Russian princes, barons and counts, field marshals, actors and movie stars, including Clark Gable and Anthony Quinn, kings and queens, sheikhs, even emperors. Franklin Roosevelt stayed here when he was governor of New York, and so, later, did Winston Churchill and John Fitzgerald Kennedy. It has been used as the setting for numerous films.

"And another interesting fact of history. Did you know that Benito Mussolini, the Italian Fascist dictator, and his mistress, Clara Petacci, were executed by Italian partisans on the shores of Lake Como, not far from here, as they tried to escape to Switzerland?"

"No," she answered, as they walked toward the reception area. She couldn't keep her eyes off the lake, now a striking bright green, a mesmerizing sight, like a million diamonds sparkling in the morning light. It was truly a setting out of a picture book. She doubted even an artist could properly capture the beauty of the scene before her.

They made a fuss over her at the front desk like she was royalty and ordered a bellman to accompany them to her room. First, Nikolai handed her a postcard.

"A keepsake. I'll have a picture book with the history of the hotel sent to your room."

"Thank you. That's very thoughtful."

When she ascended in the tiny elevator and arrived at her spacious suite at the end of the hall on the second floor, one of sixty rooms, the bellman stored her luggage in an oversized paneled wardrobe and pulled back the drapes. The view of the lake and the snow-covered mountains was breathtaking. Nikolai tipped him and stood next to her at the window, beneath an intricate ceiling painting in a room full of vintage furniture. The room was the very definition of luxury, with the feel of a private residence.

"It is beautiful," she admitted. "I've never even imagined a place like this."

"There's a tree-lined garden surrounded by woods, and a lakeside pool. Outside the gates, there's a connecting path from the villa to the village, with easy access to the shops and the port."

"Aren't you afraid I will escape, so close to town?"

"You're under constant surveillance, so no, I'm not concerned. And I know you will go nowhere without Katya. I will be by your side day and night."

"Night?"

"In the room down the hall, but if you wish—"

"That's close enough," she assured him.

She managed to rest for several hours until one of her myriad maids came in to help her dress for the ball. She felt like Cinderella. The gown the attendant laid out was stunning and fit her like a glove. She'd never seen its like. Of course, the jewelry set out to complement the gown was fabulous. The girl arranged her hair. She glanced into the full-length mirror, again hardly believing her eyes. She looked like a princess. Like Anastasia.

Nikolai, dressed in a black tuxedo, knocked at the door. With his movie star good looks, he was dazzling. He appraised her from head to toe, and his approving look signaled he was more than satisfied.

"So the band has started playing. Are you ready, your highness?"

She looked up at him and whispered, "Stay close."

"Just try and get rid of me."

Nikolai took her arm at the elbow, and they walked down the hall of the Lombardy-style villa with its balconies and views of the lake at every turn.

"We will make our entrance descending the spectacular main marble staircase beyond the *Rezzato* stone balustrade, to where gold candelabras and huge chandeliers of Murano glass light the room where everyone is waiting."

She inhaled and wondered, *"Can I do this?"* She held on tight to Nikolai.

She must have spoken the words out loud or Nikolai was attuned to her thoughts.

"Of course you can. There's no reason to be nervous. Do you trust me?"

That was the million-dollar question.

"I will be with you every step of the way. Look ahead. Don't look down. I will guide you."

She relaxed—or tried to. She walked slowly, regally, compensating for her slight limp, as if she had a book balanced on her head, like they'd practiced, like her life and her daughter's life didn't hang in the balance. She couldn't afford to fail. If she did, she could only imagine what that might mean for Katya. She glided into the ballroom, trying not to gawk at the ceiling frescoes and silken wall hangings.

"A few more steps, and then we're there."

The room was magnificent with its vast windows and oversized gilded mirrors. It had been transformed into a fairyland of sparkling lights, candlelight, and orchids. The peaks of snowclad *Monte Crocione* rose in the distance across the lake, now a calming gray in the waning light. White tablecloths, white silk balloon shades, gold-rimmed white bone china, champagne chilling in silver stands tableside, fine silver sparkling. Ferries and pleasure boats sailed by, lights on. There was a fireworks display in her honor.

"You are not impressed," Nikolai whispered, barely moving his lips, tightening his grip. "You are an aristocrat, used to this level of luxury. You are perhaps a little bored."

Bored? She was anything but. She felt like a country mouse come to the big city. She raised her head and tried her best to look haughty.

A hush fell over the crowd, and they greeted her with applause. Sounds of the piano, violin, and double bass trio floated through the air and spilled out into the garden. The musicians began by playing the powerful, patriotic strains of *Bozhe, Tsarya krahni! God Save the Tsar!* the historical anthem of the Russian Empire, according to Nikolai. Then they switched to her personal favorite, Andrea Bocelli's *Con Te Partiro*, a nod to their host country, followed by a Strauss waltz. A synchronized ballet of waiters in white tuxes and bowties danced around the room serving the guests, who raised their glasses.

"To the Empress."

She looked up but couldn't identify the dignitary. Then she realized they were toasting *her* and talking about *her*. Bowing to *her*. Even Nikolai's wife shot her a sharp, terrifying look, but then lowered her head in acknowledgment and curtsied. That must have cost her. If Nana could see her now, would she be pleased?

Nikolai's firm hand was at her back. Her spine tingled. His touch was not meant to arouse. He was playing a role. He was merely her escort, not her lover as he had once been. How could he be, with his wife in the room? No matter that she'd taken separate transportation to Bellagio, or that he'd told her they had separate bedrooms. Could he even be believed that they didn't share a room?

She snapped back to reality.

"Let us enjoy dinner. It's a seven-course meal the chef has prepared in your honor. He has won a Michelin star. He is the father of Italian molecular cuisine. Then, after we eat, we will make the rounds for introductions.

"Like they do at weddings."

"Exactly."

She imagined for a moment that this was their wedding banquet and she and Nikolai were the happy couple.

"I can't stop staring out the window. The scenery is so beautiful."

"Then you won't have noticed that people are staring at you because *you're* so beautiful. Let them stare, take no notice," Nikolai advised. "You are the woman of the hour. Act as if this pomp and circumstance does not faze you in the least."

Cameras flashed throughout the sumptuous dinner, nearly blinding her. She took it in stride. The food was delicious. By the time the festivities were in full swing, she was no longer playing a role. She *was* Empress Maria Tatyana Feodorovna.

"Now, there are some important people I want you to meet," Nicholas said. "People who made this all possible, starting with our host."

"Do I dare speak Russian to them?"

"You are almost fluent, so yes, why not?"

Nikolai had made a practice of speaking to her in

Russian since her arrival at the castle in Zurich, so she felt she had a basic command of the language.

"And if I make a mistake?"

"They will be so besotted by your beauty they will fall all over themselves to please you. To them, you are the second coming, Anastasia reborn.

"And besides, the Guardians are from all over the world, Spain, Greece, Italy, even America. There are various assortments of counts, Russian princes, British aristocrats, American politicians, prime ministers, even a movie star or two. You will definitely recognize some of them. You'd be surprised at how widespread our influence is. All the Guardians speak English, if you want to revert to your comfort zone. But you are good with languages. Don't sell yourself short."

Nikolai paraded her around the room until her head was spinning, careful not to spend too much time with any one Guardian. She could hardly keep all the names straight. She suffered the embarrassment of being put on display like some thoroughbred racehorse. She was surprised no one had pulled back her gums to check the condition of her teeth, but that didn't stop some of the older men from patting her flanks. She wondered what they would think if she started to neigh.

She hated being flaunted, but at the same time, she craved Nikolai's approval and the comfort and safety of his arms. She was falling back into his emotional trap.

By the time the ball was over, she had received a personal invitation to tour the villa and the gardens from the host and owner, several marriage proposals, and a few proposals of the indecent variety, which Nikolai, who had never been more possessive, shut down on the spot. She had a few fan girl moments of her own when she shook hands with several internationally prominent actors and actresses among the crowd.

"The hotel owner says he is a direct cousin of the Tsar and that he will amaze me with stories of the history of the villa at a private luncheon in the living room of the Royal Suite. He says it has amazing views of the lake."

Nikolai frowned. "The owner is a hotelier, not a prince. And his claim to be a Romanov is debatable. You are too good for him. If you want to see the lake, I will show it to you. There will be no private meetings. We can't afford any slip-ups. He may have a glimpse of you, no more. If you want to learn the history of the villa, I will be glad to take you out on the lake after breakfast tomorrow and teach you. Stay away from him. He has a reputation with the ladies."

"Not unlike yours," she teased.

"We've come this far together. There is no time for diversions."

She couldn't help but smile. Nikolai's jealousy was on full display.

"He is very handsome and quite charming."

"Do you enjoy torturing me, Maria Tatyana?"

She laughed. She and Nikolai were on good terms, but she wouldn't let him touch her again. He had lost that privilege forever. But being so near him, dancing with him, soaking up the romance of the evening and the ambience of their surroundings, she was tempted to fall back into their familiar pattern. And he sensed her wavering, she knew. He was just waiting for her to capitulate.

As the last guest left the dining room, she knew she

had passed the test. That evening, before he left her suite, Nikolai showed her a press release he would issue in the coming month. The dream was beginning to seem real. She would allow him to take her into his arms and kiss her, and more, a reward for her stunning performance, but instead he kissed the back of her hand, chastely. He may as well have patted her on the head like an obedient dog. He knew she was intoxicated, which made her giddy and susceptible to him, tonight of all nights, but he held back. So that was the dance they were doing with each other. Parry, thrust, parry, thrust, parry… He apologized, but he had an important late-night appointment he must attend. An assignation with his wife, perhaps?

****

THE NEW YORK TIMES INTERNATIONAL EDITION
ROMANOV RESTORED TO THE RUSSIAN THRONE
Published 18th July 2021
Written by Peter Ivanoff, CNN, St. Petersburg
The Coronation of Russian Empress Maria Tatyana Feodorovna, the last male-line heir to Tsar Nicholas II, was celebrated yesterday, 17th July 2021, in the Russian Orthodox Cathedral of Saints Peter and Paul. The cathedral houses the tombs of all Imperial Russia's rulers, including Peter the Great, Catherine the Great, and other Romanov ancestors. The Empress expressed her wish not to be coronated in the Moscow Kremlin, but instead to be crowned where the remains of Emperor Nicholas II, the last Russian monarch, Empress Alexandra Feodorovna, Grand Duchesses Tatiana, Olga, and Anastasia, who were executed on that same day in Yekaterinburg in 1918, were interred. The Romanov dynasty ruled Russia for over 300 years,

from 1613-1917.

After a magnificent processional entry into St. Petersburg, the ceremony began with the Empress seated on an historic throne in the middle of the cathedral. The Empress wore an antique diamond-and-emerald-encrusted heirloom necklace and a diamond-studded crown from the Romanov jewel collection. Afterward, there was a royal banquet and a masked ball. Thousands of people attended simultaneous festivities in St. Petersburg and Moscow, including various Russian noble families, royal guests and relatives, and Romanov descendants from around the world. Upper balcony, towers, and walls of the Kremlin were illuminated. Guests in St. Petersburg queued for hours to get a glimpse of the new Empress, reputed to be the incarnation of Grand Duchess Anastasia, and her infant daughter, Grand Duchess Ekaterina Nikolaevna, affectionately known as "Katya."

Count Nikolai Kinsky, the Empress's closest advisor, was at her side. In a show of solidarity, the newly elected President of Russia, Peter Zhukov, known as "Peter the Reformer," the anti-corruption candidate, was also in attendance.

The newly crowned Empress and her daughter have captured the hearts of the Russian people and captivated royal watchers around the world.

"The coronation, which pays homage to the last royal family of Russia and celebrates the new generation, goes a long way to erase the stain of the execution of Nicholas II, his wife, and young family," said Count Kinsky. "A new dawn is rising with the coronation of the Tsar's last living direct heir. The coronation and concurrent free election of a new

president offer the Russians a chance to wipe the slate clean and rewrite history with a happy ending to a gothic fairy tale."

As in the British monarchy, the duties of the Empress will be largely ceremonial. She and the Grand Duchess will make their home at a waterfront palace in St. Petersburg, the location of New Russia's seat of government.

Chapter Twenty-One

Bellagio, Lake Como, Italy

Back in his own suite, Nikolai ran the shower hot, eager to erase all traces of his wife from his body, *one last time*. She was so aroused by the previous evening's success she'd insisted her *husband,* her puppet, join her in bed. As an incentive, she intimated she might soon be willing to sign the divorce papers. The nauseating smell of her perfume—not to mention all her oils and lotions and powders and creams she thought would restore her youth and hide her flaws—made him want to vomit. He had to think of Maria Tatyana to get it up at all.

And he was tired of just *thinking* of her. He wanted, no needed, to rekindle the flame of their love. He'd never thought of another woman since he'd bedded her. Yet her body and her mind were hardened against him. Deep inside, he feared she wanted nothing to do with him.

It had taken everything in him to leave Maria Tatyana's suite last night. She would have welcomed him in her bed. He could see she was waiting for him to make the first move. How he longed to take her into his arms and make her his again. But he had satisfied himself with a chaste kiss on the hand. Any more intimate contact would have led to a passionate night in bed, and he had a mandatory appointment with his wife. He wanted to do things the right way, to wait until he was legally free. How could he convince Maria Tatyana of his true feelings? Of his allegiance? This obligation to his wife—his rote attempt to placate her once again for the false promise of a divorce that never came—had to stop. He swore this would be the last time he succumbed to her demands.

****

Dressed in freshly laundered and pressed dark blue jeans and a long-sleeve cotton shirt, Nikolai stopped by Maria Tatyana's suite. She answered the door, dressed in slacks and a sweater top. He breathed in the clean scent of her—her shampoo and her unique essence.

"How was your meeting last night?"

"Boring, but necessary," he replied. "But I don't want to dwell on last night. I have a surprise for you. The hotel has prepared a picnic, and the captain is waiting at the dock. We're going on a private tour of the lake. It would be a crime to come to Lake Como and not go out on the lake. You can't appreciate Lake Como unless you've seen it from the water. Come, put on a hat, and we'll go."

She grabbed a floppy hat from the wardrobe. He took her hand and led her out of the hotel and down to the dock a short walk away.

"What about Katya?"

"I know you miss her, but we'll be back in Switzerland by this evening."

"Where are the guards?"

"It's just the two of us."

The captain helped them aboard, and they sat in the boat, the sun shining on the light blue water, and a gentle wind blowing.

"First stop, Varenna," he announced. "Then Menaggio. We'll pass by Tremezzo where we can view the Villa Carlotta. Then Cernobbio, where we'll pass by the Villa d'Este. Then to the city of Como itself. On the way back, we'll sail by the Gardens of the Villa Melzi. When we pass by George Clooney's house, I'll point it out. Last night at the ball, he mentioned he would welcome us for a visit if we wanted to stop by."

"Could we?" she asked excitedly.

"Not on this trip," said Nikolai. "I told him we had urgent business in Zurich. Sorry to disappoint you, but you'll have to settle for spending the morning with me. But I promise, I'll take you back."

"With Katya?"

"With Katya."

"You seem very familiar with the lake."

"I have visited many times. When I was younger and had no money, I stayed in a lesser known hotel in Menaggio. I remember the hotel concierge asked if I would like to ride along with a famous soccer player and his family for an outing on the lake. Of course, I said yes to what I thought would be a free ride. At the end of the day, it turned out I had to pay for that very expensive excursion. The soccer player was told he'd be riding along with me, at my expense.

"My father was not very happy with me. He said I needed to marry a wealthy woman. It was around that time he arranged my marriage with Juliette, a woman from another Guardian family."

"An arranged marriage?"

"It worked out for both of us. She had the money I needed and I had a title she craved."

Maria Tatyana lay back in the boat with her hat over her face to block the sun and block out all thoughts of Nikolai's objectionable wife and her cravings.

"This is heaven. It's a perfect day."

"I'm glad you like it. It will be the first of many new memories."

"You promise we'll be back?"

"Promise. I've bought a villa here on the water, and I'm having it refurbished. It will be our home away from home."

Chapter Twenty-Two

Kinsky Palace, Zurich, Switzerland

Nikolai sat at his desk and made calls to his contacts in the Guardian network across the globe. All was ready. He would have liked more time to prepare Maria Tatyana for her new role, take better precautions for her safety, but they were out of time, out of options. If events didn't move forward fast, and his wife had her way, with Miss Cormier's help, Maria Tatyana would be usurped or worse. The thought of his love suffering the same fate as befell her unfortunate Romanov ancestors had his heart racing. Shot and bayonetted, burned and carelessly tossed down a mine shaft. He would die before he let that happen. But if he died, who would protect Maria Tatyana?

He rode the elevator up to Maria Tatyana's bedroom and found her studying the diary. He didn't want to alarm her, but he had to warn her.

"If my wife or Miss Cormier comes for you, don't go with them. Think of an excuse. A headache, a fainting spell, whatever you have to do. I've already instructed Wolfgango not to let you out of his sight. We are going to leave for St. Petersburg early, as soon as it's safe. It may be as early as tonight."

"What about Katya?"

"Wolfgango will get her from the nursery, and

we'll leave together."

"I won't go anywhere without my child," Maria Tatyana insisted.

"Understood. You have my word."

Personally, he was not as worried about Katya's safety. His wife and Natalia adored her. They would never let anything happen to her. Katya could follow. They needed her to control Maria Tatyana. But the Empress was his chief concern.

"Pack your bags. Only what you need for a short flight. The rest of your things—your gowns, shoes, and jewelry—will follow. It's frigid outside. There's a fur in the closet. And some boots that are your size."

"Will Katya—"

"Wolfgango will take care of the Grand Duchess."

"Why the rush? Has something happened?" Maria Tatyana wondered.

"No, my love, but we're not taking any chances."

Nikolai took Wolfgango aside and hastily whispered his final instructions.

"You want me to drug the Countess and Miss Cormier?" Wolfgango answered in disbelief.

"I fear they will try to do the same to the Empress. We need to get her away and out of this viper pit as soon as possible. We already have to worry about possible resistance from the Kremlin. We don't need interference from our own side."

"If Miss Cormier gets wind of this plot, she'll kill me," Wolfgango said. "Her hands are lethal weapons."

"I'm aware that she's a trained killer. So you will put something in their tea after dinner, a sedative perhaps, nothing to harm them but enough to slow them down. And then you will take the child and meet us at the airstrip behind the palace."

"I can handle that."

Maria Tatyana overheard the conversation.

"Miss Cormier is trying to kill me?"

"I won't let that happen. Do you trust me?"

"Do I have a choice?"

"Do you trust Wolfgango?"

"With my life."

He frowned, truly desolate. She trusted Wolfgango but had no use for him. She had bewitched his right-hand man.

"I've picked out your outfit," the Count said. "It's in the closet." But he made no move to exit the room.

"You can leave now while I get dressed," she said.

"No need for modesty. I've seen you without your clothes before," he remarked.

She lifted her chin stubbornly. "That was then. This is now." Could she smell the malodorous stink of his wife on his body?

Sullen, he walked toward the entrance of the suite. Wolfgango remained.

"That goes for you, too, Wolfgango," Nikolai ordered. "Give the Empress her privacy."

Wolfgango walked toward the door.

"Go to the kitchen and have the chef prepare the dinner," Nikolai said. "Then bring it up to the nursery. As soon as the women pass out, pack the child a bag with clothes, some formula, and a warm coat. It will be a long journey."

"Yes, sir."

He looked back into the bedroom and caught a tantalizing glimpse of Maria Tatyana in a sheer bra and lacy underwear and nearly flushed with desire. He couldn't stop staring at the beautiful body he'd been denied for so long. And it was all his fault. She'd lost her baby weight, but she was as ripe and curvaceous as ever. He missed her body and their closeness and promised to do whatever it took to place her back in his bed.

Chapter Twenty-Three

Nikolai anxiously awaited Wolfgango's text, and when it came, he rushed into Maria Tatyana's bedroom.

"We've got to go now. There's no time to lose."

"Where's my daughter?"

"Wolfgango will bring her to the plane."

Melody grabbed her travel bag, tucked the diary into the side pocket, and didn't object when Nikolai grabbed her hand and led her out the door.

They took a back entrance and walked down three flights of stairs. They passed some guards, but the men only saluted the count and let them through. Nikolai hustled Maria Tatyana into a waiting black Mercedes sedan, and they drove around the back to the airstrip. It was too cold to walk even a few feet. They walked up the stairs of the private jet and settled into their seats.

Melody stuffed her overnight bag into the overhead compartment. She craned her neck toward the window, looking for her daughter.

"Where is Wolfgango?" she asked, pulling off her fur-lined leather gloves.

He checked his phone, and his face paled when he read the terse message from his wife.

"Nice try, Nicky. Wolfgango won't be coming. I'm afraid he is indisposed. No worries. The future Empress is in good hands. Natalia and I will see to her."

"What's wrong?" Melody asked, noting the alarm

on Nikolai's face.

"We must get to St. Petersburg, now."

"Where's Katya?"

"I'm afraid Katya won't be coming."

Nikolai gave the pilot orders for takeoff.

Melody screamed.

"Calm yourself, Maria Tatyana. Katya will be fine. It's you I'm worried about."

Melody unbuckled her seatbelt and ran for the door of the aircraft. "I'm going after Katya, and you can't stop me."

He unstrapped his seat belt and pulled her back into his arms. "My love, we must leave her. They won't let any harm come to her. You stay with me."

Melody broke away and dashed for the door. He'd misjudged her intense devotion to Katya, again.

"Maria Tatyana, stop," he urged. "You're hysterical. We must leave Katya for now. It's for the best."

"You don't understand. If they want me dead, how can Katya be safe?"

"Your daughter will be fine."

She turned to face him, fighting him off, desperate to get back to the palace—so desperate that she did the one thing she'd promised herself she would never do. But she was out of options.

"She's yours, Nikolai. Katya is *your* daughter."

Chapter Twenty-Four

Nikolai froze in the moment that changed everything. "What did you just say?"

"I *said* Katya is *your* daughter."

"Christ," he swore. Several expressions played across his face as he digested the news. Surprise, relief that Maria Tatyana had not been with another man, then pride. But there was no time to contemplate his feelings. He sprang into action to rescue his daughter.

He barked an order to the pilot. "If I'm not back in half an hour, take off. Make sure the Empress is on the plane."

"But I want to come with—"

He pushed her firmly down in her seat. "Stay on the plane. I'll bring our daughter back. Don't ever doubt it."

Immobilized, and in a state of shock, Melody remained in her seat, fastening and unfastening her seatbelt. For the first time in a long time, she believed him.

Nikolai flew down the steps of the jet, ran to his car, and started the engine. He drove to the front of the palace and commandeered a trio of soldiers on duty. "Come with me, now, to the nursery."

He led them into the elevator and up to the top level. Wolfgango was laid out on the tile floor. Was he dead or just passed out? Katya's bag and coat were on the floor beside him.

"You," Nikolai indicated to the beefiest of the soldiers. "And you," he said, pointing to another guard. "Check him for injuries and get him onto the jet on the landing strip."

Nikolai grabbed Wolfgango's pistol from his jacket pocket, checked the cartridge to make sure the weapon was loaded, and motioned to the third soldier. "You follow me."

Storming into the nursery, he found his wife and Miss Cormier peering into the crib, cooing to Katya.

"What happened to Wolfgango?" he began.

"He'll be out for the next couple of hours," the Countess said. "Don't worry about him. Natalia brought him down like a pro."

"I'm here for my—for Katya," Nikolai stated carefully.

"You mean you want to kidnap the Grand Duchess," the Countess replied.

"I simply want to take her to St. Petersburg, early, with her mother." His eyes wandered to the crib. His daughter was standing up, smiling and gurgling, with a mop of blonde curls atop her head. He stared at her eyes—*his* eyes—he now realized. She was a stunner, like her mother. So beautiful, a miracle. And she was his. Why hadn't he noticed it before? Why hadn't he recognized their connection from the beginning? Katya was every inch his child. And he wasn't going to let anything bad happen to her. He would gladly die for her, if it came to that.

The Countess rounded on her husband. "Go on, take your whore to St. Petersburg. Katya is the true heir. She stays with us."

He rose to his full height. "Prepare the Grand Duchess for the flight. She's coming with me."

The Countess laughed. "You have no authority here. Be on your way."

He brought out Wolfgango's pistol and pointed it at the Countess.

"This gun says I do."

The Countess dismissed him as if he were an irritating gnat. "Natalia, you have my permission to—"

He pointed the gun at Natalia Cormier.

"Don't come a step closer," Nikolai warned.

"Make up your mind, Nikolai," taunted the Countess. "Which of us are you going to shoot?"

He didn't want to shoot anyone. There was too much risk of harming his daughter.

Natalia moved toward him, crouching like a tiger.

His finger tightened on the trigger.

"I *will* shoot you."

Natalia snorted. It was obvious she doubted his ability to carry through on his threat.

"Nicky, darling, have you ever shot anyone?" his wife teased. "I know you parade around with your Guardian comrades, but you always have your henchmen do your dirty work."

"I will shoot you, both of you, if you stand in my way."

She laughed and flashed a secret smile at Natalia. "You may be good in bed, but you're replaceable. Do you really want to test my resolve?"

Natalia rushed him, and he shot her in the shoulder. She cried out in pain but kept charging like a bull enraged by a matador's red flag.

The Countess screamed and ran to Natalia.

"Get the Grand Duchess," Natalia cried.

"I don't want to kill you," Nikolai warned the two women. "But I will if I have to."

Natalia assumed her aggressive position, but he anticipated her next maneuver and countered. He was also combat-trained in Krav Maga—a combination of boxing, wrestling, and street fighting. But the gun in his hand put him at a disadvantage. And, even with her injury, he knew Natalia's talent in that arena exceeded his skill level.

From the corner of his eye, he saw the Countess lift Katya out of the crib, hoping to sneak away while he was otherwise occupied. She obviously had no doubt Natalia would win the day. She had no such confidence in him. But she didn't know about his secret weapon— Katya. Natalia looked over at the baby and his wife. The adoring look she gave the Countess made him wonder about the depth and nature of their relationship. While the nanny was preoccupied, Nikolai clocked her hard in the head with the butt of Wolfgango's gun. She crumpled to the ground.

He ran toward his wife.

"You can't have her," she screeched. "She's mine."

"You're delusional. Now give her to me."

"She who holds the child, holds the crown," the Countess chanted shrilly.

"She's not a bargaining chip. Juliette, please. Give her to me." There was only so much he could do while she was holding his child.

"We are changing the order of succession," his wife announced. "Katya will be the new Empress. And I will be her guardian. She's my child now."

Nikolai exhaled and spoke quietly, deliberately, but

with import. "No, Juliette, she's *mine*."

The Countess looked at the child and then at Nikolai, and her mouth opened in surprise. Examining her closely, she saw the resemblance neither of them had noticed before.

"Y-yours?"

"She's my blood. She's my daughter. I'm not leaving without her."

Juliette countered. "You won't shoot me while I'm holding her."

"You're right," he reasoned. "I don't want to hurt either of you."

He activated the safety and pocketed his pistol. "I have a guard at the door. You're out of options. Now give her to me."

The Countess was seething. "You won't get away with this. I'll have you thrown out of the Guardians. Banished to Siberia, or worse. You'll never see Maria Tatyana or your child again."

"You won't do that. Maria Tatyana and Katya are the reason we're here. You don't want any harm to come to either of them."

What had he ever seen in her? She was evil and needy, nasty and dangerous to her core.

"Hand over my daughter," he pleaded. "If you ever cared for me, let me have her." But he could not predict what his wife might do. She was a madwoman. What if she threw Katya out the window? Sweat poured from his forehead, and it was freezing outside.

The Countess held Katya but made no move to bolt. He walked over to her and placed a hand on Juliette's cheek like he was gentling a horse. "I'm grateful for everything you've done for me."

"I don't want your gratitude," she sniffled. "I want your love."

"You say you love me, Juliette. I only want to hold my daughter. For the first time. She's innocent."

Juliette was deflated, defeated. He had no trouble wresting the child from her arms.

Nikolai pressed the baby's warm body against his chest, and tears moistened his cheeks. "Come, Katya," he crooned. "Come to Papa."

He took a moment to examine her, count her fingers and toes and touch her nose. She was a miracle. A perfect creation. And she was his. His heart swelled.

He rushed out of the room and grabbed the bag Wolfgango had prepared for the journey. Katya was as light as a feather. He was running late, but he drove cautiously with his precious cargo.

Thank God the plane was still there.

He climbed aboard, and Maria Tatyana jumped out of her seat. "Katya," she cried and tore the child out of his arms.

Katya gurgled with happiness to be reunited with her mother.

Wolfgango was slumped in a seat and strapped in. Nikolai checked for signs of life. His friend was still breathing. He instructed the pilot to take off. He made sure Maria Tatyana and Katya were strapped in safely before he fastened his own seatbelt.

He would likely spend the entire trip gazing into his daughter's eyes and thanking Heaven for this most amazing and unexpected gift. His gratitude was reflected in the adoring look he gave to Maria Tatyana. She smiled to see father and daughter together at last.

Chapter Twenty-Five

Zurich to St. Petersburg

Maria Tatyana appeared to be dozing, but she had a fierce hold on Katya. When they reached cruising altitude, Nikolai unbuckled his seatbelt and gently pried Katya from her mother's arms. Maria Tatyana stirred but then fell into a deep sleep. Wolfgango was still passed out.

Nikolai sat back in his seat and bounced little Katya on his knee.

"Whee!" He laughed quietly, making noises and blowing warm puffs of air into his daughter's face. She was laughing. He loved making her smile. She seemed to recognize him. What a gentle nature she had. What a sweet disposition. He came late to this fatherhood business, but he had every intention of making up for lost time. One day soon, she would be calling him Papa. His protective instincts reached the stratosphere.

"My daughter," he thought proudly. So Maria Tatyana hadn't betrayed him. She hadn't slept with another man, a conclusion to which he had quickly and inaccurately jumped. He'd gotten her pregnant and she left school to move back in with her grandmother and prepared to have the baby. But whenever he spoke to the woman, she never revealed that he had fathered a child. Either she didn't know Katya's paternity or she was trying to protect her granddaughter from him. Both women had essentially shut him out of their lives. He should be angry for all the time lost with his daughter, but he wasn't. He could understand why Maria Tatyana had left him. He was a married man. It was a loveless, complicated marriage, but nevertheless, Maria Tatyana was the injured party.

He was determined to make it up to her. He would no longer live with Juliette, and he was going to make the divorce permanent and win back Maria Tatyana's heart. A daughter needs her father, and he was determined to be there for her, whether or not Maria Tatyana wanted him as a lover. That was a father's right. Now that he knew Katya was his daughter, he vowed to protect her at all costs.

Did he really want her to suffer the burden of her mother's heritage? Or would he rather she grow up like any normal girl, unencumbered and safe? But he was a Guardian. His mission and duty were ingrained in him. He needed to have a talk with Maria Tatyana soon to see how she felt. What she wanted out of life. Because events were spiraling out of his control. His daughter was a wild card. He would sacrifice his life for her, give up his mission, if it came to that. Maria Tatyana had grown up unaware of her birthright. That would not happen to his daughter.

The Romanov heirs were being attacked on all fronts. Katya would need his protection from the enemies of the Guardians outside, and within from his estranged wife and Natalia. Evil forces were working against them. Juliette had been stunned when she realized he was serious about his plans to divorce her, but he knew she wasn't finished with him. She wasn't the type to give up easily. And as far as Natalia, he had stirred up a hornet's nest. There was no love lost between himself and the nanny. She would come for him, and he didn't want Maria Tatyana or Katya caught in the crossfire.

Katya was getting sleepy. She laid her head on his broad shoulder, and he began patting her back and rubbing it in a circular motion like he'd seen Maria Tatyana do. Asleep, she grew heavy in his arms, but he could sit like this for hours. She was so tiny, so helpless. He would stand between her and whatever came their way. Sniffing, he detected a malodorous smell. But could he contend with a dirty diaper? He chuckled. He would do anything for Katya, no matter how distasteful. Well, almost anything.

Chapter Twenty-Six

St. Petersburg, New Russia

The jet came in for an approach to the private airstrip and made a smooth landing. Katya was still asleep in his arms. His back was aching, but he didn't care. He wondered how Maria Tatyana and all other mothers did it. He looked over at the future Empress. She was so beautiful, even in slumber. He unbuckled his seatbelt and carried Katya over to her mother.

"Wake up, sleepyhead," he whispered, nudging her gently. "Your daughter needs to be changed."

She crinkled her nose when she detected the familiar smell. "Ah, so it's *my* daughter, now. Cleanup on Aisle Four." Melody laughed. "Are we here already?"

"We have arrived," he confirmed. They were laughing and joking like any married couple. This could be their life if their lives were normal.

****

Melody saw Nikolai holding Katya, her tiny cheek resting on his broad shoulder, and for a moment, her heart melted. She could see he had genuine feelings for his daughter. She reached out her arms, and he placed Katya gently into them so the baby remained asleep.

Wolfgango stirred.

Nikolai made a call, and when they deplaned, a

sleek black Mercedes SUV was waiting for them on the tarmac. A doctor in the vehicle was waiting to examine Wolfgango.

"See that this man gets off the plane and take him to a room in the palace as soon as he gets checked out," Nikolai ordered.

"Where are we?" asked Maria Tatyana.

"St. Petersburg. At a private airstrip behind your new home."

"What about customs?" Maria Tatyana asked.

"We bypass that. You're no longer an ordinary citizen. Remember, you're the Empress of New Russia."

"I'm still having trouble digesting that."

"Well, get used to it. We're moving into your new palace tonight. Tomorrow, I'll be taking you and Katya on a private tour of St. Petersburg."

"But I thought the capital of Russia was Moscow."

"That has all changed. We're making our home in St. Petersburg. We're going back to the way things were, before 'the Tsar' came to power." And by "the Tsar" she knew Nikolai referred to the former Russian leader who no longer wielded absolute and autocratic power. But Nikolai warned it would be dangerous to underestimate him.

"You and Ekaterina represent a new generation. You will capture the hearts of the people. It's as if you're bringing back the Grand Duchess Anastasia to her rightful place. Once we release the royal portrait, the world will go wild. You'll trend to the moon. We even have plans to release a royal commemorative stamp for the coronation."

"It's a lot to live up to."

"But I know you can do it."

"What am I supposed to do with the rest of my life? Wave at the crowds?"

"A lot of women would love to take your place, but only you were born for this role. The sky's the limit. You can become as involved in politics as you please. You can make a difference. You now have a good grounding in Russian politics, history, economics, and language. I should know. I was your teacher. I know you don't think of Russia as your country. But you read the diaries. You know where you came from. Your ancestor could have been, should have been, the Tsarina. She bore a royal child. Now you have the power to alter history."

"If Ekaterina had been crowned along with Nicky, she and her child would have been murdered at Ipatiev House," Melody pointed out.

"Thank God that didn't happen."

Nikolai placed a reassuring hand on her shoulder.

"You must take your proper place in history, restore a true Romanov to the throne."

She sighed. It all sounded so right. She was beginning to buy into the whole fantasy. Like it was meant to happen. She did identify with the girl in the diary. They had both fallen in love with the wrong men. And from those unions, daughters were born. She was carrying on a long tradition of Romanov women, women who remained in the background but who, through her, would be restored to their rightful places.

"I don't see that I have a choice," she said.

"So you're willing to truly commit to our cause?"

"In doing so, I'd also be committing Katya's life, too. Now that you know Katya is your daughter, do you still feel it's the right thing to do?"

"Yes, more than ever. I believe in the Guardians' mission. It is her destiny. Now that I know Katya is mine, I—"

"What?" she asked, looking up at him.

"I want to make you mine, too." Then came the words of apology for everything he had put her through, the betrayal, and for the burden of raising Katya alone.

"Is it too late for us?" he asked.

She let out a breath. She still loved him, would probably always love him. But could she trust him? It was obvious he adored Katya.

"I won't rule it out, but I'm not making any promises," she said. *Until I understand your real motives. Do you love me or are you just using me? Do you plan to make me your bride to reign alongside me, or to control me in order to control New Russia? Would you still love me if I weren't Maria Tatyana and I didn't look like your ideal, Anastasia? Or will I simply serve as your mistress?*

"Maybe, in time," she added. "Who can know the future?"

He leaned over and kissed her gently, and she responded by kissing him back.

"That's all I ask for. A chance."

"That's all I can promise now." She reluctantly broke off the kiss. "Katya will be awake soon."

She was grateful to be allowed total access to her daughter. Nikolai had arranged that. As long as she did things his way, they were safe. If they ran, now that people were aware of their identities, they wouldn't find safe harbor anywhere in the outside world. They would always be targets. Staying cocooned in St.

Petersburg in the palace and under the Guardians' protection was the only way to guarantee their survival. That is what Nikolai explained to her. The Guardians had a long reach. So, for the time being, she would continue to play her role and keep a tight rein on her heart as well as her kingdom.

Chapter Twenty-Seven

St. Petersburg, New Russia
Three months later

Nikolai strode into the royal nursery, anxious to spend time with his daughter. How strange and wonderful those words sounded. During these past three months he had been happy beyond all expectations. The time spent with Maria Tatyana and Katya had been a precious gift. He'd been able to make up for lost time by spending as much of the day with his daughter as possible while Maria Tatyana was busy with her ceremonial duties and her charitable work.

The Russian people adored their Empress, and she was beloved and admired around the world. Just today in the newspapers, she was being compared to the late Princess Diana for her style, her grace, and her good works. Now that the Countess and Miss Cormier were barred from the palace, on his orders, he felt unencumbered, and he and Maria Tatyana were growing closer. She hadn't let him back into her bed yet, but he was hopeful. He could be patient. She was worth the wait.

His eyes focused lovingly on the Grand Duchess, his Katya, before they wandered over to Wolfgango, lying immobile, his body sprawled on the marble floor. Not again, Nikolai thought.

"Wolfgango!" He shook his unresponsive friend, then dialed an emergency number. "I need a doctor at once in the royal nursery."

Wolfgango began to regain consciousness. Blood was seeping out of his side.

"Who did this to you?"

Wolfgango groaned.

"What happened?"

"The Empress. I'm sorry."

"What about the Empress?"

"They took her."

"No, the Empress is scheduled to make an appearance at the fundraising for the Children's Charity in town and then on to dedicate a new hospital."

"She was here with Katya when they came for her. I tried to stop them, but she—"

"She who?" Nikolai shouted to Wolfgango impatiently.

"Miss Cormier. She shot me, and they took the Empress."

"How is that possible? Miss Cormier is not allowed in the palace."

"She broke in with soldiers."

"Did they hurt Katya?"

"No."

The Count lifted his daughter and pressed her to him. "Thank God, Katya. Thank God you're all right. Thank God they didn't take you."

The doctor appeared at Wolfgango's side.

"Please, help him, he's been shot," Nikolai said.

He leaned over Wolfgango. "Did they say where they were taking her?"

"No. But Miss Cormier kept saying over and over,

'History repeats itself.' "

"History repeats itself?" Nikolai stared blankly at Wolfgango, who was starting to slip out of consciousness. "That makes no sense at all." Something Maria Tatyana had once mentioned triggered a vague but fleeting thought.

The Count placed his daughter back in the crib and called for a woman to watch the child and another guard to be placed outside the nursery.

"How many of them were there?" Nikolai asked Wolfgango.

"There was Miss Cormier, the Countess, and three guards," Wolfgango managed, the color seeping from his face.

"My wife was here, in the palace?"

"Yes."

A stretcher arrived, and Wolfgango was placed on it, accompanied by the court physician.

Nikolai grasped his friend's hand. "You're going to be okay."

"Don't worry about me. Find the Empress."

Nikolai placed another call to his event planner. Maybe Wolfgango was mistaken. Maybe Maria Tatyana was going about her business, unharmed. Maybe they hadn't taken her yet. He clung to that hope.

"Is the Empress still at the fundraiser?"

"She never showed up. We've been calling her appointment secretary. She has no idea what happened."

It was true then. Maria Tatyana had been kidnapped by Miss Cormier, and his wife was possibly involved. Natalia was a born assassin. A treasonous bitch. They didn't kill the Empress outright when they could have. They left the Grand Duchess in her crib. What did that mean? That his wife and Natalia were following through with their plan to make the Grand Duchess the heir to the throne? That Maria Tatyana was expendable? If they got rid of her, they could function as the child's guardians. They still had influence in the Guardian organization.

Where did that leave him in their plans? The Countess refused to sign the divorce papers he'd drawn up. Would they use the Empress as a bargaining chip to keep him in line? It would be an ultimatum, then—stay married to his wife or they would dispose of the Empress and eventually him. Would they really dare to threaten Maria Tatyana's life? The answer was clear. He must find her.

He replayed Wolfgango's words in his mind, furrowing his brow. "History repeats itself." History. Didn't Maria Tatyana say something about Ipatiev House, the site where the Tsar and his family were executed? When the ugly truth dawned on him, his hand flew to his heart. Please God, this cannot be happening. There was only one place they could have taken her that made sense. If he was wrong and he couldn't get to her in time to save her, he would lose her forever. And Katya would lose her mother.

Chapter Twenty-Eight

The former site of Ipatiev House

She was tied at the waist to a hard wooden chair in the dark basement of a cavernous building, illuminated only by the eerie glow of moonlight. There were no street noises. They must be in the countryside. They had blindfolded her on the journey so she couldn't track her location. But they needn't have bothered. She knew virtually nothing about Russian geography. The land was so vast, she could be anywhere. She wore no gag. Her hands were free and the blindfold was off, so she could clearly see her captor—her worst nightmare.

The last thing she clearly remembered was being in the nursery, screaming Wolfgango's name, trying to fight off the intruders. Wolfgango had tried to come to her aid, but before he could get to her, Miss Cormier had shot him. He was bleeding out. She hoped to God he survived and that he hadn't given his life in their defense.

Miss Cormier had lifted Katya out of her crib and tossed her up and down in her arms, pausing at an open window, dangling her in midair.

"Katya," she breathed, unable to make a sound she was so paralyzed with fear.

"If you go with us willingly, I will not harm Katya," Miss Cormier announced. "It's your choice to make. Put up a fight and I'll drop her."

"Put her back in her crib, please," Melody begged. "I won't scream. I won't fight you. Just let my baby live." She knew she was putting her fate in the hands of a monster. But she would not risk her daughter's life. Surely Miss Cormier had counted on that.

The nanny smiled and placed Katya back into her crib.

"Mama," called Katya, her little arms flailing.

She had spoken her first word. *Mama.*

"Let me say goodbye," Melody pleaded.

The Countess entered the room and nodded.

"Let them have this final moment together," she allowed.

Melody walked slowly over to Katya, not wanting to alarm her. She held her tightly and whispered all her love, enough words to last a lifetime. "Goodbye, my princess. Mama loves you so much."

"Touching," the Countess observed rigidly. Melody doubted the woman had an emotional bone in her body.

She let go of her daughter and glared at Nikolai's wife.

Three guards arrived and marched her out at gunpoint. As they left the castle, they placed a hood over her head and shoved her roughly into the back of a car. The hood was a necessity when they were out in public. Her face was now the most recognizable face on the planet.

Miss Cormier sat in the back seat next to her. Melody heard her unwrap a package. She'd heard that sound of paper crinkling before. The nanny was preparing a syringe, her weapon of choice, to knock her out.

"I am going with you. There's no need to drug me."

"I'm taking no chances."

"Where are you taking me?"

"You'll find out when we get there."

They transferred her from the car to a private plane. They didn't go through airport security. It was about a two-hour flight. Then back to a car. She tried to remain alert as they rumbled down the highway, but the motion of the car coupled with the drug lulled her to sleep. Would she spend her final hours in slumber? She fought to stay awake. She prayed Katya was safe.

The movement of the car stopped. It was dark and eerily quiet. They must be somewhere very remote.

"Okay, you can take off the hood," instructed Miss Cormier. "We've reached our destination." Two guards led her roughly up a wide flight of stone stairs into a building. Her limp was back, more pronounced than ever.

Melody hadn't eaten or drunk anything since she'd been abducted, and she swayed on her feet.

"Hold her up. She should see."

"Where are we?" Melody asked. "Is this a church?"

"Yes, it is indeed a church," explained Miss Cormier eagerly. "It's called the Church on Blood in Honor of All Saints Resplendent. It was built on the site where the Romanovs were executed. You would know it as the Ipatiev House or a house of special purpose. It was known as the last palace of the Tsar. There nothing left of the house today. It was demolished in 1977. You might find these exhibits fascinating. How much do you know about the way the Imperial family died?"

"Only what's written in the history books.*" Of course she knew the story. How many times had Nikolai drummed it into her head?*

"You may recall the discovery of a heap of charred bones in a mine shaft," Miss Cormier said. "Among the remains were diamonds and platinum crosses belonging to the empress, her four daughters, and the Tsarevitch. The family was cut down in a hail of bullets. When they didn't all die right away, they were stabbed with bayonets and hit with the butt ends of Bolshevik rifles. Then the bodies were burnt, covered in sulfuric acid, and dumped down a mine shaft."

"A horrific way to die," Melody said, turning to face the nanny. "I thought the truck broke down and they were buried at the side of the road. And I recall reading that their bodies weren't all discovered together, that the remains of Crown Prince Alexei and Grand Duchess Maria weren't discovered until 2007."

"Excellent memory. Yes, the bodies of Maria and Alexei were missing. Some say it was Anastasia's and not Maria's body that was missing. Details are sketchy—there are variations in the story—but in 1991, during a construction project, workers found nine skeletons in a shallow grave in Yekaterinburg. When the bones were proved to be those of the Tsar and Tsarina and three of his children, their doctor and three servants, the remains of the royal family were buried in the family crypt in the Peter and Paul Cathedral in a ceremony in St. Petersburg.

"They were canonized as martyrs for the faith. The rest of the remains were found not far from where the others were discovered. The people are clamoring for the bodies to be buried with the rest of the family in St. Petersburg. But enough history. We need to move on to the lower floor. We need to be out by the time the church opens this morning."

Miss Cormier sensed her next question.

"You can scream bloody murder. No one will hear you."

"Why aren't my hands tied?"

"You need to sign your abdication papers."

"Abdication?"

"Yes, just like Tsar Nicholas II did. He stepped down in favor of his brother, who didn't accept the position. You'll be stepping down in favor of your daughter."

"I never wanted this," Melody said. *How could she ever have thought she could be a Romanov ruler?* The past three months had been like a dream. She had reveled in her new role. She believed she was making a contribution. She believed she was the connection with her Romanov relatives, that she would fulfill their dreams. But she and Nikolai had tempted fate by trying to change history. And now she would pay the price.

"An accident of birth," said the nanny. "I understand. I have an illustrious—some might say an infamous—relative too. Have you ever heard of Yakov Mikhailovich Yurovsky?"

Melody shook her head.

"Most people haven't. He headed up the operation to keep the Romanovs locked up. He was the Bolshevik who led the firing squad. The man who finally put an end to the monarchists. A job well done, but he received no glory for doing it. I am simply finishing the job."

"I thought you were a Guardian."

"I was playing a role. The Tsar had no business ruling Russia. He didn't have the brains or the guts to do the job. He was the true enemy of the people. And his blood runs in your veins."

Suddenly, the room flooded with lights. It took time for Melody's eyes to adjust to the brightness. Two cameras were focused on her to get all the angles. Someone hooked her up with a lavalier microphone.

"Smile. We want you to look your best. The crew will be *shooting* a documentary."

Miss Cormier explained how things would work.

"First, you'll sign the abdication papers I've prepared. They are much like the original manifesto Tsar Nicholas II signed. It says that in the name of dearly beloved Russia, you renounce the throne of New Russia on behalf of and in favor of your daughter Ekaterina Nikolaevna and her guardian, Countess Juliette Orlov Kinsky. After that, supreme power in New Russia passes to the Countess."

Miss Cormier signaled a guard to shove a small wooden desk in front of her chair, handed Melody a pen, and thrust the document in front of her, ordering her to sign.

"And if I don't?"

"It makes no difference in the end. I thought you'd want to do your best for your daughter. She will rule New Russia."

"With you by her side?"

"And the Countess. Who better?"

"What about Nikolai?"

"For some reason, the Countess chooses to keep him around, for now. He is not worthy of her."

Maria Tatyana took a heavy breath, read over the document, and signed, ever conscious of the soldiers, their rifles at the ready. Did it make a difference that she signed the document under duress? So did Tsar Nicholas. What choice did she have? She only hoped Nikolai would be there to care for Katya so she'd have at least one parent to love her. He would have to love their daughter enough for both of them. And she knew he would. Nikolai had come to adore his daughter. She was only sorry it had taken her so long to admit her feelings for him.

If he were here now, she wouldn't hesitate to tell him how she felt. He had betrayed her in the past with his wife, the Countess. Perhaps she was behind this abduction. Perhaps this was her end goal from the beginning.

She thought briefly of Rabbi Slick. If she had stayed in Pennsylvania, they might have started dating. It might have led to something more. She and Katya could have led a normal life, a safe life, a Romanov-free existence. But instead, her daughter's future was tied to Nikolai and the Guardians, who were nowhere to be found in her time of need. Were they aware of this traitor in their midst? Was Nikolai complicit? Was he aware that he, too, was expendable?

"And now the whole world can tune in and watch you die," Miss Cormier stated.

"I did what you asked. Why do you want to kill me?"

"It's a fitting end."

Of course, Miss Cormier had this ending in mind from the beginning. She was a false Guardian. It was high drama. A reenactment of the final moments of the

Tsar and his family on the same spot, more than a century apart. The curse of the Romanovs revisited. But it wasn't the end of the Romanov dynasty. There was Katya, and she would thrive.

Melody's mouth was parched. Her head ached. She couldn't believe she was going to die in this basement prison before she got a chance to see Katya again. She hoped her daughter would remember her. She hoped Nikolai would keep her memory alive.

"Did you know it took a full thirty minutes for the Romanovs to die?" uttered Miss Cormier. "Your death will only take seconds. Too bad it can't be prolonged. But we will follow the course of history as much as possible."

She realized the full import of what Miss Cormier was saying. The nanny intended to execute her and document it for all the world to see. She had a sudden flash to a page on the Internet, the wallpaper in the basement of Ipatiev House, riddled with pockmarks, bullets, gouges in the floor. Screams fairly echoed off the screen. Nicholas and Alexandra must have turned to each other suddenly, reaching to shield their son. The four daughters, including Anastasia, would have hugged each other once they realized their fate in those final moments of chaos and agony. In contrast, she was totally alone. No one would be coming to save her either. What would they do with her body? Would anyone ever find her remains? She wished she didn't know what horrors awaited her. She hoped the end would be quick and painless. She would give her crown to return to Downingtown, Pennsylvania, to an anonymous life as ordinary Melody Segal.

A tiny tear slipped down her cheek. But that was as

far as she would display her emotions. She held her head up regally. After all, she was an Empress. She was determined to die with dignity. She wondered if Marie Antoinette had held her head high before it was unceremoniously severed and dropped into a basket.

Her final thoughts were of Katya. Would she truly be safe? Would they protect her, or would she fall victim to the same fate her ancestors suffered? Could she as a mother have done more to protect her innocent child? A child that would grow up without her mother's love.

She imagined all the moments she would miss, like a film playing in her head. Katya taking her first steps to her papa, graduating college, falling in love (hopefully not with another Guardian), walking down the aisle, playing with a child of her own. Melody smiled.

Miss Cormier looked puzzled.

"There won't be a last-minute reprieve, if that's what you're thinking. No one knows where you are."

Wasn't the hero supposed to ride to the heroine's rescue at the last moment? Rescue the maiden, or the princess, or in this case, the empress? In all the modern romances, the heroine saves herself. That's not the way this final scenario would play out. She was helpless to avert disaster.

In the final moments, the Countess came into view, haughty and triumphant.

"Pardon me if I don't stay for the finale," she said. "But I want you to know, I will never sign those divorce papers. Nicky will never be free. We will raise Katya together with the assistance of Natalia."

Was there a special relationship between the

Countess and Miss Cormier? It seemed so, the way they acted when they were around each other, huddled together, touching hands, heads nodding toward each other. She prayed Nikolai would find some way to be free of the she-beast he was shackled to. She wondered if he knew the part his wife was playing in this execution. Was it her idea or Miss Cormier's?

Would they actually go through with it? Would they really execute her in cold blood like they did the Tsar and his family? She was terrified they would. She could hear the sound of her heartbeat amplified. She was having a full-blown panic attack. She couldn't breathe. She feared she would die of fright before they had the chance to cut her down in a hail of bullets.

Miss Cormier lifted her hand to give the command. Hatred flared in her eyes. What had she done to deserve the woman's anger? Fallen in love? Then the guards raised their rifles in unison to open fire. She closed her eyes tightly so they couldn't see the hope fade from her face. She couldn't bear to confront her own mortality. She held her breath.

Then she heard the bullets ping. Where was she hit? How long would it take to die? She hoped it would be over soon. She sagged in her chair, mercifully blacking out.

Chapter Twenty-Nine

IZVESTIA

October 7, 2021—The world is mourning the death of Russian Empress Maria Tatyana Feodorovna, the last male-line heir to Tsar Nicholas II, at the hands of anarchists. Shot by firing squad, the Empress was murdered on the anniversary of the October revolution by self-proclaimed neo-Bolsheviks after she was forced to abdicate the throne live on camera. The location of her remains is unknown, and the mysterious disappearance of her daughter, Grand Duchess Ekaterina Nikolaevna, from the Palace is unexplained. She is presumed dead, but her body has not yet been recovered.

Viewers around the globe watched in horror as the Empress was placed before a firing squad in the basement of the Church of Blood in Honor of All Saints Resplendent, the site upon which the Ipatiev House, the last Palace of the Tsar, once stood. The Empress bravely held her head high, eyes shuttered against her killers. Mercifully, cameras stopped rolling seconds before her execution. Government sources report that in the interim, Count Nikolai Kinsky, also of Romanov blood, will remain in the government, supporting the administration of President Peter Zhukov. The Count is in mourning and unavailable for comment.

The perpetrators have been rounded up and shot or

arrested. Ironically, the deceased ringleader, Natalia Cormier, was the descendant of Yakov Mikhailovich Yurovsky, the man in charge of the murder of Tsar Nicholas II and his family in 1918. Materials found in her apartment indicated she had been planning the execution for some time.

In a related story, the Countess Juliette Orlov Kinsky has signed divorce papers from her husband, Count Nikolai Kinsky, and she has retired from the social scene. Friends cite a severe case of nerves over the execution.

In other news, the discovery of the Tsar's Lost Shipment of Gold has been reported. Details are sketchy, but the shipment, missing for a century, and discovered in an undisclosed location in Omsk, Siberia, has been remanded to the Russian Treasury and will be used to fund infrastructure and social services for the people of New Russia.

Chapter Thirty

Downingtown, Pennsylvania
Three months later

"Rabbi Rosenberg, Temple Beth Tov."

Melody still had the business card with the rabbi's private number imprinted on it, and she was glad he answered on the first ring. She might have lost her nerve if she'd had to wait any longer. Slick's Southern drawl resonated as deep and sexy as she remembered it. She pictured him in body-hugging jeans and a tight black T-shirt, lounging in his office at the synagogue, his white cowboy hat hanging on the coat rack, at the ready for when the rabbi performed his good-guy deeds in his congregation and the community.

"Slick?"

"Who is this?"

"It's me. Melody Segal."

"Melody!"

And then he took the Lord's name in vain in a very un-rabbi-like way.

"Where have you been? I've been calling you for months. There was never any answer. I tried to track you down. There was no one at your house. It was as if you'd fallen off the face of the earth."

"Nana always used to say, 'You won't find what you're looking for until it's ready to be found.' "

"And are you…ready to be found?"

She hesitated before she decided how to answer that loaded question. "I think I am."

"Where were you all this time?"

"I was out of the country for a while. Staying below the radar. Actually, I was visiting Katya's father."

She recalled the happy months she and Katya had spent on Nikolai's frequent visits to their hideaway on Lake Como. She had been tempted to sleep with him a number of times, but she was holding out for more than a part-time relationship. Nicky was still committed to helping govern the New Russia. And she could no longer be by his side or show her face in public.

"Are you still involved with him?" the rabbi asked warily.

"Not in the way you're thinking. He has other priorities. He's very busy at the moment. He has a pretty high-profile position in government, and he has no time for romantic entanglements. And, anyway, we're just friends now. But we keep in touch for Katya's sake."

"If Ekaterina were mine, I wouldn't want to spend a minute away from her. And if you were mine, well, I can tell you, I'd never let you out of my sight."

"That's really sweet."

"I know this sounds crazy, but you weren't in New Russia by any chance, were you?"

She choked but managed to laugh. "New Russia? Of all places. No, why would you think that?"

"Well, you're going to think I'm insane, but you know that Russian Empress Maria Tatyana Feodorovna, the one who was assassinated… I could have sworn—I mean, she looked just like you, and I thought… I mean, I was worried that… Let's just say I've had a lot of sleepless nights wondering, worrying, and praying. I almost hopped a flight to St. Petersburg to check it out."

"I get that a lot. I favor her, but no, it's just plain me."

"You could be her twin. I was so convinced it was you. When I saw the execution on television, I think my heart stopped. I thought I'd lost you forever."

"But a Jewish Empress of Russia? That's pretty improbable."

"It was awful what happened to her. Just when her life was beginning. And they never found her daughter."

"No. Unfortunately, not every story can have a happy ending." She hated to lie to a rabbi, and she would tell him the truth if they started seeing each other seriously. But how could she explain the unexplainable? For now, the less said, the better. The fewer people who knew the secret, the safer she and Katya would be. She had dyed her hair and had it restyled, but she might still be recognizable as a Romanov.

"How is Ekaterina?"

"Katya is fine, thanks for asking."

"It's so good to hear from you."

"You, too. I was afraid you might have forgotten me."

"Never. I told you I'd be waiting, and I meant it."

"I'm glad to hear that. Um, I was wondering…if you're not busy, if you'd like to join Katya and me for Friday night dinner before services. I'm making brisket. My grandmother's recipe. And matzoh ball soup. After dinner, I thought Katya and I could come to services."

"That would be great. I mean yes, definitely. Is Katya too young to be out that late?"

How could she explain she was never going to let Katya out of her sight again? It would be a long time before she trusted another nanny or babysitter.

"I've just gotten back into town. I don't know any babysitters. She'll just sleep through services. She's very well behaved. She never cries. She's a princess."

"Well, I'll be glad to meet her. What time would you like me to be there?"

"Around five thirty? That will give us time to have dinner and talk and get to the synagogue in time for your eight o'clock service."

"I'll be there, although I'm not sure I can wait that long. Can I bring anything?"

"Just yourself. That's all I need."

Melody hung up the phone and smiled. Fingering her rose gold necklace, her touchstone, she felt Nana's presence, matchmaking from above. The diamond-and-emerald-necklace the Tsar had bestowed on the first Katya was gone. Nikolai had offered it to her as he offered his love and commitment, but she had declined them all for now. He said he would save them for Katya, for when she came of age. At the same time she would present her daughter with the diary, the history of her heritage.

Melody loved when Nikolai made up stories to tell their daughter. Her favorite was the one about the beautiful girl who lived in the small Russian village of Downingtown, who didn't know she was a Grand Duchess. He hoped she'd remember the story when she and Katya returned to the United States.

They had spent a lot of family time in the Italian villa. Lake Como was like a dream. But she had to wake up to reality. She would not keep Nikolai from his daughter, but she would make her own life with Katya. There was too much to forgive. He wasn't behind her abduction, but he wasn't true to her and had lied about being married and sleeping with his wife for whatever reasons.

She could never fully trust his motives. He had come to her rescue at the very last minute before the execution. And he would always be her first love and Katya's father. But he had made his choice. He was a Guardian, first, a man second. The New Russia needed him to help steer the ship.

He swore he would give up his life with the Guardians for her, and he claimed he had, in terms of his personal happiness after her staged death. He reasoned that if they were together, and on the throne, she and Katya would always be targets. And he would not allow that. He could have ruled by proxy with Katya, but he refused to separate mother and daughter, *his* daughter, again. She promised to send pictures so he could track her progress.

At the same time, he left the door open for Katya so that if one day things weren't right in New Russia, the Guardians could call on her to take her rightful place. Melody still referred to her daughter as her *little princess*, but she decided to be honest with her daughter about her birthright as soon as she was old enough to hear the truth, so she would be prepared for that eventuality. She didn't want Katya to be blindsided like she had been. When her daughter was old enough, she would make her own decisions.

Meanwhile she was more than happy to have this quality time alone with Katya, away from prying nannies, jealous wives, and the unwelcome glare of the spotlight. She needed a proper chance to breathe, to bond with her daughter, to bask in the simple life. But she promised Nikolai she wasn't closing any doors. She wanted to see where a relationship with Slick would take them. See if she could be happy. She owed that to Katya.

Affairs of state in New Russia seemed to be humming along without an empress and her heir. Romanovs of every stripe were beginning to migrate back to the Motherland, prowling onto the social scene to fill the royal void. Back to the business of being Romanovs, purchasing dachas, priceless jewels, and box seats at the ballet, and frequenting all the trendy bars and clubs.

To all the world, the Empress Maria Tatyana was dead, and her daughter Katya would forever remain missing. Long live Melody Segal. It would remain one of the great unsolved mysteries. Nikolai had arranged all that. He was their protector, but for one to survive, the other had to sacrifice.

And he had stepped up. He professed his love for her and wanted the three of them to be a family. But he knew they would never be safe from opposing forces, those unknown enemies coiled inside or outside the Guardian nest, waiting to spring. One day, when they least expected it, their lives would again hang in the balance. Like the lives of her parents and grandmother. He loved his newfound family enough to give them up. But she suspected he also craved power, maybe more than love. And that was not good enough for her or for

Katya.

On the other hand, there was something true and reassuring and steady about Slick. She was anxious to open her heart to joy and to the possibility of a new, unencumbered love, without all the drama and intrigue. Would it be the same kind of all-consuming love or lust she'd felt for Nikolai? Maybe not. Maybe love the second time around could never burn as bright. But it could be love, just the same. She desperately wanted that to be true. She believed in happy endings.

She had followed in the footsteps of her ancestors. Ekaterina's lover, the Tsar, had fathered her child, yet she married and seemed relatively happy with Pyotr and their new family. And a Guardian had fathered a child with Nana out of wedlock, yet Nana had eventually been happily married to another man. A Guardian was her birth father, yet her mother had later married someone else, though their lives had been cut short. Nikolai was her Guardian, her lover, the father of Katya, but she was not destined to spend her life with him, if she chose to marry Slick.

Was she up to the task? If she could be an Empress, she could be a *Rebbetzin*, a rabbi's wife. Nana would definitely approve. She could feel her grandmother smiling down from Heaven.

Part Four
Downingtown, Pennsylvania
Twenty-three years later

"These things I warmly wish for you—
Someone to love…
And a guardian angel
Always near."
~Irish Blessing

Chapter Thirty-One

Downingtown, Pennsylvania
Twenty-Three Years Later

"Katya, get dressed. You don't want to be late to services. Your father is expecting you."

Katya scowled and grunted something nonsensical to her mother.

She pulled her head under the duvet cover. My *stepfather*, she wanted to say. Which was unfair because Rabbi Slick (Dad, as she called him) had raised her from infancy. For all intents and purposes he *was* her father. But she knew the truth. Her real father, her *Papa*, was Count Nikolai Kinsky. She didn't see him often, but when she did it was wonderful. She treasured the summers she spent at Lake Como, just the two of them, and the occasional "mother-daughter" trips she and her mom took to meet her father on the sly somewhere fabulous around the world. She and her mother would jet off to London, Paris, Zurich, or Nice, incognito, stay at private residences owned by Guardian families, eat at the finest restaurants, go sailing, shopping, or just soak up the atmosphere. Papa was fun. He threw caution to the wind. She felt comfortable around him because she was like him. With Papa, she could be herself. Grand Duchess Ekaterina Nikolaevna. Papa supplied her with the latest designer clothes, all the money she needed, anything in the world her heart desired.

When she was in Downingtown, she was under constant supervision. She was the obedient, diligent rabbi's daughter who did her homework on time and never broke the rules, much less bent them.

It was a Saturday, her first day home from college graduation, and all she wanted to do was sleep in. She'd forgotten how rigid her *step*father's schedule was. He conducted Friday night services, Saturday morning services, and Havdalah services Saturday evening. Not to mention Sunday school classes, celebrated all the Jewish holidays (there were a lot of those) and went on sick visits and offered personal counseling and religious programming to congregants. Rabbi Slick was very popular, especially with the women in the congregation.

Her friends were jealous that the dreamy rabbi was her father. He was true to her mother, but he'd had every opportunity to stray if he'd wanted to. She didn't know how her mother lived with it. And her mother had her own part to play as a *Rebbetzin*—attend services and sisterhood functions, do charitable work... The list went on.

Rabbi Slick didn't have a clue who she was or what she did during her summers abroad. Mom had decided to keep the truth from him, for his own protection, but she and Papa had taken her aside, shown her the diaries and the sparkling diamond-and-emerald necklace, and talked about her place in the world.

From the time she was a young girl, her birth parents had explained her destiny, the historical chain of events, and the fact that she was an important link in that chain. She and her mother had been called on once to serve, but something had gone terribly wrong. She was too young then to remember it. But in case the time was right again, they had prepared her, with Russian history and language lessons, ballet appreciation, and all the lore that surrounded New Russia and the Romanovs. She'd read the diary, heard the stories of the women who had come before her. She was ready, as ready as she would ever be.

It had been some pretty heady stuff to learn she was a Romanov. On the downside, she couldn't tell a soul.

When she was with her real parents, she detected a spark between them. Papa was in love with her mother. There was no doubt about that. You could see it in his eyes as his gaze followed her every movement and in the sparkle in her eyes whenever she was near him. To her knowledge, they had never acted on their feelings. Her mother had never betrayed her marriage vows, but there was a closeness, a genuine friendship, and more, she thought, between them.

Mama was what Rabbi Slick called "a woman of valor," the song in praise of a good wife, sung on Friday nights in synagogue by husbands to honor their wives for making the house a home. As a rabbi's daughter, she was also expected to be respectable.

Her mother did love Rabbi Slick, and she seemed happy with her simple life of service, but Katya wanted more. More excitement, more meaning. Just more.

She had earned a political science degree from an Ivy League school, but what use was that in the real world? She had one job and one job only, to wait for someone to come or something monumental to happen.

The problem was, something monumental had

already happened that might have altered her parents' cosmic plan.

"Katya, stop moping around," her mother called through the door. "Please come out. We're about to leave for services. You've already missed breakfast."

At the sound of the word breakfast, Katya hurried to the toilet and vomited.

"Katya, are you in there?"

"Mom, I'm not feeling well. I can't go."

"We're sponsoring the Oneg Shabbat today. Your father wants to show off his beautiful daughter, a college graduate. He's so proud of you."

Wiping her mouth with a hand towel, Katya felt anything but beautiful. She couldn't face her mother. She would sense that something was wrong, terribly wrong. They had some kind of psychic connection. If her dad ever found out, he would go ballistic, and he was normally a calm man. She knew very well her stepfather would not be proud that his precious daughter had come home from college pregnant, although Rabbi Slick was maddeningly understanding. He'd married her mother under similar circumstances. History does repeat itself, after all.

"Katya?" her mother called again, annoyance creeping into her voice.

Katya partially opened her bedroom door and stuck her head out.

Melody frowned. "What's wrong? You haven't washed your hair. You're not dressed. You look so pale. Are you ill?"

"Tell Dad I won't be able to make it."

"Why not? You know how important today is for your dad."

Katya sighed.

Melody nudged the door open, and Katya stepped back. Far enough so her mother could get a closer look. In her sheer nightgown, Katya's newly rounded belly was on full display.

Her mother's head tilted in puzzlement. "Katya?" she whispered. She stared at her daughter but was unable to make sense of what she was seeing.

"Are you—? You're not—?"

Katya shrugged. "I didn't want you to know."

Melody exhaled and struggled to regain her composure. "Did you think you could hide it from me?"

Katya shrugged again.

"How far along are you?"

"Maybe three months or so."

Melody shook her head. "Who is the boy?"

Katya walked to the bed and sat down. "His name is Dax."

"Dax what?"

"Just Dax. It's his initials. It stands for Damien Apollo Xerogeanes."

Melody shut the door behind her and joined her daughter on the bed.

"Oh, that explains it. He's a Greek god."

"Mom. Don't make me laugh." She could tell her mother Dax was Greek and that he looked how she imagined a Greek god would look.

"Believe me, I don't find this funny. Do you know anything about him?"

"Not really."

"Does he know about the baby?"

"Not really."

"Not really or no?"

"No."

"Have you been in touch with him?"

"No."

"Is he a student?"

"No."

"Then how did you two meet?"

"At a party off campus."

"Do you at least know how to get in touch with him?"

Katya shook her head. "I thought he might get in touch with me."

"Did you exchange information?"

"Mom, it wasn't an auto accident."

"More like a car crash," Melody said. "Let me understand this. You slept with someone you didn't know, and you were like two ships passing in the night? Were there drugs at the party?"

"No, but we might have been drinking."

"You *might* have been drinking?"

Tears pooled in Katya's eyes. "I thought maybe—"

"Or you *didn't* think."

"I thought maybe he was my Guardian."

Melody sighed. She and Nikolai had agreed to inform Katya about her heritage. But, in her opinion, he had gone overboard, as he tended to do. Nikolai had been filling the girl's head with fanciful Guardian lore her whole life. And she had been waiting for someone who might never come.

In the case of all the other Romanov girls, their Guardians had come unbidden before they realized who they were. In Katya's case, Nikolai had been preparing her for her eventual role on the world stage since she was a young girl. He thought he was doing the right thing. But Katya had obviously bought into what she thought was her destiny with her knight in shining armor, and it had become a self-fulfilling prophecy.

"Let me think," Melody said, rubbing her mouth. "We're going to have to tell your father."

"Don't tell Dad. He'll be so disappointed."

"I'm not talking about the rabbi. I'm talking about your Papa."

"Do we have to?"

"I don't see any other way. Maybe he knows who this Dax person is, or who his parents are. He'll know what to do."

"Do you think Dax is my Guardian?"

Melody frowned. "I have no idea."

Rabbi Slick called from the hallway. "Girls, are you about ready to roll? We don't want to miss this rodeo."

Melody rolled her eyes. "Your father is such a Texan."

"I can't go," Katya pleaded.

"Okay, I'll make up some excuse. But when I get back, we're going to have to make some decisions. I hate to leave you alone."

"I'll be okay."

Melody covered her daughter's hands with her own. "And don't worry. Everything will turn out all right."

****

Melody got through services somehow and circulated among the congregation at the Oneg Shabbat. She watched the women gather around her husband like flies to honey, like he was some kind of rock star. She was still getting used to the fact that her handsome

243

husband seemed to attract ladies of all ages. She knew he was committed only to her, but that didn't stop them from flocking to his side.

Then she made her excuses to Slick and asked a friend to drop her at the house so the rabbi could stay at the synagogue with his "worshippers."

When she got home, she dropped her purse on the end table, collapsed on the couch, and pulled out her phone to dial Nikolai's number. She'd told Katya that everything would be all right. But it was not. They were still living in the house she had inherited from Nana. All the memories came rushing back. She hated that her daughter was going through what she had gone through all those years ago. Pregnant and unmarried. And who was this Dax person?

"Hello," Nikolai answered.

"Nikolai, it's Melody."

"Maria Tatyana," he said, sounding surprised and happy to hear from her.

"Where are you?"

"In St. Petersburg."

"I need to see you."

"Are you and Katya coming for a visit? Where do you want to meet?"

"Can you come to us?"

"Is something wrong?"

"Yes," she said, explaining the situation in a rush.

"My God. how did this happen? Who is this boy?"

"That's what I need you to find out. She has some kind of silly notion that he is her Guardian." She passed on the pertinent information to Nikolai.

"I was afraid this would happen. I need to make some phone calls. But I'll be there as soon as I can get

244

away."

"Hurry," Melody said.

She tiptoed down the hall to check on her daughter and cracked the door open to a dark room. Katya was sleeping. That was good. She'd have some time to think about the situation before discussing it with her daughter. If Nikolai was coming, she'd have to tell Slick.

Slick knew Katya spent her summers with her real father, but he didn't know that those mother-daughter trips she and Katya took to Europe were excuses for extended family time. She had been lying to her husband all these years. And now it was time for the truth.

She had no idea how Slick would react. She'd been deceiving him all along. She'd never told him who she really was. He'd suspected, but she'd put all those concerns to rest. Now they were coming home to roost. History was repeating itself.

Chapter Thirty-Two

Maybe she *was* following the grand plan. After all, the first Katya, her fourth-great-grandmother, had ended up pregnant out of wedlock and married another man, not the man of her dreams. The same thing had happened to many of the other women down the line when their Guardians showed up. Her own mother had followed the same path.

All she had to do was protect her virginity until her Guardian came along—and she couldn't even manage that. Was Dax her Guardian? Who knew? How was she supposed to tell whether he was or wasn't? What did a Guardian look like? Dashing and handsome, smart and sexy, like Papa? Or dependable and patient, centered and true, like Rabbi Slick? There was no Guardian rulebook to follow. She had simply followed her heart and given in to passion without a thought to the consequences. She was the Romanov vessel. Everyone was depending on her. And she had slept with and procreated with the first good-looking guy who had taken an interest in her.

In her defense, she had been drinking, a lot. She tended to do that when she was moody. Graduation was looming and she had no idea what life had in store for her. She was tired of waiting for her elusive Guardian to show up. She was impatient and wanted to control her own destiny. So when she received an invitation to a party off campus, she was eager to accept. To discard all thoughts of finals and her future, to just have some fun.

And when a mysterious stranger walked into the room, she was unprepared for her reaction. He looked around as if searching for something or someone. Then his gaze landed on her, and he smiled and strode over.

She'd heard of and read about love at first sight. Connecting across a crowded room, a thunderbolt delivered by Cupid's arrow, *être le coup de foudre*, and all that romantic lore. She thought this must be the way it happened. When she'd first seen him, she had been overwhelmed, quite in shock, and then when he crossed the room and took her hands in his, she felt faint. She could feel her heart beating erratically.

"I think I've been looking for you all my life." Those were his first words to her. That's how it started. Was it just a cheesy pick-up line? Could he be her Guardian, or was he just a predator? They talked. Most of the night. About everything and nothing.

She'd asked him if he'd ever been to New Russia. He had. Where was he from? Greece. They had a few more cocktails, which loosened their tongues.

And then he said, "Let's get out of here." After he'd pulled her close and kissed her thoroughly in front of everyone. His meaning couldn't have been more clear. And she'd responded.

Why had she gone with him? Why had she sat nervously across from him in his late model sportscar, and followed him to his apartment, like a lamb to the slaughter? He could have been a serial killer. Or a serial lover.

When they got to his bedroom, he began

undressing her, eager to be closer, kissing her hungrily. When she mumbled something about taking precautions, and this being her first time, he'd said, "I'll protect you."

If that wasn't classic Guardian speak, she didn't know what was.

Then she gave herself up to him with abandon. Again and again. After their first wild coupling, he was tender and sweet. Whispering words of love, making promises. She was the most beautiful girl he'd ever seen, he couldn't believe he'd finally found her. He'd even spoken of love. Then they went to sleep tangled in the sheets, his arm draped possessively across her naked breasts. When she woke up late the next morning he was gone. No note, no evidence he'd ever been there.

Was Dax even his real name? Had she given him her name? Told him anything about herself, where he could find her? She couldn't remember who had invited her to the party. What an idiot she'd been. He'd just targeted her, used her for a night's pleasure, and she was never going to see him again. She couldn't lay the blame completely at his feet. She had been a willing partner.

Somehow, she'd managed to get back to her apartment and, some time later, to take her finals. Then she just wandered through her life in a daze, until she was wracked with morning sickness and realized something was not right. She bought a home pregnancy test from the local drugstore near campus and wasn't surprised the test was positive. Nothing to do but go home and face the consequences.

Chapter Thirty-Three

Melody paced the living room until she threatened to wear out the Persian carpet. It was time to face the music.

Slick's car pulled into the driveway. When he walked into the living room, he kissed her and cocked his head. "What's wrong?"

"How do you know something is wrong?"

"Because I know you. Now, out with it. Is it Katya? Is she still feeling sick?"

Melody hung her head. "She's not sick. She's...it's about Katya, but not completely. Slick, I have a confession."

"Is this a rabbinical confession or a marital confession?"

She pursed her lips. "A marital confession."

"Go on. People say I'm a good listener."

Melody sighed. Slick was a good listener, a good husband, a good man. The man in the white hat. Her personal white knight. And she had deceived him throughout their marriage.

"Promise you won't hate me," she began.

"Come over here," he said, sitting down beside her and gathering her into his arms. "You can tell me anything and I won't hate you. I could never hate you."

"Where do I start?"

"The beginning is usually the best place."

She sat up, moved his arms away, and turned to face him.

"Remember when I came to your office, then disappeared for so long, and you thought I looked like—in fact, you thought I *was* that Empress, Maria Tatyana Feodorovna, who had been executed in New Russia?"

"Yes. But that was more than twenty years ago. What does that have to do with us today?"

"Well, you were right. That was me."

Slick looked at her in disbelief.

"You're Maria Tatyana Feodorovna?"

"No, I'm Melody Rosenberg, your wife, and very happy to be."

"How is that possible? And her daughter, Ekaterina, your daughter?"

"Our Katya."

"But I saw them execute you on television."

"I was sitting there about to be executed when Nikolai and his soldiers got there in time to rescue me. We wanted the world to think I was dead, and that Katya had disappeared and was assumed dead, because it was no longer safe for us in New Russia. That allowed us to hide away so no one would come looking for us."

Slick was quiet, incredulous. "And all these years, after we were married, you didn't trust me enough to confide in me?"

"I'd planned to tell you, but I hardly understood it myself. How was I going to explain it to you? You never would have believed me."

"You're wrong. I would have believed you because I believe in you, and I thought you believed in our love."

"I do, but let me start at the beginning."

Melody recounted the whole story about the diary, the necklace, and the nanny. The Romanov legacy. How in this very room Nikolai had appeared and confirmed that Katya had been kidnapped, the flight to Switzerland, the Guardians, and everything that followed.

Melody sighed. "I did it to protect us, to make sure we weren't hunted down."

"I don't know what to say. I was your safety net? Your fallback? Your second choice?"

"No, that's not true," Melody protested.

"Why didn't you just stay with Nikolai?"

"Because you were the man I wanted to be with, the one I wanted to raise our daughter with."

"What else have you been hiding from me?"

Melody kneaded her hands together.

"You know Katya spends every summer with Nikolai, but never in New Russia. What you don't know is when Katya and I take our mother-daughter trips, we're actually going to meet Nikolai to spend some quality family time together."

Slick turned away. "I thought I was your family."

Melody grabbed his chin and turned his face toward her.

"Honey, you are, but I wanted Katya to know her father and feel like she was part of his life too."

"I would have understood. What I don't understand is why you felt the need to lie to me. To treat me like a fool. I guess it must have been a big come-down, having to live with me, here, instead of in a palace."

Melody took his hands in hers. "You know I love

you. I've been happy with you all these years."

He pushed her hands away. "What's this really all about? Are you leaving me?"

"No, of course not. But Nikolai is on his way here. He's taking the Super Jet from Europe, so he should be here this evening. I asked him to stay with us."

"What if I don't want him here? Why is he coming?"

"Because there's more."

"More I don't know about?" Slick got up from the couch and began to pace the room.

"Yes, it's about Katya." Melody paused. "She's pregnant."

Slick stopped in his tracks and turned toward her with a look like he had been punched in the gut. The color drained from his face.

"Katya?"

"Yes, I just found out this morning. That's why she couldn't come to services with us."

"How did this happen?" Slick asked, raising his voice.

Melody sighed. "The usual way, I guess."

"That's not what I meant."

"We were honest with Katya about her heritage, from the beginning. She was the Grand Duchess. Even you refer to her as your princess. Nikolai regaled her with stories of her illustrious ancestors. She had expectations. If New Russia ever needed her, she could resurface."

"So you and Katya were going to save the world."

"Just do our duty."

"You don't really believe all this, do you?"

"I can show you the diary."

"But what does the pregnancy have to do with any of this?"

"She thought the boy she slept with was her Guardian. But she doesn't know for sure."

"She thought?" he shouted. "Her Guardian? Doesn't she know who she went to bed with?"

"No, I don't think so."

Slick was furious. She had spent her entire married life living with calm, measured, reasonable Rabbi Slick, and now that man was gone. Whether it was because of her lies or her daughter's predicament, or both, she didn't know. She'd depended on Slick for his moderate disposition. He had enabled her to live life on an even keel, to provide structure and stability in her daughter's life after living with Nikolai's impulsive, chaotic temperament.

"I'm going to find out how this happened. Is Katya in her room?"

"Yes, but don't go in there until you've calmed down," Melody said.

"You want me to be calm? My daughter is pregnant by a man she knows nothing about except for the fact that he *might* be her Guardian. Do you know how ridiculous that sounds?"

Slick marched into the hallway and knocked loudly on Katya's door.

"I want to talk to you, young lady," he shouted.

When there was no answer he opened the door and walked in.

Katya sat on the bed in tears, distraught.

"I'm sorry, Daddy. I'm sorry for everything. I'm stupid."

"You're not stupid."

"But I've ruined your reputation."

Slick exhaled and walked over to the bed, sat down and enfolded Katya in his arms.

"You haven't ruined anything, Princess. And I don't care a thing about what people say or think about me. I only care about you, sweetheart. What can I do? How can I help you?"

"Don't be mad at me," Katya pouted. "Oh, Daddy, what am I going to do?"

"Everything will be all right," he said, rocking her back and forth. "I'll make sure of it."

But for the life of him, he couldn't figure out how he could accomplish that.

Chapter Thirty-Four

Nikolai arrived just in time for dinner. Melody made crispy fried chicken, crunchy green beans with slivered almonds, and yellow rice, and she, Nikolai, Slick, and Katya sat around the dining room table like nothing was wrong. Like this was an ordinary day. An ordinary situation.

On the surface, Slick and Nikolai were polite to each other, but Slick was seething. She could tell he was feeling usurped in his own home. Katya was glad to see her Papa, but she was quiet. She didn't want to be disloyal to Slick. Everyone was talking about everything but the elephant in the room. How was the Count's flight over? How was the Super Jet? How was the weather in New Russia? Congratulations all around on Katya's graduation. Katya thanked Papa for her over-the-top graduation gifts—a priceless string of pearls and a yacht waiting in the boat slip behind their house at Lake Como.

Melody hoped Nikolai had some answers. The Count was usually handy in a crisis, but they'd never faced a situation quite like this. After dessert, she showed Nikolai to the guest room, where Slick had deposited his luggage. He closed the door, took her into his arms, and held her tight.

"I've missed you," he whispered. He leaned in to kiss her.

She held her hand out flat against his chest to stop him.

"It's good to see you, too, Nikolai, but this is my home, with my husband. You need to respect that."

Nikolai released her. "If that's what you want," he said. "What a mess."

"We can agree on that much," she said. "I hope you have some ideas about what to do next, because I'm fresh out of solutions."

"What does the learned rabbi say?"

"He had plenty to say until he actually confronted Katya. Then he caved when she turned on the tears. He still thinks of her as his little princess, and he can never stay mad at her or refuse her."

"And you think I can?"

"Well, somebody has to be the adult. I of all people can understand the situation she's in. I just can't believe it's happening again. This is a curse, Nikolai. Let's all go into the living room, and we can hash it out. And no more hugging or kissing. Is that understood?"

"I can't stop loving you, Maria Tatyana," he said, rubbing the inside of her elbow, "or touching you."

"What we had between us was over a long time ago. Just keep your hands to yourself. And call me Melody, please."

She walked to the door, opened it, and he followed.

They all congregated in the living room, Melody and Slick on the couch, Katya and Nikolai on separate matching wing chairs across from them.

Nikolai had wanted to chat in private with Maria Tatyana, but she insisted Slick be included in the discussion. Actually, Slick had insisted.

"I'm not leaving you alone with that man. Not for a

minute. I see the way he looks at you, like a hungry wolf."

"He looks that way at all women. And how is that different from the way all the women in the congregation look at you? It's as if I don't even exist."

"But you know you're the only woman I want."

"Exactly. I do know that. And Nikolai wants every woman he looks at. That's why I'm married to you."

"Do you think Katya should be here when we talk?"

"Of course. She's the reason we're all here."

When they got to the living room, Melody started the conversation.

"Nikolai, have you been able to find out anything about this boy Dax?"

"I took the first flight to the States, but I was able to learn some things, and I have people investigating. It turns out that Damien Apollo Xerogeanes *is* the son of a Guardian, a former Guardian."

"Dax is a Guardian?" Katya exclaimed.

"I'm not sure. His father is or was. He was involved in the attempt on your mother's life all those years ago. He was shot along with the other soldiers who kidnapped the Empress."

"Then he's a traitor, a false Guardian," Melody said. "Like Miss Cormier."

"Possibly. When his father was killed, he was raised by an uncle, who's also a Guardian. The uncle lives in Greece, so that's where Dax was raised. Whether or not he's part of the network, we don't know. Is he out to avenge his father? Did his uncle put him up to it? Or did he just wander into that party and walk out with our daughter?"

"He didn't travel all the way from Greece to attend an off-campus party in the United States," Melody said. "He targeted Katya. I'm sure of it."

"I'm not," Nikolai said. "The boy's brother also attended the university where Katya graduated. His uncle checks out. But New Russia is changing again. Oligarchy is creeping back in. It's looking like our next president might be a dictator. Dax's uncle is Greek born, but he's a New Russian oligarch, and he craves more power. He wants a seat at the table. This may be the way he gets a foot in the door. Or the whole thing may just be an innocent coincidence."

"Nikolai, this is not a coincidence," Melody insisted.

"How could he know who I am?" Katya wondered. "Everyone thinks I'm dead or that I disappeared."

"Katya, I'm sure there are people who know all about you, probably where you are at all times," Nikolai said. "We can't be sure if this boy targeted you, what he wants, or why."

"But if he wants me, and he knows where to find me, then why hasn't he called or written or tried to get in touch? Why when we…when we were together did he leave the next morning without a word? It's been nearly three months."

"Katya, sweetheart, I'm so sorry," her mother said. "I can't explain it."

"Well, the boy is not going to get away with it," Nikolai stated. "He is going to answer to me. I have arranged a meeting with him and his uncle when I return to New Russia, and I will get to the bottom of this. That is, if you want to see him again."

Everyone turned to Katya.

"I just want to know why he left me, or why he sought me out in the first place."

"You'll get your answers."

"I want to come with you. I want to face him."

"Then I'm coming too," Melody said.

"And I'll join you," the rabbi said.

"Slick you can't just take off for Europe. Who knows how much time this will require?"

"I'll get my assistant rabbi to take my classes and conduct services. We haven't had a family vacation in years. And I've never been to New Russia."

He would be thinking of all the "family vacations," she and Katya had taken with Nikolai, Melody thought.

"This is not a vacation," scolded Nikolai. "We have serious business to negotiate. And we're not meeting in New Russia. The boy and his uncle are going to meet on my turf in Bellagio. Maria Tatyana— er, Melody—you cannot be at the meeting. Everyone thinks you're dead."

"I'll be listening in the next room, then. I will not be left behind."

"And Katya, you are not to make an appearance until I'm convinced of this boy's motives. No one has any idea who you really are. Once your identity is revealed, you'll be exposed, as will your mother."

"Yes, Papa."

Chapter Thirty-Five

Bellagio, Lake Como, Italy

"Is it strange, being here with me at his house?" Slick asked as they lay in bed in one of the many spacious guest rooms on the third floor of the villa with a full lake view.

"A little," Melody admitted.

"Is this where you sleep when I'm not here?"

"No, I sleep in a suite on the second floor."

"Near Nikolai's bedroom?"

"Yes," Melody admitted. "But Nikolai has given you the best room. He's showing off."

"It is beautiful here. I'd love to come back someday, just you and me."

"I'd like that," Melody said.

"Come over here," Slick whispered, reaching for her.

"I am here."

"Closer. I want to admire the view."

"Then you're looking in the wrong direction. The beautiful vista is out the window."

"The view in here is much more stunning. Why don't you take off your nightgown?"

"Slick," she admonished. "They'll be expecting us for breakfast. If we don't show up, they'll be wondering."

"Then let them wonder." Slick removed her nightgown and tossed it on the floor. He drew her in and kissed her passionately before his hands moved to fondle her breasts.

"Slick, I don't think…"

"Don't think."

He licked her nipples, one at a time, then brought them into his mouth before his hands moved lower. She moved restlessly, then shuddered, crying out his name.

He moved to mount her and, once inside, rode her, his hands on her breasts, his mouth hungrily on her lips, until he cried out and spilled his seed into her body. Drained, he plopped his long, lanky body next to hers.

"It's been a long time," he said. "Too long."

"I'd thought you might have forgotten how," she said sarcastically.

"Well, I've been neglecting you. I've been so busy with the needs of the congregation, I haven't been paying enough attention to your needs. I've lost sight of my most important responsibility, keeping you satisfied."

"I'm not complaining, but was this about sticking it to Nikolai?"

"No, it was all about sticking it to you."

"Ha, ha. You're jealous."

"Of course I am. I'm never going to let you out of my sight, not for a minute."

"I'm going to hold you to that. But now we need to shower and get dressed."

"Would you like some company in the shower? It looks big enough to hold a symphony. How would you feel about an encore?"

"I would very much like that," Melody said,

jumping out of bed, Slick close on her heels.

****

"Are you ready, Katya? He'll be here soon."

"What are you going to say to him, Papa?"

"I don't know. What do you want me to say?"

"I'm mad at him for the way he treated me," Katya said, biting her lip. "But I very much want to see him again. Are you going to force him to marry me?" She sounded almost hopeful.

"Katya, this boy must do right by you. But he is going to have to fight for you if he wants you. I'm not going to give away my greatest treasure to just anyone. He must be worthy of you and earn your love, if that's how you feel about him. Only you can know if he is *the one*. This is an important decision you must make, one that will affect the rest of your life. And it's not just about the boy. If he is your Guardian, then you will be called on to take your rightful place in the world."

"Oh, Papa." She threw herself into Nikolai's arms. "When should I come in?"

"You will know when the time is right, *if* the time is right. You can wait with your mother in the next room, and you'll hear everything."

After breakfast, Melody joined Katya in her room. "Your father has laid out a magnificent gown for you to wear, should you decide to make an appearance. I will fix your hair. You will be a vision. A true Grand Duchess. That boy will be sorry he ever scorned you. He will see what he is missing. We will make him pay. Your father will see to it."

Katya hugged her mother.

"Are you nervous?"

"Yes, he's all I've been thinking about."

"Let's see if he is the man you think he is. I hear their car outside. Let's take our places."

Chapter Thirty-Six

Dax and his uncle were met at the door by a butler
and led to a pavilion where Nikolai was waiting,
overlooking the sparkling lake.

"Count Kinsky, how nice of you to invite us to
your beautiful home. What a spectacular view of the
lake."

"It's why I bought the place. I've really enjoyed
living here. It's my getaway when the pressures of
governing New Russia become overwhelming."

"May I present my nephew Dax, although I think
of him as a son. I've raised him and his brother since
they were boys, since the unfortunate death of my
brother."

"Yes," said Nikolai flatly. "That was a most
unfortunate incident."

His guest's expression was inscrutable. Did the
man agree that the "execution" of the Empress was
unfortunate, or was he lamenting the death of his
brother as a result of the incident? It was hard to tell
where the man's loyalties lay or ascertain the nephew's
feelings about his father's actions.

Dax stepped forward and shook hands with
Nikolai. "Count Kinsky, it's an honor to meet you. I've
heard a lot about you."

So the boy had manners.

"I don't know much about you, though."

"Not much to tell."

"My nephew is just being modest. He is a member of one of the top legal firms in St. Petersburg. He specializes in mergers and acquisitions law."

"Very impressive," Nikolai acknowledged with a slight frown. Maybe that's why you were so skillful in merging with my daughter, he thought bitterly. "Why don't you have a seat."

The guests sat on the couch facing Lake Como. The Count sat with his back to the water so he could study the two men. His intention was to convey the impression of absolute wealth and power.

"So, young Dax, what are your plans?" Nikolai began.

"Plans, sir?"

"Yes, what do you plan to do with the rest of your life?"

"He aspires to join the Ministry of Justice," Dax's uncle answered.

"Is the boy not capable of answering for himself?" Nikolai said aloud.

The inquisition lasted for about twenty minutes before Nikolai got to the heart of the matter.

****

In an adjoining room, Katya and her mother whispered.

"Oh, my," said Melody, fanning herself with a magazine. "He *does* look like a Greek god. I think I'm having the vapors. He has the face of an angel and the look of a devil. And that body! I think he's the most handsome man I've ever seen. Was he as good as he looks?"

"Mother!"

"I may be your mother, but I'm not dead yet. I still have eyes, don't I? And an active imagination. He reminds me of the way your Papa looked when we first met. Just one look was all it took, as the song goes."

"So you believe in love at first sight?"

"That's the way it happened for me."

Katya got a faraway look, remembering the night she and Dax had spent together. Seeing him again this close brought the memories flooding back. She rubbed her neck.

"But you married someone else," Katya pointed out. "Eventually, the heat cooled down."

"There will always be a spark between your Papa and me. But I refuse to let him fan the flames because I am completely in love with my husband."

The morning bedroom romp followed by the incendiary shower scene flashed in her mind. She was still breathless. The heat was still there after all these years. She had a feeling Slick's nascent amorous affection would be on display every night they spent under Nikolai's roof. She'd sent her husband on a ferry tour around the lake while she kept watch over her daughter.

"Mother, shush, Papa is talking again."

****

"I'll get straight to the point of why I asked you here," the Count said, glaring at Dax. "A few months ago, you walked into an off-campus party at the university and, not much later, after plying her with liquor, walked out with a girl. Ekaterina Rosenberg."

Dax looked puzzled. "Katya?"

"Yes. And where did you take her?"

"We went back to my brother's apartment." He had

the good grace to look ashamed.

"I don't understand," Dax's uncle interrupted. "What does this have to do with anything?"

"I'm asking the questions, and I'm speaking to your nephew. I want answers and I want the truth."

Dax nodded.

"And you took that young girl back to your brother's apartment and spent the night with her, when you were both inebriated. Is that correct?"

Dax nodded again.

"And what happened after that?"

"What do you mean?"

"What I mean is *after* you slept with her? After you took her virginity."

"I...we...I didn't mean...I didn't think—"

"You didn't mean to take her virginity? It's obvious you didn't think or use protection. And *then* what did you do?"

"I—"

"I'll tell you what you did. You left her. You used her, stole her precious gift, and snuck out without even saying goodbye. Is that the way a gentleman behaves?"

"How do you know all this?" Dax asked.

"I know all this because that girl you took advantage of is my *daughter*."

Dax stared at Nikolai openmouthed, dangling like a fish on a hook, speechless.

Nikolai got up and placed himself directly in front of Dax, blocking his view of the lake.

"Is that the way it happened? Because if it isn't, please enlighten me."

Dax ran a hand up his forehead, pushing back the untamed dark black bangs from his face.

"Obviously, this little interlude meant nothing to you. You seem to have conveniently forgotten it. But now I am going to tell *you* what will happen. As it turns out, because of your recklessness, my daughter is pregnant with your child. And as much as I can't stand the sight of you, you are going to make this right. You are going to marry her and give her child a name. After the child is born, you will get a divorce, without a settlement, and you will sign away all rights to her child. Do I make myself clear?"

Dax's jaw dropped. "She's pregnant?"

"That's right. Now what do you have to say for yourself?"

The room was quiet.

"I'm waiting," Nikolai said, veering dangerously closer to Dax.

"I'm her Guardian," Dax said softly.

"I didn't hear you," Nikolai shouted.

"I said I'm her Guardian!" Dax shouted back.

Nikolai reached into his suit jacket and pulled out a revolver, shaking it in Dax's direction. "It's loaded, and I will use it, just like I used it on your traitorous father."

"You killed my father?"

"He kidnapped the woman I loved and stole the life I was meant to have."

"They never told me exactly who it was. Are you sure?"

"I should know. I was there. How can you be certain you're her Guardian? And if you lie to me, I'll shoot you on the spot."

Dax's uncle stepped between them, willing to take the bullet. "I told him, after my brother told me. His faction was in favor of the young Grand Duchess taking over the throne. His son was to be her Guardian. It was all in a letter he left me in the event anything should ever happen to him."

"So you knew about the kidnapping in advance?"

"No," Dax's uncle protested vehemently. "I was as shocked and horrified as you were. Nevertheless, Dax is your daughter's Guardian. When the Grand Duchess went missing, I didn't know what to do. So I waited until Dax was old enough to know the truth. I trained him, to honor my brother's wishes. And we waited."

"How do you know Dax is the legitimate Guardian?"

"Has anyone else surfaced since the abdication, er, execution?"

Nikolai paused. His hand shook, but he kept the gun firmly pointed in Dax's direction.

"Papa, enough," Katya cried, stepping out from the anteroom.

"Katya, are you sure?" her mother whispered.

"I'm sure," Katya responded, waving her mother back.

"I want to talk to Dax alone."

Nikolai frowned but stepped away from a shocked Dax. "You two can walk outside by the lake. But I have my eye on you, Damien Apollo Xerogeanes. If you make one wrong move, I will kill you where you stand."

Chapter Thirty-Seven

Katya led Dax out the door of the pavilion and down the bluestone path to her Papa's private lake front. They passed the dock where her new yacht was moored and sat down on a bright green bench facing the water. A slight breeze shifted in the air. They bathed in the sun shining directly overhead. It was a magical day.

"Katya," Dax said, turning to face her, staring adoringly into her eyes. "Is it really you? I wasn't sure I would ever see you again."

"I have to apologize for my Papa. I don't think he would have used the gun." Katya lifted the hem of her floor-length gown and folded her hands demurely over her lap.

"I deserve it," Dax said, leaning back on the bench. The lake cast its spell like it always did.

"You are so beautiful, a vision. Like the painting of the goddess Venus emerging from the sea."

"I'm not looking for flattery. Just the truth. You said you were my Guardian. What did you mean by that?"

"First, let me say how sorry I am for leaving you alone in the apartment. I had an appointment to settle my brother's account at the college administration building. He spent the night at his girlfriend's apartment, and he was meeting me there. You looked so peaceful asleep in bed, I didn't want to wake you, although I was tempted. You had the most adorable smile. You looked very…satisfied."

Katya blushed.

"I had no idea how to find you," Dax continued. "We hadn't exchanged information. I knew your name was Katya, but I didn't have your last name. I thought you'd be there waiting when I came back. I should have left a note. I didn't think."

"I thought for sure you would find me. And then I found out I was pregnant. But I don't care what my father said. You are under no obligation to marry me. I was just as much to blame for what happened. I had too much to drink. I knew what I was doing when I went with you. I wanted to. I'm not sorry."

"Katya…" Dax sighed, reaching for her hands and holding them tight. "When I walked into that party, I wasn't looking for anything or anyone. I just wanted to pass the time, and then I saw you, and I swear my heart literally stopped. It was like, I have to meet that girl. I have to be near that girl. I have to be with that girl."

Katya squeezed his hand and smiled. "I felt the same way when I first saw you. I wished you would come over, and then you did."

"You looked so familiar to me, like Anastasia— you know, the Russian Grand Duchess."

Katya smiled. "A lot of people say that."

"Especially now, in that dress. I knew I had no right to touch you. I am spoken for. But my brain told me one thing and my heart another."

Katya's breath caught in her throat. "So you are engaged?"

"No, promised. It's like I told your father. I'm a Guardian. My whole life I have been pledged to someone, a girl who disappeared many years ago when she was just a child. A Grand Duchess. But I have been trained my whole life to protect her. I supposed she was dead, like her mother, the Empress. What was worse was that my father was one of the soldiers responsible for the execution of the Empress.

"When we came together, it felt right. I thought maybe there could be something between us. But in the morning I knew I couldn't stay with you, couldn't hurt you. I didn't know how to explain. It wasn't something you could put in a note. I thought I was falling in love, but I was obligated to someone else. I wanted to tell you, but when I got back to the apartment you were gone from my life. There hasn't been a moment since then when I stopped thinking about you.

"And now I've found you again, and my uncle has confirmed who you are. You look just like your departed mother, he says. I know we are meant for each other. And I will love and protect you and our child, for the rest of my life, whether or not we're married."

Dax leaned over and kissed Katya sweetly on the lips in the warmth of the sun. "My Katya."

She pulled out of his embrace. "Doesn't it bother you that my father killed your father?"

"He had no choice. My father fell in with a false Guardian who preferred you on the throne. My family was shamed. But I went to live with my uncle, and I have tried to stay in the shadows but live a life of honor, without blemish. A life within the law."

"I believe you. But I really don't know you. And I don't like the idea of being forced into a marriage."

Dax looked at Katya's slightly swollen belly and placed a hand on the tiny mound. "But you're carrying our child. We must get married. I refuse to bring shame to you or your father."

"My child needs a name, so I will marry you. But my father says then we will divorce and you will have nothing to do with the child. He is not convinced your intentions are honorable. I have a role to play. And if you are my Guardian, then you know I must meet my obligation. I have been training for this role my entire life. It is time for the Grand Duchess to reappear."

"But Katya, now more than ever, I want to be with you. I will never desert you or our child. I will fight for us. I would die for you."

He caressed Katya's face. "Katya, look at me. Tell me you feel what I feel."

Katya yearned for Dax. She longed to give herself to him again. She thought she did love him, but her father was her guide in all things royal, and she would follow his counsel, not her heart.

Katya and Dax basked in the sun for another hour, staring at the lake, sometimes silent, sometimes talking, always watching the boats dotting the water and the spectacular mountain view. Katya was tempted to sail away with Dax, to live a life of freedom, away from the spotlight. Why couldn't she find happiness with her Guardian? But in the end, they walked back into the pavilion and approached Nikolai.

"Papa, I have made my decision. I will marry Dax to give my child a name. Then when the child is born, we will divorce, and I will be ready to take my place and wear the crown."

Nikolai hugged Katya. "You're doing the right thing. I'm very proud of you. We will hold the wedding here at the end of the week, with only family. Then you will separate until the marriage is over. We have much to do. Dax and his uncle can stay at one of the hotels in Bellagio until then. You needn't see him again until the wedding."

He turned to Dax. "You and your uncle can show yourselves out."

"Katya," Dax whispered, beseeching her to look at him, rubbing his hand lightly over her hers.

She shivered once, slightly, before regaining her composure.

"This will be a marriage in more than name only, I promise you."

Ever since she was a little girl, she had dreamed of being Cinderella, living in a fairytale castle with her Prince Charming. But it seemed she and her child were destined to live alone.

Katya turned her head away from Dax, lifted her chin, and practiced her best Grand Duchess smile that her Papa had taught her in this very room, summer after summer.

"That can never be. You will never have me. We will never be together."

Chapter Thirty-Eight

The Wedding
Bellagio, Lake Como, Italy

The day dawned bright and cool. The water sparkled like diamonds. Mama and Papa handled all the arrangements, leaving her alone with her thoughts. She hadn't seen Dax in four days. She was very much looking forward to seeing him again, for however brief a time. Would they spend the night at the villa, a nearby hotel, or would they whisk her away before she and Dax could consummate the marriage? If they were legally married, why shouldn't they be together, even for one night?

Mama had picked out the most magnificent gown from the Romanov collection, a frothy white silk gown seeded with pearls.

"And you must wear Nana's emerald-and-diamond necklace," said her mother, bringing out the piece in its blue velvet box and fastening the jewels around Katya's neck. "If there ever was an occasion to wear this heirloom, it is your wedding day."

"It is so beautiful," Katya breathed, touching the necklace, mesmerized by her reflection in the freestanding mirror.

"You are beautiful. I'm sorry this will not be the wedding of your dreams, with an orchestra, distinguished guests from around the world, a spread fit for a queen, lavish gifts, and champagne flowing."

"No champagne?" Katya asked, smiling.

"Of course we'll have champagne in crystal glasses," her mother assured. "Darling, tell me how you're feeling."

Katya paced restlessly. "I am happy to be marrying Dax. I wish it were a serious commitment, that we could really be together."

"I can see that you're in love, although you just met the boy. And I can understand what you see in him. If your Nana were here, she would say he's too good-looking for his own good.

"But we can't be sure of his allegiance. Are he and his uncle false Guardians? What are their true motives? Do they plan to profit from their association with us? Are they after money or power? If so, your life is in danger. So is mine, once people find out I'm still alive. Can we trust them? I don't want you to go through what I went through. I keep reliving in my mind the events leading up to the execution. The thought of never seeing you again… I couldn't live with myself if I put you back in danger."

"I don't think Dax would put me in danger. He's my Guardian."

"But how can we be certain? Your father thinks he's doing the right thing by denying him access to you until we can be sure. He doesn't want you to be hurt. Now, come see the pavilion. I think I've purchased every flower in Bellagio. The caterers have arrived. Wait until you see the cake. The wedding will take place inside, and then it will spill out onto the patio and down to the lake."

Melody led Katya into the pavilion, into a fairyland.

"Mama, it's beautiful."

"Your Papa had a big hand in the planning. Even though he calls it a fake wedding, he still wanted it to be memorable for you. And your dad will perform the marriage ceremony. After all, he is a rabbi."

"It's perfect."

"I hear a car pull up, so off to your room. It's bad luck to see the groom before the wedding. You'll want to make an entrance. I'm right behind you."

Nikolai had argued that Maria Tatyana should not show her face. She'd been in hiding all these years, he reasoned, and once her daughter ascended to the throne, she could return, when he could officially offer her more protection, but she refused to miss her daughter's wedding.

"She'll marry again," Nikolai said.

"Don't be so sure about that. Do you want her to go through life without love?"

"That boy is not right for her."

"Only Katya can decide that. She's her own woman. And she will have her way."

"We'll see about that."

Melody smiled. Her daughter was a strong-willed woman and she would prevail.

"By the way, you look beautiful, Maria Tatyana."

She wore a simple but smart ivory suit with a strand of pearls Nikolai had given her from the royal treasury when they were in St. Petersburg.

"Thank you," she replied, "and you make a handsome father of the bride, but it's Melody, remember?"

"I remember a lot of things," he said, his eyes clouding. "We never had a wedding."

"We weren't married."

"But now our daughter is getting married. Our little Katya. And soon she'll be having a baby of her own."

"I can't wait. I'm looking forward to being a grandmother."

"That will keep us tied together forever."

"Melody, come help me get into my robe," Slick called, not content to leave his wife alone with the count for a moment longer than necessary.

She turned to Nikolai. "I have to go, but I'll see you in a few minutes when we walk our daughter down the aisle."

"Where did the time go?" he wondered, taking her hands into his. "If you don't mind me asking, why didn't you and the Rabbi have any children?"

A look of pain flitted across Melody's face before she composed herself. "We would have loved that, but it wasn't meant to be. I'd better be going. I need to look in on Katya."

"And your husband."

"And my husband."

Melody entered her suite and helped Slick into his black robe. "Why don't you welcome the groom and his uncle. I'll be in with Katya. Then Nikolai and I will walk her out when the music begins."

"The father of the bride."

"You know Katya thinks of you as her father, and you will be marrying them. That's a big honor." She kissed Slick on the cheek before he went out the door.

In Katya's room, Melody found her daughter gazing into the mirror.

"Oh, my, you look amazing in that dress. The women who did your hair and makeup, well, you almost look like…"

"Anastasia. I know. Dax is fixated on the Grand Duchess."

"As was your father, and probably every Guardian through the generations. Just remember, you're every bit as beautiful and serene as she was. And you are the Grand Duchess now. Soon to be Empress."

"But you won't be there."

"I'll be wherever you need me. Slick will understand."

"Promise?"

"Promise. Now let's go and meet your groom."

"They will be shocked to see that you're still alive."

"I refuse to miss your wedding, no matter the consequences. And if we can't trust them, then we might as well find out now."

The strains of the bridal music could be heard from upstairs. Katya stepped down the circular staircase, floating like a dream, in her royal gown and jewels, her mother and father holding her up on either side. She wouldn't have made it on her own. She'd heard that a bride never remembered much about her wedding day. She could understand that. She'd been too nervous to eat breakfast. Her stomach was doing backflips, and her mind was working overtime.

Was she doing the right thing? Did Dax really care for her, or was he more interested in the prestige she had to offer? Was he marrying Katya, the woman, or Katya, the Romanov heir, or his dream woman, Anastasia? Well, it was too late for second-guessing.

This was really happening.

When she reached the last stairstep, she saw Dax and her heart lurched. Oh, my, he was so handsome in his red-and-gold pre-revolution regimental Life Hussar uniform. Had it belonged to a past Guardian from the former Imperial Russian Army or to one of his relatives, his traitorous father perhaps?

Her eyes roamed from the short single-breasted jacket with high collar trimmed in fine fur and gold braid cords, fringe, and lace, to the belt at his waist, his form-fitting cream breeches and low boots. The outfit was complete with a pair of pistols and his sword.

She kissed her parents as they handed her off to the groom. He held her hands and whispered, "You are the most beautiful sight I have ever seen."

Katya smiled.

For a moment, both the groom and his uncle were flabbergasted when they saw Maria Tatyana escorting the bride down the aisle. They were speechless, and they stared open-mouthed at the Empress, but said nothing.

The music stopped, and Rabbi Slick began the ceremony. They stood under a makeshift *chuppah* and observed all the traditions of a Jewish wedding, down to the groom stepping on the glass. He read his vows, pledging to love, honor, protect, and serve her and love their child. Her voice wavered as she recited her hastily written vows. He had procured two plain gold rings, but then he surprised her with a magnificent antique ring, a large square pale green emerald in a platinum setting of pavé diamonds.

"Your engagement ring," he said.

"I wasn't expecting this," Katya answered. "It's

beautiful."

"It's a family heirloom."

"I will treasure it."

They looked into each other's eyes and saw love reflected. Was that enough? Rabbi Slick told Dax he could kiss his bride, and he swept her into his arms and kissed her until she was dizzy. Was the earth moving? She held on to Dax until her head stopped spinning.

Then the ceremony was over, and they walked hand in hand outside to enjoy the brunch, champagne, and cake. A while later, a photographer took pictures of the happy couple and the family outside by the lake.

Nikolai took the groom aside. "Don't get too comfortable," he warned.

"Sir, I love your daughter."

"You just met my daughter. How can you say you love her?"

"I've never been so sure of anything in my life."

"Those are just words."

Melody came over and kissed Dax. "Welcome to the family."

The Count beetled his eyebrows.

"Your highness, we thought, we all thought—"

"If you or your uncle breathe a word of this to anyone, the wedding will be annulled and you both will be arrested," Nikolai vowed. "We will reveal the Empress to the public when the time is right."

"Of course," Dax's uncle promised, gaping at the Empress.

"Let's have a champagne toast," Melody said, wishing the couple health and happiness.

Then Dax's uncle took a turn, followed by Rabbi Slick.

Nikolai raised a glass. "To Ekaterina and her child."

Dax and Katya toasted each other. The drinks kept flowing.

A few hours later, the newlyweds came to Nikolai and Melody.

"I have booked a senior suite at the Grand Hotel Villa Serbelloni," Dax announced.

"That was not the agreement," said Nikolai, narrowing his eyes. "You won't be taking my daughter anywhere."

"Nikolai," Melody protested. "They're married. Give them one night alone."

"The marriage must be consummated," Dax's uncle agreed.

"That ship has sailed," Nikolai said, indicating his daughter's baby bump.

"Count Kinsky, your daughter and I will be at The Grand Hotel Villa Serbelloni across the lake if you need us." Dax was adamant.

"Katya?" the Count objected, imploring his daughter to stay.

"Daddy, I want to go with him. Dax and I need to talk, to make plans about the baby. This may be the only time we have together before we leave for St. Petersburg."

"Katya, have you been drinking?"

"A little," she said, swaying on her silver sequined heels, grasping at Dax to steady herself.

"What about you, young man?"

"It's our wedding day."

"I'll have my driver take you around to the hotel."

"I've already made arrangements, sir."

Melody put her hand on Nikolai's arm. "Remember how it felt when we were young? That anything was possible? Let them have their night."

"That's what I'm afraid of."

"I will protect her," Dax promised.

"Like you protected her when she got pregnant?"

"Papa, please," Katya scolded. She reached up and placed a kiss on his cheek and hugged her mother and Slick.

"You'll be back tomorrow?" Nikolai asked.

"I'll bring her back to you, as promised," Dax said. "Come on, wife." Dax steered a slightly tipsy Katya out the front door into the glorious sunlight, arm in arm, to where the limousine awaited.

"But my bags, Dax."

"Don't worry, sweetheart, your luggage is already in the car." Then he leaned in to his bride, kissed her passionately, and whispered, "But you won't need any clothes tonight, darling."

Katya giggled like a naughty schoolgirl and clung to Dax, while Nikolai seethed silently.

Chapter Thirty-Nine

Senior Suite, The Grand Hotel Villa Serbelloni

The bellman stored Dax's and Katya's luggage in the oversized wardrobe of the sumptuous senior suite. He opened the curtains and the windows to beautiful views of both Lake Como and the hotel's lavish gardens. He gave a well-rehearsed explanation of how the air conditioning, shower in the private bathroom, and flat-screened TV worked, showed Dax the minibar and the safe, and left a card with the WiFi code. He asked Dax to call if he needed anything. Dax tipped him handsomely and thanked him profusely, but it was obvious to Katya and the bellman that Dax wanted him to make himself scarce. It was their honeymoon, after all.

When the bellman left, Dax locked the door and walked over to his bride.

Katya and Dax stood in front of the window, gaping at the magnificent view of the mountains surrounding the water. No matter how many times Katya had seen the lake, it never failed to move her. There was just something magical about a water view that soothed the soul. She remembered her mother telling her about her "coming out" Guardian gala, a test she had to pass before she became Empress. Now she was at the same hotel, about to step into the role of wife and, ultimately, Empress.

Dax moved to close the windows, but Katya stopped him. "Leave the windows open. I love the breeze and the scent of flowers from the garden."

"Your wish is my command, your highness," Dax said, bowing.

"Don't call me that." Katya laughed.

"Well, you are a Grand Duchess about to become Empress, and I am your loyal subject."

Katya turned to survey the suite. It was decorated in her favorite shades of green. The gold chandelier was positioned above the arrangement of a red velvet couch and chairs. An antique writing table and chair stood between the two windows, in front of a mahogany mirror. On the table was a bottle of champagne chilling in a silver bucket, beside an assortment of gourmet cookies and chocolates.

"As if we needed more champagne," Katya said.

Impossible to ignore was the king-sized bed.

Dax folded her into his arms. She held out her left hand and glanced up at her engagement ring sparkling in the sun. She was a married woman, with all that entailed. Both of them vibrated in anticipation. It was only natural to be nervous about the honeymoon. It had been a while since she and Dax had been together that way. But she'd dreamed of him every minute of every day they'd been apart. Would it be awkward? Or would it be like ripping off a Band-Aid® for a moment of pain and maybe a nighttime of pleasure? She was excited and unsure at the same time. Her husband would have to set the pace.

"First, Mrs. X, we need to remove that gown. We wouldn't want it to get wrinkled. And if you don't lose the dress very soon, I might have to rip it off you."

"Dax," Katya chided.

He dipped his hand slowly down the bodice of her dress and stroked her nipples, making them tighten.

"Dax." Katya's breath caught in her throat.

He turned her around, and as he pulled the zipper he planted soft, wet kisses down her back. Katya shivered. The dress fell around her legs. She stepped out of the gown, and he scooped it up and spread it across a chair. Now she was wearing only a lace bra and panties.

He took care removing his elaborate Hussar uniform, the pistols, and the sword. When he turned back to her, he was completely naked.

"Now," he said, unclipping her bra and fondling her ample breasts. He ran the inside of his hands across her nipples and then removed her panties, cupping her buttocks, grinding his erection against her. She shivered again.

"Are you cold, my love?"

"No." For the first time in a long time she felt free, sexy, and loved. Maybe it was the champagne, maybe it was the nearness of Dax. He picked her up and carried her over to the bed. He tossed off the excess pillows and threw back the duvet cover and the top sheet and pulled her close.

"It's been so long. I've missed you. If we only have one night, then I want to make it count." He smoothed his hands across her belly.

"I can't believe we created this," he marveled. "I can't wait to meet him or her."

"If history is any indication, it will be a girl. It always is with the first one."

"I will love the child, either way, because I love you."

Then he kissed her lips hungrily and began to explore every inch of her, first with his fingertips, then his lips, wetting her breasts and making her wet when he touched her lightly in her special place.

He covered her with his body. She rocked and bucked beneath him, but he kept up the torture until she screamed his name. "Dax, please!"

"Dax please what?" he said, smiling against her lips.

"You know what I mean," Katya said, writhing restlessly.

"I do know, but I want to hear you say it."

Katya blew out a breath in frustration. "I want you," Katya pleaded.

"Where do you want me?" he inquired, increasing the pressure. "Say what you mean."

"I want you inside me," Katya cried.

"Right now?" he asked.

"For God's sake, yes!" she shouted impatiently.

He wasted no time plunging into her, gaining rhythm as they both rode the wave of passion. It seemed to go on forever, until they both exploded, crying each other's names, and Dax slowed his pace and plopped back down on the bed, staring at the ceiling, sated, grabbing Katya's hand.

"Wow, just wow," he said. "That was—"

"For me, too."

"I love you, Katya. I loved you from the moment I saw you, and I will love you forever."

"I love you too, Dax."

"I'm sorry about the words, I mean, making you

say them. I've been having erotic dreams about being with you ever since that night, and I might have gotten carried away. Now let's take it slower. Let me make love to you."

Later that night, Dax said, "I forgot all about dinner. I made a reservation at the Mistral Restaurant. It has a Michelin Star and live music. We're having the seven-course dinner. What time is it?"

"I have no idea," she answered. "Are you hungry?"

"Only for you," he murmured. "But I guess we should get dressed and go down there."

"Then we can come back here for dessert," Katya said.

"I like the sound of that."

"Then maybe later, we'll go down to the spa."

"Katya, thank you for marrying me. I don't care what your father says. I will never leave you."

"Let's see what the future holds. For now, my love, we are together. Let's not waste a minute."

The next morning, after brunch at the hotel, Dax took her down to the dock for a private boat tour of the lake. She sat back against him between his legs, and they basked in the sun and murmured words of love to each other.

"I called your house and spoke to your mother. Thank God your father didn't answer the phone. I told her I need another night with you. She understood."

"Papa will not be happy."

"Katya, it's our life. And I don't want this to end."

When they returned to the hotel, they showered together and fell into a deep sleep on the bed. When they woke, they made love again. They couldn't get enough of each other.

"I will miss you, miss seeing you, miss this," Katya said, cuddled naked in Dax's arms.

"I'm going to speak to your father. I won't allow this to happen. He wants to separate us until the baby comes and then, if I pass his test, he intends to parade me around St. Petersburg like some puppet husband until the divorce is finalized."

"Papa will change his mind. I'll work on him."

"But he will keep you from me until our child is born. How will I live without you?"

"We will find a way. Papa says if you really love me, you will wait."

"Of course I will wait, forever if I have to, but why shouldn't we be together like a man and wife?"

Katya couldn't think of one reason why not.

****

On the other side of the lake

"I thought we agreed on one night," Nikolai said, hands clasped behind his back, pacing across the pavilion.

"*You* agreed on one night. Your *son-in-law* wanted an entire week, not unreasonable for a man in love on his honeymoon," Melody said.

"Stop calling him that," Nikolai ranted.

"Well, that's what he is."

"One more night? What does he think he's going to accomplish in one night?"

Melody stifled a laugh. "Well, he was pretty productive the first night they spent together."

Nikolai stopped in his tracks and turned to Melody. "You think this is a joke?"

She held her hand over her face but couldn't hide a smile. "You are adorable when you don't get your way.

How often does that happen?"

"What do we really know about this boy? He says he's her Guardian. We have no proof that's the case. His uncle is growing richer off the people. New Russia is falling back into its old bad habits with all the oligarchs taking control of industry, the land, and the banks, and with it, the government. All of our good work will be destroyed. And with Katya in his nephew's bed, he will have ultimate control."

"Guardian or not, she's in love with him. And there's nothing you can do about it. It seems your daughter is as obstinate as her father."

"The moment they get back, we are taking Katya to St. Petersburg."

"Which is where Dax lives. How long do you think you can keep them apart?"

"For as long as it takes me to expose him as a charlatan, a false Guardian, like his father and his uncle."

"What if Dax is different? What if he's not anything like his father?"

"He's bewitched her. She's innocent and needs protection."

"She's not so innocent, and she can protect herself. She knows her own mind. She knows she wants to take her place on the throne. I was coerced into the role. She had a choice, and she made it. Are you going to release the bridal photos?"

"When the time is right. The world will need to see she was legitimately married."

"Before they divorce?"

"That's the plan. While they're apart, I will commission her ceremonial portrait. When she ascends the throne, we will display it."

"You can't just banish Dax from her life. He's going to be her child's father. Don't you remember how you felt when you had to live apart from Katya?"

"That was not what I wanted. I had to do it to protect you and my daughter. And then you married the rabbi."

"I did, yes, because I loved him, and we've been very happy."

"You would have been happier with me."

"And I might not have survived. Where is Slick now?"

"He's out on the lake. I've had my captain take our guest out on the yacht and told him not to rush back. I might have mentioned that you and I would meet him for lunch in Como."

"Will we?"

"Of course not. It was the only way to get him on the boat."

"Nikolai, you're impossible."

"The man won't let you out of his sight. How else can I spend any time alone with you?"

"It's not a good idea for us to spend time alone."

"Why not? Are you afraid you'll be tempted? Admit it, you still want me."

"You're delusional."

"I still remember how it was between us."

"When I was your student and you were my professor. I was young and vulnerable and you took advantage. And then I became your creation. I'm not sure you were ever in love with me, just the idea of me."

"That's not true. I loved you then and I love you

now. Will you come away with me, with our daughter, back to New Russia where you belong? You can see your grandchild grow up. We can be together."

"What about Slick?"

"He can go back to Downingville."

"Downing*town*," Melody said.

"To his small life. You were meant for greatness."

"Nikolai, I am very satisfied with my life and my husband. I never wanted to be in the spotlight. I never wanted the crown. You wanted it for me."

Nikolai grabbed her to him and kissed her with all the pent-up passion he'd felt since he last held her in his arms more than two decades ago. She kissed him back.

"There, you see? You still feel something for me. Come to my room so I can show you how much I love you."

Melody shook her head and pushed him away. "You caught me in a weak moment. It was all the excitement of the wedding."

"Tell me Slick is as good a lover as I was."

Melody thought of the scene in her bedroom the first night of their arrival at Nikolai's villa. It had been a long time since they'd been together that way, but it had been very satisfying. She promised herself she wouldn't let the time between those moments grow too long."

"Sex isn't the only thing that makes a good marriage. Slick is a good man."

"And I'm evil?"

She had thought about this many times over the years.

"Not evil, just complex. We didn't want the same things."

"I never betrayed you after my divorce. I stayed true to you."

"You were never with another woman? I find that impossible to believe."

"I had needs, of course, but I never pursued a committed relationship."

"And that was one of our problems."

"Maria Tatyana," he said, gazing into her eyes.

"Melody."

"Give me another chance. We could live together as a family."

"I would never leave Slick."

"So that's it."

"As far as the two of us, yes. But don't deny our daughter her chance for happiness. Stop trying to control her like you tried to control me. Think of what might have been between us, if you had loved me enough to leave New Russia and your royal responsibilities. We would be together today."

"I did it to save you."

"Be honest, Nikolai. You did it because you craved power."

"I craved you. I still do."

"Let the children have the happy ending we were denied."

Nikolai paused.

"That boy will have to prove himself to me first."

"If you keep them apart, she will resent you."

"It's my job to keep her safe."

"That job belongs to Dax now."

Nikolai stormed out of the room and down the hall into his suite.

Chapter Forty

St. Petersburg, New Russia
Six months later

IZVESTIA
St. Petersburg—Church bells chimed throughout New Russia and citizens around the country and the world are celebrating the birth of Grand Duchess Natassja, born to Empress Ekaterina Nikolaevna, who shocked the world when she resurfaced after a decades-long disappearance. The Empress and her dashing husband, attorney Damien Apollo Xerogeanes, known as Dax, who were secretly married in the popular tourist town of Bellagio, Lake Como, Italy, welcomed their daughter after a year of marriage.

The former Empress Maria Tatyana Feodorovna, who the world thought was murdered by anarchists, was by her bedside. The former Empress was actually rescued by Count Nikolai Kinsky after she signed the abdication papers in favor of her daughter and before she was allegedly shot by a firing squad on camera. In what was considered the mystery of the century, Count Kinsky, also of Romanov blood, father of the Empress, reports that his daughter and her mother were in seclusion in the United States until it was deemed safe for Ekaterina to return to New Russia to assume the throne.

Ekaterina Xerogeanes, known as "Empress X" by her Chatter *followers, is back from the hospital and resting comfortably at the palace. The royal family released a picture of the heir and her parents and issued this statement: "My husband and I are overjoyed to welcome Grand Duchess Natassja into the world. Her name means resurrection and her arrival signals a rebirth of the Romanov monarchy to New Russia and better times ahead for the people of New Russia."*

Chapter Forty-One

The Last Guardian
St. Petersburg, New Russia

"She's a real beauty, just like her mother," Dax commented, watching his daughter suckle eagerly at his wife's breast.

"She is fabulous, isn't she," Katya agreed, reclining on her bed. "She has your eyes."

"And your mouth," Dax said. "Is that a smile?"

"Probably just gas," Katya said. "I think it's too early for a newborn to smile."

"But she's our daughter, so of course she is advanced."

Katya laughed, while the baby's mouth slipped off her nipple and the child drifted off to sleep. She patted the newborn's back until she burped.

"There. All done. Could you take her back to the crib?"

"Of course," Dax said, lifting his daughter out of her mother's arms and strolling around the room with her until he finally deposited her in the crib.

Then he turned to Katya. "How are you feeling?"

"Never better."

"How long do you think your father will let me stay this time?" Dax wondered.

"I don't want you to leave, ever. My father will not

dictate how I live my life, how we live our lives. The baby and I need you."

"I'm expecting a guard to come in at any moment and tear us apart again."

"I'm the Empress, and I won't allow that to happen."

"He's allowing me to stay so we can make a show of posing together, the new royal family. We still have to make our balcony appearance."

"My father has had enough time to check you out during the pregnancy. I think he's satisfied, but he's too stubborn to admit it."

"I know he has reservations about my uncle's business holdings. He's afraid my uncle was in league with my father all those years ago."

"There's no evidence of that."

"My uncle has given him assurances that his associates are perfectly content with the monarchy."

Katya patted the bed beside her. "Come sit with me."

Dax sat on the other side of the bed and inched his way toward his wife. He held her as she sighed. He leaned in to kiss her lips. She responded.

"I've missed you," she whispered. "It was so lonely without you. My mother and the rabbi came to visit a lot, and I'm glad they were here for the birth, and my mom has agreed to extend her stay, but I don't want to raise Nastassja alone."

"You can always hire a nanny," Dax said.

"That isn't even funny. I've insisted the baby sleep in here with me, not in the nursery. I will never let another woman raise her."

"I don't know how I managed without you all these

months. I've answered all your father's objections. You've no idea all the hoops I've had to jump through—my motives questioned, my morals attacked, my reputation threatened. But I won't give up on us. He's even offered to buy me off."

"I hope he offered a lot."

"He did, but I didn't take the bait."

"What fault is he finding?"

"He questions whether I am your true Guardian."

"No one else has stepped forward."

"All I have to go by is a letter from my father, an enemy of the state. He says if I were a true Guardian there would have been some kind of succession plan. Who will come after me, who will be our daughter's Guardian? There was no mention of that in my father's letter."

"How can anyone know that?"

"It's been that way in the past."

"Perhaps you are the very last Guardian," Katya suggested.

Dax shrugged his shoulders, keeping a tight hold on his wife. "You and Nastassja can always come away with me."

"Give up the throne?"

"Your mother did."

"That wasn't her choice. And she didn't end up with her Guardian."

"I will never desert you. I am pledged to protect you for the rest of your life."

"That's a promise I'm going to hold you to."

"Do you love me, Katya?"

"I do."

"Then fight for us."

The bedroom door opened, and Nikolai and Melody entered.

"Is this a bad time? The grandparents are here bearing gifts."

"Come in, Papa, Mom. I've just fed her and put her down to sleep."

"Then we'll just watch her," Melody said, peeking into the crib at her new granddaughter.

"Wouldn't you like us to hire someone to care for her in the nursery?" Nikolai asked. "Then you can get your beauty rest and have some privacy."

Melody turned to face Nikolai and narrowed her eyes. "You can't be serious. A nanny? Didn't you learn your lesson with Miss Cormier? I raised Katya by myself, and my daughter will do the same for her child."

"Katya will have many responsibilities. She won't be able to care for the child twenty-four hours a day."

"I will do whatever I have to do to protect Natassja," Katya said.

"And I will do whatever I have to do to protect Katya and our child," Dax said, rising up to confront Nikolai.

"Your usefulness is coming to an end," Nikolai said.

"Papa, I love my husband and I want him with me. If Dax goes, Natassja and I go. I will not separate her from her father. Did you like being separated from Mom and me?"

"Of course not. That's a choice I made to keep you both safe."

"Well, I've made up my mind. I will walk away if you banish Dax."

"You will walk away from the throne of New Russia? Your people love you. Think of all the good you could accomplish."

"Do you want me to be happy?"

"Of course."

"I can't be happy without Dax. You've kept us apart for too long. My heart will break if Dax is not with me. It's my choice, and I am the Empress."

Melody put her hand lightly on Nikolai's elbow. "Nikolai, don't deny our daughter your blessing. History is repeating itself. You sacrificed our family for the sake of your duty. Don't make the same mistake and destroy your daughter's life."

Nikolai's features softened.

"If not for Katya, do it for me," she coaxed.

"I could never resist you, Maria Tatyana. I mean, Melody."

"Maria Tatyana will do."

Nikolai turned to Katya. "If this boy makes you happy, then who am I to interfere with destiny?"

"Papa, thank you," cried Katya. Nikolai hugged her. Then he turned to Dax.

"Welcome to the family, son. I expect you to live up to your commitment and be a true Guardian to my daughter."

"I love Katya, and I would give my life for her. You can count on me." He extended his hand to Nikolai, who shook it. Then he put his arm around Katya. "I swear my allegiance to you my Empress, my one true love, and to our child and all of our children to come."

"And I pledge my love to you, my husband, for the rest of our lives."

Author's Note

There really is a lost shipment of the Tsar's gold hidden somewhere in Siberia. The exact location of the bullion, missing for almost a century, and worth an estimated $80 billion at today's prices, remains a mystery for the ages.

I have visited all the setting locations in the book. My summer as a resort reservationist in Downingtown, Pennsylvania, was similar to the movie *Dirty Dancing.*

Bellagio, on Lake Como, Italy, is perhaps the most beautiful place in the world. I patterned the villa in the book after the hotel where we stayed called the Grand Hotel Villa Serbelloni. On the same trip, we also spent some time in Zurich, Switzerland.

I was charmed by St. Petersburg, Russia, with such amazing sights as the Hermitage Museum, Catherine Palace, The Peter and Paul Fortress, and the Peter and Paul Cathedral, the final resting place of the Russian Tsars. I have always been fascinated by the tragic story of the Romanovs, the last imperial family of Russia.

Acknowledgments

I was inspired to write the novel when a member of my book club, Marilyn Tuckman, brought in a rose gold charm on a necklace passed down from her great-grandmother to her grandmother to her mother (who was born in Siberia) to Marilyn, and I thought, "What if this necklace held the key to the location of the Tsar's lost shipment of gold?" The location of the missing bullion remains a mystery for the ages.

The family story is that a relative found a gold nugget during the Alaskan Gold Rush and had it fashioned into this necklace. Marilyn has a picture of her mom (in Siberia) wearing it when she was a little girl. Her aunt said it was her mother's prized possession. It traveled with them from Siberia to China to Mexico and then to Nashville, when they finally got to America. The actual necklace was inscribed in Russian: *To our daughter as a memento from her parents.*

Thank you for purchasing
this publication of The Wild Rose Press, Inc.

For questions or more information
contact us at
info@thewildrosepress.com.

The Wild Rose Press, Inc.
www.thewildrosepress.com